PATCHWORK

A NOVEL

AUGUST
press

AUGUST

Acknowledgements

This novel has been a long time in the making and has gone through many revisions to reach its present form. Thanks once again to my writers' critique group in Titusville who read it chapter by chapter in its earliest drafts and offered invaluable advice and encouragement. To Cathy Boyle, Irene Herring, Joe Richardson, Leslie Talley, and Kim Wendt, my heartfelt appreciation for being my first readers and morale boosters.

Thanks also to my family, many of whom read earlier drafts of the novel and also offered their encouragement. To my mother Doris Everett and my late father Murphy Everett, who always offered their unwavering support, and to my sisters Libby, Ann, and Lynn, my brother Bill and my late brother Jim, whose sudden and unexpected passing last year left a void in all our lives, a sincere thank you for all that you have meant to me over the years. It is truly our childhoods that set us on the path to what we will become, and it is from my childhood memories and impressions that so much of my writing is drawn.

Finally, thanks to my husband, Bill and to my three children, Matt, Amy, and Will, for also being my readers, cheerleaders, and go-to aides whenever I need them. A special thank you goes to my daughter Amy Teed, who took the cover photo, a detail from a feed sack quilt handmade by my maternal grandmother, Odessa Caulk Williams, sometime in the early part of the 1900s and handed down to me. The quilt, which has gone through much use and many washings, is falling apart now, but it will remain a treasured part of my heritage. And to my son Matt, who formatted the novel for me and prepared it for publication, doing all those technical things that are beyond my expertise, my deepest appreciation. I could not have done it without you.

To my grandchildren, I hope someday you'll read this novel and come away with a deeper understanding of and appreciation for family and heritage. The old saying that we choose our friends but we can't choose our family is all-too-true, but no matter how far away we may go or how much our paths diverge as we mature, our past will always be with us. It is family that is our earliest influence and our last refuge.

PATCHWORK

A NOVEL

Chapter 1

Friday, July 11, 1952

As the Greyhound bus slowed for another railroad crossing, I lifted Benny's head, damp and itchy against my leg, and shifted it to a new spot, careful not to wake him up. Out my window I could see a faded sign on the right: Valdosta—10 miles—and beyond it, at the crossroads, a tiny, wood-frame general store, its white paint peeling, a red Coca Cola sign dangling precariously above the rusty screen door.

Almost home, and the familiarity of the scene tightened the sour knot in my stomach. As the bus picked up speed again, I could hear through my open window the plaintive call of a whippoorwill, and my hand stopped its soothing motion on Benny's back as I concentrated on the sound. I hadn't heard any whippoorwills in New York, and I hadn't realized I'd missed them until now, until I was almost home again.

The word "home" stuck in my throat and churned my stomach. After six-and-a-half years away, I didn't know what to expect, but at least I wouldn't be facing them all alone. I had Benny now, my center for the last six years, and with him as a buffer, I'd make it through this visit. Let anybody dare to say one word against this child of mine, and I'd bare my claws and fight to the last breath anyone who tried to hurt him. If it had to be Benny and me against the world, that's how it would be.

My fingers closed over the telegram sticking out of my purse.

Only six words: "Daddy had stroke. Come home. Mama." I couldn't refuse. It was time for Benny to know he had family—and time for them to acknowledge his existence. I tried to imagine Daddy pale and helpless in a hospital bed, but that image kept being supplanted with those last horrible weeks at home—his tight, thin-lipped frown and steely blue eyes, as fierce as God, as he pounded the Bible and hurled those terrible accusations at me. He couldn't die on me now without seeing Benny or acknowledging how good a job I'd done as his mother. He'd have to acknowledge his own grandson, his own bloodline, who had some of the same McCormick stubbornness as his grandfather. He owed me that, at least.

During the night Benny had dozed fitfully, his head on my lap, while I had stared out the bus window watching the miles recede into darkness. We'd had to make a transfer in Raleigh, North Carolina, in the middle of the night, and I'd had to wake him, leaving him whiny and grumpy. Then I had developed a pounding headache that had kept me awake until dawn. Evening again now and I'd been awake for thirty-six hours straight.

I rubbed Benny's back briskly. "Benbo. Time to wake up." But Benny only burrowed his head deeper into my leg.

"Ouch! That hurts." I lifted him into a sitting position, his head still lolling against me. In Valdosta, we would have to change buses one last time, for the final thirty-mile ride that would take us over the state line into Florida and to the Pine Lake station. "We're almost to Grandma's."

Benny raised his head and rubbed at his eyes. "I'm hungry."

"Me, too. We'll get a sandwich at the bus station."

But when we disembarked, only a rack of limp-looking bags of chips and cookies stood beside a vending machine of nickel bottles of Coca-Cola. I reached into my purse for some change. "Want a Co-Cola, Benny?" I bought two bottles from the machine and picked up a package of ginger snaps from the rack. "We'll get something at Grandma's. It's not much farther."

As the bus headed south, I leaned back and closed my eyes, just for a minute. I was dead tired.

"Mommy, wake up!" Benny was pulling on my arm.

"What? Where are we?" The bus had stopped and all around us passengers were gathering belongings off overhead racks. I was disoriented for a moment until I looked out my window and saw the giant rotating ice cream cone across the street at the Dairy Delight.

"Wait." I told Benny. "Stay close to me." Grabbing the paper bag I'd hurriedly packed with Benny's books and toys, I kept one hand on his shoulder as I followed him down the aisle.

"You did come." The voice came from my right as Benny and I descended the steps. "I was about to give up on you."

"Roy!" I looked up gratefully into the face of my older brother—blue McCormick eyes and ruddy cheeks beneath a green cap with "John Deere" stitched in yellow on its brim. I noticed that his navy T-shirt was stretched over the beginning of a paunch, a softness that wasn't there six-and-a-half years ago when I left home. "Am I glad to see you!"

I tried shifting the paper bag so that I could touch Roy's arm, but he had already stepped away toward the suitcases being unloaded at the side of the bus. I spoke to his back. "I didn't know if anybody would be here to meet me or not. How's Daddy?"

Roy kept his eyes on the suitcases. "He ain't kicked the bucket yet. So if you come for a funeral, you'll have to wait a while. One of these yours?"

I pointed out the cheap cardboard valise I'd borrowed from Rita next door, and he picked it up and jerked his head toward the gravel lot behind the station. "I'm over here."

Squeezing Benny's hand tighter, I followed Roy's stiff back. When we were kids and I'd gotten into trouble for one thing or another, I'd always been able to count on Roy to stick up for me, but now he seemed angry and unforgiving. Had I made a mistake coming here, thinking foolishly that six years of distance could have made a difference in anyone's mind?

Roy stopped at the back of what was either a dark-blue or a black pickup—its exact color camouflaged beneath a thick, talcum-powder coating of July dust—and slung the valise over the tailgate. "Let's go."

I set the paper bag beside the suitcase. "Wait a minute." Roy could be as angry at me as he wanted, but I was not going to let him treat my son this way. I pulled Benny in front of me and put my hands on his shoulders. "This is my son Benjamin. Benny, this is Uncle Roy, Mommy's big brother. Can you say hello?"

"Yeah, I assumed as much. Hey, there, sport." Roy ruffled Benny's hair a little but didn't wait for an answer before heading for the driver's side of the truck. "Well, let's get a move on. I ain't got all night."

I opened the passenger door but didn't get inside. "Maybe Benny and I should go back to New York right now, so as not to trouble you or anybody else with our presence."

"Don't go getting on your high horse." Roy's voice was weary, without inflection. "Mama's waiting for you at home. Get in."

He turned the key in the ignition as I boosted Benny in ahead of me and climbed in after him. Now that I was here, I had no other choice but to make the best of it. "I knew coming back was a mistake. I knew it would be like this."

Roy pulled into the street before answering. "Your mistake was stealing that money and running away. If you ask me, coming back is the first right thing you done in a long time. Running off to New York to live with Yankee strangers. You ain't raising no Yankee kid here, are you? You a Yankee, sport?"

Benny looked at me, his lip quivering.

I pulled him into my lap, away from Roy. "He doesn't know what you're talking about."

"Never mind." Roy touched Benny's knee. "Don't you worry, sport. We'll get the Yankee out of you in no time. You got Southern blood, boy. Don't forget it."

"The Civil War ended a long time ago. What's all this about Yankees?"

"You tell me. You're the one living with 'em."

I clasped both hands around Benny. "You really know how to lay out the welcome mat, don't you? Daddy's going to pull through, then?"

"You disappointed?"

I tried to read Roy's expression in profile. "No. Of course not. I want to set things right between us, for Benny's sake."

"You're a few years too late for that, don't you think?"

"I couldn't come back before. It's been over six years, and I'm still terrified at the thought of facing him again. Look." I held up one hand, and we both watched it tremble in what little light was left of the day.

"Not much to be scared of right now. He's in pretty bad shape. Can't talk or move his left side none."

I leaned my head back against the seat and willed my eyes to stay open. "You know what? When I was about Benny's age, I thought Daddy was somebody straight out of the Bible. Remember that picture in the Sunday school room of Isaac standing in front of a field of sheep, holding a staff? He had this iron gray beard and these bright piercing eyes, just like Daddy's. I couldn't figure out what Daddy had done with all his sheep, for I'd seen only hogs and cows in our fields. But Miss Flora Lee said it was Isaac, and that was Daddy's name. Then when she told us about Abraham being ready to kill Isaac as a sacrifice to God, I lived in deathly fear that Daddy would do the same thing to one of us if God asked him to. I don't know how long I believed that, or when I stopped believing it. Maybe I never did. Maybe that's why I ran away to New York."

Roy grinned. "He probably would have."

"I don't know if I can do this, face everybody again. I'm afraid I'm going to be sick."

"You ain't the only one nervous. Mama's sitting at home on pins and needles, jittery as all get-out. She can't wait to see you."

"How's she doing? I know she's worried sick about Daddy."

"That, among other things. She ain't had it easy these last few years."

"You mean me?"

"If the shoe fits." Roy paused before continuing. "You nearbout killed her, in case you didn't know, running off like you did with

11

no word about where you were, if you were alive or dead."

I looked down to see if Benny was listening to this exchange, but his head was nodding forward. I shifted his position so that he could rest against my shoulder and kept my voice low so as not to wake him. "I didn't mean to worry her. But I was afraid to write for the longest time, afraid of what Daddy would do if he knew the truth. I've wanted so much for her to meet Benny, to get to know him."

"She ain't talked about nothing else since she got word you was coming. And I guess I better warn you she ain't the only one waiting to get a gander at him. You should have heard everybody earlier, speculating—"

"If anybody says—"

"You'll take 'em on, right? Welcome back, Sis. You ain't changed a bit."

I studied Roy's profile in the near darkness, looking for the old Roy, the big brother I had once counted on to take my side. "Thanks. You mean it?"

"That you ain't changed?"

"No, the welcome part. You really mean it?"

"You're home, ain't you, where you belong?" Roy made a fist and extended his arm to cover the distance between us, giving me a light sock on the shoulder.

"I don't know where I belong any more." I leaned my head against the window frame. I was so tired that speaking was an effort. "You said everybody. Who all's there?"

"Well, let's see." Roy counted off on his fingers. "There's Grace. She's been here since Wednesday."

I relaxed. Grace I was eager to see. A half-sister to Roy and Geneva and me, she'd been a teenager by the time I was born, and I'd considered her almost a second mother, a less busy mother who had time for games and stories. Grace was the person I'd contacted first after Benny's birth, and she'd been the conduit between Mama and me during those first difficult months when I'd been afraid to send letters directly home. "How is Grace? Gosh, it'll be good to see her again."

"Fine and dandy. You know Grace. She's been sticking right to Mama ever since she got here, getting her to eat and rest some between running back and forth to the hospital."

"That's good. Who else?"

"Well, Neva and Tom drove up yesterday with their two young'uns."

Geneva. I stiffened. "I guess she's the same as ever?"

"Put on a few pounds with the two kids, but otherwise the same. You two ain't still feuding, are you?" Roy's tone was gently teasing.

"Not me." Geneva was three years younger than Roy, two years older than me. All my life I'd worn Neva's hand-me-downs, been compared to Neva (her ladylike behavior, her good grades at school), been the brunt of Neva's bossiness. "But if she starts in—"

Roy laughed. "You still threatening to beat her up?"

"No, but if she makes any snooty remarks about Benny—"

Roy turned off the highway onto the dirt road leading to the farm. "Almost there."

"What about Simon?" He was the only one still unaccounted for. Another half-sibling, Simon was a toddler when he and Grace were left motherless by the death of Daddy's first wife. When Daddy married again, Mama had taken Grace and Simon to her bosom, and nobody who didn't know the family history would ever suspect that the two of them weren't just as much her children as the three younger ones born to her.

"He don't know about the stroke yet. He's on a trucking run up into the Carolinas, and we can't get hold of him till he gets back. All we can do is hope nothing don't happen between now and then. Anyway, we'll stop at Mama's so's she can see you made it here safe and sound. Then after you say howdy to everybody, we figured you two could sleep at our house tonight. Mama's got all her beds full already. If that's okay with you."

"The way I feel right now, a bed anywhere would be fine. I'm not particular." My eyes kept closing, and I kept forcing them open again.

"That's what I figured. Actually, it was Julia's idea to get you away from the crowd."

"Gosh, I forgot to ask. How is Julia? Mama wrote she's expecting again."

"Yep, any day now. Between checking on her and Daddy, I been on the run all week. I could use some shut-eye myself right about now, like this 'un." Roy motioned at Benny.

I looked down and readjusted Benny's head against my shoulder. "He hasn't slept much since we left home. And I haven't slept at all. I don't know how much longer I can keep my eyes open."

Roy pulled up in front of the house and turned off the engine. "I'll get you in and out quick as I can. Ready?"

I took a deep breath. "I guess. Ready or not, huh?" I climbed out, hefting Benny over one hip, his head against my neck, his fists rubbing at his eyes. Roy reached for him, but Benny drew back, clinging to me.

"Look who the cat dragged up," Roy called as we started up the porch steps.

The front screen door was pushed open and Grace ran across the porch. "It's Lacey," she yelled behind her. "She's here. Gracious, girl, let me look at you. I can't believe it. And this must be Benny."

I gratefully returned Grace's hug with one arm, Benny squeezed between us like the filling of a sandwich. "Grace! You don't know how good . . ."

Grace held the screen door open for us to enter. "Mama, Lacey's here! For real!"

Mama came out of the kitchen, wiping her sudsy hands on her apron. Taken aback by how gray her hair had become, how tired and lined her face looked, I stopped just inside the door.

"Hey, Mama." I lowered Benny, now semi-awake, onto the floor beside me.

"Lacey. You're here." Mama's voice broke. "I didn't know if I'd live to see the day..."

I held out my arms, and I could feel her body shaking as I

14

hugged her. "It's all right, Mama. I'm here. You said come home, so I did." I held on for a while longer, the knot in my throat growing so big that my vocal cords couldn't squeeze out any more words. *You nearly killed her,* Roy had said in the truck, and a fist of guilt gripped at my chest, squeezing all the air out of me. Finally, I stepped away, took a deep breath, and pushed Benny in front of me. "This is Benny. He fell asleep in the truck on the way here. Benny, this is Grandma that I've been telling you about. Can you say hello?"

Benny turned his head into my skirt and Mama rubbed one hand against his back. "Such a big boy. I know all of this is new to him."

"We're both exhausted," I said. "We were on the bus since early yesterday morning."

"Come on and sit down." Mama put one hand on my arm. "You must both be plumb wore out."

I took the seat on the sofa that Mama led me to, pulling Benny into my lap, and Mama sat beside me. Grace pulled up a chair on my other side and bent forward. "Hello, Benny. We've been waiting a long time to see you, haven't we, Mama?"

"We sure have." Mama laid one hand on Benny's leg, but he drew back and buried his face against my neck. Mama withdrew her hand. "I didn't know if you could get away—with your job and everything. And it's such a long trip. But I thought you'd want to know, even if you couldn't come."

"Mama, of course I'd come. I wanted to come before, but ..." I left the sentence unfinished. "How's Daddy? Roy says he's better."

"Well, look who's here!" Geneva swished into the room from somewhere down the hall. "If it isn't my long-lost little sister in the flesh! Hello, Lacey. How are you?"

I looked up. Roy said Neva had added a few pounds with motherhood, but they agreed with her. In her floral shirtwaist and sandals, her perfectly coifed hairdo, she looked like an advertisement for the Junior Woman's Club brochure. "Hi, Neva." I raked one hand through my own disheveled hair and pulled at my rumpled denim skirt that was bunched up beneath Benny's legs. I tried to move him aside so that I could stand.

"No, don't get up. I see your hands are full." Geneva waved me back down. "We weren't sure you would come. I told Mama not to get her hopes up too high. And this must be—?"

"This is Benjamin."

Geneva bent and peered into Benny's face, half-hidden against my shoulder. "Such dark hair. My goodness, he's got brown eyes. He doesn't look anything like you, does he? He must take after—"

I hugged Benny tighter. "He's worn out right now. We both are."

The screen door banged as Roy stepped inside. "Lacey, you ready to go? I gotta get home and check on Julia."

"Yes, I'm ready." I touched the back of Mama's hand and then slid Benny off my lap. "Mama, I'm really beat. I haven't slept for two days. I'll see you first thing tomorrow."

Chapter 2

Saturday, July 12, 1952

I woke the next morning to sunlight streaming into the east window of the bedroom, and children's voices somewhere outside. Turning onto my side, I closed my eyes against the brightness and let myself drift back toward sleep. I didn't remember much about the ride back to Roy's house or what happened afterward. I remembered Julia, hugely pregnant, greeting me at the door, and then the softness of the bed, the relief of lying down, Benny curled beside me. I reached behind me to check on Benny, to see if he was still asleep.

My fingers found only a wrinkled sheet. Instantly alert, I turned onto my back and searched the room with my eyes, feeling a moment of irrational panic. Where was Benny? He wasn't used to being away from me, certainly not in a strange place among people he didn't know. I bolted to my feet, surprised to find myself still in the clothes I'd been wearing the past two days. Apparently we'd both fallen into bed last night without changing into nightclothes or brushing our teeth.

In the kitchen, signs of breakfast were still on the table, but no one was around. The children's voices sounded closer now, just outside. I crossed the room, my whole body going limp with relief as I spied Benny through the back screen door, no more than ten feet away, standing beneath a small scrub oak. Beside him, another boy about the same size was kneeling in the grass, his arms around a large black and tan German shepherd. As I pushed the latch, a tall, slender girl in a pink-flowered sundress reached for Benny's hand. Katie? She'd been a dimpled, round-faced toddler when I left home, and now she had transformed into a willowy eight-year-old, her straight honey-colored hair falling halfway down her back. The boy stood and said something to Benny. This was my first glimpse of Roy, Jr., but I'd have known him anywhere. He was a miniature version of Roy—the same square build, the same coarse rust-colored hair with a cowlick that wouldn't lie down, the same ruddy chipmunk cheeks. Benny took a step backward, resisting whatever Katie and Roy, Jr. had in mind.

I pushed open the screen door and stepped outside. "Hey, Benbo. How long have you been up?"

Benny ran to me. "I went to look for the bathroom, and the lady said to be quiet and let you sleep. Then she told them other kids to take me outside and show me their dog. His name is Champ."

"Is that so?" I caught Benny up in a hug. "*Those* other kids are your cousins. Remember Uncle Roy from last night? Mommy's big brother? Those are Uncle Roy's children. We're at his house now."

"Morning, Lacey!" Julia came around the corner of the chicken house with a basket of freshly gathered eggs. "I hope the children didn't wake you. I tried to keep them quiet."

"No, I didn't hear a thing." I reached for Benny's hand and followed Julia inside. "You need a bath," I told him. "And so do I."

"How about some scrambled eggs first?" Julia set the basket on the counter. "Benny wouldn't eat earlier. Maybe he'll eat something with you."

"That sounds great, but not until I get cleaned up and into some fresh clothes." With one hand I attempted to stick my blouse back into my skirt, which was a mass of wrinkles, while running my other hand through my limp, oily hair, resisting the urge to scratch at my scalp. "I must look a mess."

Julia laughed sympathetically. "You were both asleep on your feet when you got here last night. Benny can go back outside with Katie and Roy, Jr. while you get a bath, and then you can have breakfast together. I'll go ahead and scramble some more eggs. There's grits on the stove and biscuits keeping warm in the oven."

"Oh, no, don't go to any trouble for me. I can scramble my own eggs once I'm decent. You look like you need to sit down and take it easy. Roy says you're due any day now."

"Overdue." Julia put one hand on her stomach and sank into a kitchen chair. "This one's as stubborn as the rest of the McCormicks. He's taking his own sweet time."

"He?"

"It's gotta be a boy. A girl wouldn't kick this much."

❋   ❋   ❋

When I returned to the kitchen, I found Julia at the stove and breakfast waiting for us on the table. "Yum, that smells delicious. But you didn't have to do that. I don't want to cause you any extra work."

"It's no trouble. Why don't you and Benny eat while it's hot, and then he can have his bath?"

"Okay, but you have to let me do the dishes." Through the back screen door, I could see that Katie and Roy, Jr. had somehow coaxed Benny into petting the big dog that he had seemed afraid of earlier. He was stroking its back gently as Roy, Jr. held it around the neck. Katie, on Benny's other side, had one arm draped protectively over his shoulder. Maybe this visit wouldn't be as difficult as I'd envisioned. Benny would show everybody— we'd both show everybody—what a great kid he was.

Julia sat opposite us as we ate. "Benny's so tall. He's like Katie—all arms and legs."

"I know." I couldn't keep the pride I felt from showing in my voice. "He's growing so fast. I can't believe he'll be starting school in the fall." I cleaned my plate and then polished off the rest of Benny's as well. "Um-m, this is good. I haven't eaten like this in years."

❊   ❊   ❊

By eleven o'clock, I was squeezed into the cab of Roy's pickup along with Roy and Julia, Benny on my lap and Julia balancing a macaroni and cheese casserole over her rounded stomach. Katie and Roy, Jr. were behind us in the open truck bed. "Hospital visiting hours start at one," Roy announced. "I guess you'll want to go, seeing as that's why you came back."

"Yes, of course." I wiped one hand across my forehead, clammy suddenly with perspiration. "We can't all go in at once, though, can we?"

"Only two at a time, and then only for a few minutes. You get first dibs, I guess. The rest of us saw him yesterday."

I clasped my hands tightly together around Benny to keep them from shaking as Roy pulled up beside the house and parked next to a fancy new wood-paneled station wagon. Just what I'd expect Neva and Tom to be driving. I hadn't noticed it last night, but then it had been dark, and I hardly remembered anything of what had happened while we were at Mama's.

Stepping down from the truck, I took a moment to look around at the familiar panorama of house and outbuildings. In the daylight, I could see that the house, too, had aged in the nearly seven years I'd been gone. Its unpainted wood siding seemed more faded, and one front section of its tin roof was loose at the seam, a corner bent up as if ready to take flight in the next stiff wind. Off to the left, beside the corncrib, Daddy's same old Allis Chalmers tractor was parked in its usual spot, and beyond the crib was the grove of pecan trees, with Mama's chicken house and its surrounding fenced enclosure built beneath in their shade.

"Not much looks different," I said to Roy.

"Least they got indoor plumbing now." Roy grinned. "I closed in part of the back porch for a bathroom."

"Mama wrote me about that. I bet she did somersaults."

"Almost. 'Course Daddy didn't think they needed it."

Catching Benny's hand, I followed Roy and Julia up the steps.

The three rocking chairs and hanging porch swing hadn't shifted position since I left, but a white metal glider at the other end of the porch was new, its bright sheen a stark contrast to the dark, time-worn rockers. A man who'd been sitting in the swing stood and came toward us.

"Lacey, you remember Tom, don't you? Neva's husband?" Roy asked.

"Of course. Hello." The last time I'd seen Tom Baker I'd been a sophomore in high school. That had been before he left for the army and before he and Geneva started corresponding. By the time he returned home from the Pacific, I had already fled to New York. The man standing in front of me looked so different from the quiet, lanky boy I remembered from high school that I hardly recognized him.

"Hello, Lacey." He stuck out his right hand. "It's been a long time." His voice was different, too, from what I remembered, deeper and more self-confident, and I blushed as I returned his handshake. Since Dwayne, I'd been wary of men, especially handsome ones, and I looked off to one side, avoiding direct eye contact.

As we exchanged greetings, two children burst out the front door and ran to greet Katie and Roy, Jr., but then they all disappeared around the corner of the house before I got a good look at them. Benny turned his head to watch them but didn't let go of my hand as I followed Julia inside, leaving Roy on the front porch with Tom.

In the kitchen, Grace was tending something in a huge enamel pot on the stove, stirring with one hand and lifting her apron with the other to wipe off the sweat beading on her forehead. As soon as she saw me, she put down her spoon and came toward me with both hands outstretched, calling over her shoulder. "Here's Lacey back, Mama. And Julia. My gracious, girl, you look ready to pop. You brought food?"

Julia handed Grace the dish of macaroni and cheese. "I didn't want to come empty-handed, not with my brood."

Grace shooed Julia toward the living room. "Honey, you go sit down right now, out of this heat." She called again out the back door. "Mama, Lacey's back."

Mama came in through the back porch, a dishtowel thrown over her shoulder, three freshly picked tomatoes in her hands. She stopped and searched my face as if seeing me for the first time. "You're really here. I thought maybe I was dreaming last night."

I took the tomatoes from Mama and laid them on the counter. "Yes, Mama, I'm really here. Don't go getting all weepy on me now."

Mama put her arms around me. "I didn't know if I'd ever see you again."

"Now, Mama. It's okay." I patted her back. "I'm here now."

When we finally separated and she stepped back to examine me, a frown crinkled her forehead. "You look pale. Have you been taking care of yourself?"

"I'm fine, Mama. I live in the city, remember? No Florida sun up there."

"And you cut off all your beautiful red hair."

"Not all." I put one hand up to my new pixie haircut, done last week by my friend Rita as we sat talking in her kitchen. "It's the new style. Besides, it'll grow back."

Mama bent forward to get a closer look at Benny. "Well, let me see this big boy of yours."

Benny buried his face against my skirt, and I was trying to untangle him when Geneva stuck her head in the door. "Well, hello again, long-lost sister." She started toward me but stopped just short of giving me a hug, her hand reaching instead toward the back of Benny's head. "And who do we have here? Looks like the cat's got his tongue. Is he always this bashful?"

"Everything's strange to him right now. He needs a while to adjust."

"Poor little thing," Geneva clucked maternally. "Torn away from home like that and plopped down smack dab in the middle of a bunch of strangers. No wonder he feels confused." Her worried show of sympathy brightened into a smile. "Anyway,

Lacey, we're all so thrilled you're here. That's all Mama talked about yesterday. 'Do you think Lacey will really come?' Of course, we wish the circumstances could be better. Poor Daddy. He looks so helpless in that hospital bed. Mama has been beside herself with worry. Haven't you, Mama?"

"Well, I have to admit—"

"I told everybody months ago," Geneva continued, not giving Mama time to finish her sentence, "last time we were up for a visit, that his color didn't look good, that he looked like he had lost weight. Didn't I tell you that, Mama? But of course you wouldn't know about that, Lacey, being way up there in New York and out of touch with the family for all this time."

I opened my mouth for a retort but then thought better of it. No need to get into an argument with Neva right now, certainly not with Benny right here. I turned to Grace, still busy at the stove. "Anything I can do to help?"

❅   ❅   ❅

When dinner was ready, the children lined up first. Roy and Tom had made a special table for them on the back porch by placing a six-foot length of wide board between two concrete blocks.

I took a fried chicken drumstick, some macaroni and cheese, and a piece of white bread for Benny. Everything else on the table—the fried okra, the stewed summer squash, the fresh butter beans flavored with salt pork, even the squares of cornbread—would be unfamiliar to him. When I took his plate and glass of milk out to the porch, Katie scooted over and patted the place beside her. "Benny can sit by me."

The boy who put his plate down beside Roy, Jr.'s and plopped onto the floor opposite Benny had to be Tommy, Geneva's oldest. He would be five now, going on six, about eight months younger than Benny. Tom had come home from the war sometime in early 1946 and he and Geneva had gotten married almost immediately afterward. I had re-established contact with Mama by letter from New York in early May, a week or so after Benny's birth, and by late summer she was writing that Geneva was pregnant and expecting a Christmas baby. Roy, Jr. was born that same year, too, only a week or so after Benny, so all three boy cousins were near the same age, all scheduled to be starting school this fall.

With Benny settled beside Katie, I was able to get my first good look at Tommy. Shorter than Benny, he was more like Roy, Jr. with his stockier build and bright blue eyes. He kept up a running stream of chatter to Roy, Jr., beside him, accompanying his words with enthusiastic hand gestures. Geneva brought out a plate for Sarah and put it down on the other side of Katie, her crinolines swishing past me as she headed back to the kitchen. Sarah must be about three now, maybe four, at that stage of morphing from cute toddler to self-aware little girl. Her strawberry-blonde hair framed her face in an angelic halo of soft curls, but her light, creamy complexion would almost certainly mean freckles in a few years—the curse of the McCormicks.

Tommy turned his attention from Roy, Jr. to Benny. "Who are you?" he asked. "What's your name?"

Before I could react, Katie answered for him. "This is Benny. He's our cousin and he lives in New York City."

"Lacey, come on," Grace called from the dining room. "We're ready to eat."

"Coming." I gave Benny a touch on the shoulder. "I'll be right inside, okay?"

"For gosh sakes." Geneva's voice dripped with disapproval. "What do you do in New York when you go to work? You do have a job, don't you?"

I slid into the remaining vacant chair and waited for Roy to say grace before answering. "I work for my landlady. She runs a children's nursery in the basement of the apartment building. I keep books for her and help with the kids. So Benny's there all day, and I don't have to leave him. When he starts school in September, I plan to get back into full-time office work."

"I think it's important for mothers to be home with their children when they're young," Geneva pronounced as the platter of fried chicken made its way around the table. "Those first years are so crucial. But children have to learn independence, too, to be prepared for school, you know. That's why I enrolled Tommy in a private kindergarten last fall. He went three hours every morning, from nine to twelve. He knows his alphabet and numbers already and can write his name. I was afraid, with him being the youngest in his class, that he might have trouble keeping up, but his teacher said not to worry. He's one of the brightest she's ever taught, and he shows real leadership qualities, too." She beamed and glanced sideways at Tom for confirmation, but Tom was busy buttering a biscuit.

I sipped my sweet iced tea. "Benny's with other kids every day, all day. The older ones learn their alphabet and numbers. Benny's reading already."

"Is that so?" Geneva raised her eyebrows in surprise. "Well, you want to be careful you don't push him too far too soon. Children pushed too fast lose their natural curiosity and their love for learning."

"Oh, I don't push—"

"So, Lacey, tell us more about New York," Grace interrupted. "What's it like living in the big city?"

I turned my attention to Grace, ignoring Neva for the rest of the meal. So she wanted to carry the sibling rivalry into the next generation, did she? Well, that was fine by me. I'd put Benny up against her kids any day.

Ruth Rodgers

Chapter 3

After dinner, Grace shooed Mama and Julia off to cooler spots while she, Geneva, and I cleared the table and washed the dishes. Roy and Tom headed to the barn in search of a tire and a rope for a promised swing on the front yard oak, and all the kids, except for Benny, trooped out after them. Benny hung around the kitchen, not wanting to be too far away from me.

"Go on out with him, Lacey," Grace urged. "We can finish up in here."

"In a minute. I don't want to leave you with all the work."

By the time I dried the last pot and walked onto the porch with Benny, the men were heading back to the house, Sarah astride Tom's shoulders. Behind them Katie was lugging a length of stout rope, and Roy, Jr. and Tommy were rolling an old truck tire between them.

As Roy tied the rope around a brick from the flower bed and threw it over the biggest branch of the oak, Benny edged down the steps and over to where the other children were gathered, and I sat on the porch glider beside Julia, who was cooling herself with a cardboard fan.

"Ought to be visiting hours by now," Roy said as Grace and Geneva joined the rest of us on the porch, Grace in the rocker next to Mama's and Geneva in the swing. "Me and Julia will stay here with all the young'uns while the rest of you go."

"I'll stay with you and keep an eye on our two," Tom said. "I'll leave the visiting to Neva."

"Are all the menfolk staying?" Mama asked. "Who's going to drive?"

"I will," Geneva walked down the steps and held out one hand, palm up, in Tom's direction. "We can take our wagon."

Tom tossed her the car keys and then pulled out his wallet. "Bring us back some cold Co-Cola's, too. Enough for everybody." He handed Geneva a five-dollar bill.

"I don't think I should leave Benny," I whispered to Julia beside me on the glider. "This is all new to him. I can wait and go later."

"He'll be okay," Julia whispered back. "He did fine at our house this morning."

Roy, Jr. and Tommy were already clamoring for the first turn on the swing. The thought of leaving Benny alone in unfamiliar surroundings with people he'd just met while I rode into town ten miles away was making me feel queasy. Or was it the thought of seeing Daddy again that was churning my stomach so? Nevertheless, I had no choice but to go. I'd come all this way to set things right between Daddy and me, and I couldn't back out now.

I walked down the steps and led Benny away from the other children. "Honey, remember what I told you on the bus about my daddy being sick? Some of us are going to the hospital to visit him, just for a little while. Can you stay here and play with the other kids on the swing while Mommy's gone? Uncle Roy and Aunt Julia will look out for you."

As Benny looked around at the crowd of strangers in the yard and on the porch, his chin trembled and he reached for my skirt. I turned toward Roy. "I'll wait and go tomorrow, when there aren't so many others. When Benny's had more time to adjust."

"Benny'll be fine." Roy's frown was disapproving. "You came all this way. You're not weaseling out now, are you?"

"Come on, everybody who's going." Neva jangled the keys in her hand. "Mama, you sit up front with me."

"Come on, Lacey," Grace called. "We won't be gone long. He'll hardly have time to miss you."

I looked at Grace, then back at Benny, torn with indecision.

"Hey, Benny, guess what? You're first in line for the swing." Roy grabbed Benny up and stuck his legs through the tire. "I'll show you what to do."

Benny began to whimper, and I turned back toward him.

"Go on, Sis." Roy's voice was stern. "Benny and me are gonna test out this contraption."

I gave Benny a kiss on the forehead. "Be good now. Mommy will be right back." I followed Grace to the car, but as I got into the back seat, I turned my face toward the window so that no one could see my wet eyes.

Geneva led the way into the hospital and swished up to the Visitors check-in desk for the two allotted passes. She handed one to Mama and waved the other one in the air. "Who wants to go first with Mama? Lacey? You're the only one who hasn't seen him yet."

My knees suddenly weak, I reached for something to hold on to. "I'll wait. You go ahead."

"We'll tell him you're here, then," Geneva said brightly, "to prepare him, you know. Too big a surprise might be bad for his heart. Come on, Mama."

I sat beside Grace on one of the two sofas in the small lobby and picked up a well-thumbed issue of an old *Collier's* magazine. "All the way down on the bus, I kept rehearsing what I'd say to him," I told Grace. "But now. . ."

"Don't worry. I'll go with you." Grace patted my hand. "You don't need to say much of anything right now. He's barely conscious. We don't know how much he understands."

I was still holding the unopened magazine when Geneva and Mama returned. "He's looking better," Geneva reported. "He tried to say something to Mama, but we couldn't understand him."

"I told him you were here," Mama said to me. "I know he'll be tickled pick you came all this way to see him."

I didn't share Mama's optimism as I followed Grace down the

hall to the half-open doorway of Daddy's room. Grace went right up to the bed, but I stopped several feet away, brought up short by the sight of this almost stranger's pale, crease-mapped face, eyes closed, one side of his mouth drooping like a loose string on a marionette.

Grace touched him on the shoulder. "Daddy? You awake?"

Daddy opened his eyes.

"I brought someone to see you." Grace motioned for me to come closer. "Look who's here."

"Hello, Daddy." I could barely manage a whisper.

Daddy's eyes turned toward me, but his expression didn't show any recognition.

"It's Lacey come all the way from New York City to see you," Grace said.

The furrow in Daddy's brow seemed to deepen as his eyes focused on me. I couldn't tell what he was thinking or if he even knew who I was. I took another step closer. "Mama asked me to come. She sent me a telegram."

Daddy's eyes blinked a few times and then remained closed, but I kept talking, determined to say what I came to say. "Benny came with me. He's not here at the hospital, but he's back at the house. Roy and Julia are watching him. He's a great kid. I want you to meet him when you're better."

Daddy's eyes fluttered open for a second and then closed again.

"We're doing fine up in New York, Benny and me. I wanted you to know that."

"We're all here, Daddy," Grace said. "All except Simon. And he'll be here soon as he gets back from his trucking run. You don't have to worry about a thing. We've got things covered." She touched the back of his hand, but Daddy's eyes remained closed.

"He needs his rest," Grace whispered to me. "We'd better go."

I stepped up to the bed railing. Over the past two days I'd steeled myself for this meeting, planning how I'd demand his apology for all those horrible names he had called me and make him acknowledge his grandson, who was every bit as much of a McCormick as the other grandchildren, but now I felt only a deep emptiness, a reluctant tug of sympathy for the frail old man that he had become in my absence. "You take care, Daddy," I said. "I'll see you later."

"Daddy was happy to see you, wasn't he?" Mama asked when we returned to the lobby. "Could you tell?"

"He looked so old. And so tired." I really hadn't been able to read anything on Daddy's face except for age and illness. Had he closed his eyes to deliberately shut me out or was keeping them open simply too much effort? I didn't know. All I knew was that I didn't want him to die without meeting Benny.

※　※　※

Half an hour later, as we pulled up beside the house, I anxiously scanned the front yard. Roy, Jr. was pushing Tommy in circles on the tire. Roy and Julia were on the glider, and Tom was stretched out in the porch swing. Benny was nowhere in sight.

"Where's Benny?" I directed the question to Roy.

"Inside somewhere with Katie." Roy gestured with his thumb. "He fell off the tire a little while ago and scratched his knee on a root. He's okay. Katie's off mothering him."

"He's hurt?" Some watcher Roy had turned out to be. I imagined tears, blood, an angry red gash across his kneecap. "I'd better check on him."

"He's fine, I told you."

"We got Co-Colas for the grownups and grape and orange Nehis for the kids," Geneva announced, handing the car keys to Tom. "They're in the back of the wagon. Where's Sarah?"

"Inside. She fell asleep a little while ago." Tom stood to get the drinks from the car.

"How's Daddy?" Roy asked. "Any change?"

As Neva began to give the latest details, I slipped inside to look for Benny. He and Katie were on the back porch, Benny sitting on the pine board that had served as their lunch table and Katie standing in front of him, holding out two closed fists for Benny to guess which one was hiding something.

"Hey, Benbo, I'm back."

At the sound of my voice, Benny looked up, his face crumpling into a sob. I rushed over and caught him up in a hug. "I told you I'd be back soon, didn't I?"

"He scratched his knee," Katie said, "but Mama washed it. Then I took care of him."

"Thanks, Katie. That was sweet of you." I examined Benny's knee. A thin red scratch had barely broken the skin. "What happened?" I asked him. "Did you fall? Did one of the other kids push you?"

"He stumbled getting out of the swing," Katie said.

Benny sniffled and wiped one hand across his nose, and I gathered him up in a hug. "You run on, Katie. There are cold sodas around front for everybody. Benny and I will be out in a minute." I held tight to Benny, choking back tears, needing the warmth of his small body right now as much as he needed me. "I'm sorry, Benbo, for going off like that and leaving you, but the hospital lets only grownups visit. I'm here now." I straightened and reached for his hand. "Aunt Neva bought cold sodas for everyone. You want a cold soda pop? That'll make you feel better."

On the porch, I popped open a Coca-Cola for myself and an orange Nehi for Benny before taking the last vacant rocker. Roy and Julia were in the glider, and Neva had joined Tom in the swing, where she was leaning into him and whispering something in his ear. I moved my chair closer to Mama's and took long, cool sips of my soda as the various conversations swirled around me, letting myself meld again into the sound of familiar voices, the swish of cardboard fans, the creak of the swing's chains, the rocker rungs clicking a rhythmic pattern against the wooden floor. Katie had taken a seat on the brick steps beside Tommy and Roy, Jr., but Benny remained close to my side as if to make sure I wouldn't disappear on him again.

Roy downed the last swig of his soda and walked down the steps. "Now who's ready for another push in this McCormick special?" He caught the tire and started it swinging in a wide circle.

Roy, Jr. and Tommy jumped up and waved their hands in the air. "Me. Me." Benny followed the arc of the tire with his eyes but didn't move from his position beside me. He still had some orange soda in the bottom of his bottle.

"Whoa, one at a time. Who's finished with their drink? Ladies first. Come on, Katie."

Katie climbed into the tire and wrapped her arms around the sides. Roy pulled it back and let go. Benny drained the last of his Nehi.

"You're next, Benny." Roy gave Katie another push.

"He's a crybaby," Roy, Jr. said. "He don't want to swing. I want the next turn."

I stiffened and looked at Roy. His lips were straight, but his eyes seemed to me to glint with amusement. I glared at him, waiting for him to demand that his son apologize.

"Crybaby," Tommy echoed. "He's scared of a swing."

I looked toward Neva, but she was saying something to Grace about new floral wallpaper in Sarah's bedroom. I gripped the arms of my chair, ready to jump up and intervene, but Benny set his empty bottle on the floor and propped both hands on his hips in an attitude of confrontation. "Am not."

"Are so," Roy, Jr. said.

"Scaredy cat," Tommy taunted.

"Am not." Benny walked down the steps and over to Roy.

"Atta boy, Benny. You show 'em." Roy grinned at me. "We'll make a McCormick out of him yet." After stopping the swing for Katie to get off, he lifted Benny into the tire and made sure he had a tight grip around it. "Ready?"

Benny nodded, and Roy gave him a gentle push. I held my breath.

"Harder?"

Benny nodded again, and Roy gave him a slightly harder push. Neva was still talking to Grace about wallpaper, and Tom had leaned back in the swing and closed his eyes.

When Roy finally stopped the tire, Benny slid off by himself and took a seat on the step beside Tommy, their knees touching, while Roy, Jr. took a turn.

"See, Sis." Roy gave me a broad smile. "You got nothing to worry about."

After a few more minutes of swinging, Roy announced that he had to go feed his hogs and check on his cows in the pasture. "Anybody want to ride along?"

Roy, Jr. and Tommy jumped up immediately and ran for the truck, with Roy, Jr. self-importantly announcing that it was his job to open and close the gates as the truck passed through each one.

"Hey, Benny," Roy asked. "You want to come help us?"

Benny looked at me, but I shook my head. I had no idea how Benny would react around farm animals, since he had never been around any. "He'd better stay with me."

"He's welcome to come," Roy said. "I'll watch out for him."

"No thanks."

Roy shrugged. "Suit yourself. Hop in, Katie Did, or you're gonna get left."

"I'll stay with Benny." Katie moved down a step to sit beside him.

Tom stood and stretched. "I guess I'll ride along with you and leave the women here to gossip."

As the men drove off, Geneva jumped up to collect the empty bottles and put them back in the crate. "Tommy's taking swimming lessons this summer," she announced to the group at large "You should see him, Mama. He swims like a fish."

"That's good," Mama answered. "That's one thing I never learned how to do."

"We're thinking of buying a membership in the country club. That way we can use the pool any time we want."

I tried to think of some recent accomplishment of Benny's to add to the conversation, but I couldn't think of a thing. I didn't have the money or the time to enroll Benny in swimming or any other classes. Then I remembered the drawing he had done on the bus coming down, a crayon self-portrait he'd made at my urging as a gift for Grandma.

Slipping quietly into the living room, I took the folded paper out of my purse. The drawing did look like him—spirals of curly black hair, dark, round eyes, and a thin red mouth curved into a wide smile. The ears were too big, and the arms were longer than the legs, but all in all he had done a good job. Beneath the picture he had printed his full first name, Benjamin, with a bright green crayon.

Of course, the drawing couldn't compare to the recent studio portrait of Neva's family I'd noticed earlier on the mantel. I walked over to examine it more closely. A fake backdrop of a fireplace and Christmas stockings—Neva and Sarah in matching red sweaters, Tom and Tommy in navy blue blazers. They were all beaming for the camera, Sarah sitting on Tom's lap, Neva standing behind Tommy, her hands on his shoulders. I could hear Neva still talking outside as I examined the other photos on the mantel—a hinged double frame holding school portraits of Grace's two girls—the oldest, Sharon, in high school now and Rebecca not that far behind—and a smaller frame holding last year's school picture of Katie. Second grade, she would have been—going into third. Beside Katie's photo was a recent snapshot of Roy, Jr. in his back yard, standing with one hand reaching down to stroke the head of their big dog—the same dog the kids had been playing with this morning. There was no picture of Benny anywhere in sight.

Anger rose in me, jangling like the lid of a boiling teakettle. The lack of a photo wasn't due to Mama not having one to display. I'd sent her a snapshot of Benny every year, from his first birthday up to his sixth. Each April we'd walk five blocks to the nearest Woolworth's and snap strips of photos in the booth—snapshots of Benny, of me, of the two of us together. And where were they now? What had Mama done with them? Why wasn't Benny on display with the other grandchildren? I didn't have to ask why. I knew. Mama might pretend that Daddy would be overjoyed to see me again, but I knew that nothing had changed. And nothing ever would.

By the time I returned to the porch Neva had moved on to talking about signing Sarah up for dance classes in the fall when Tommy started school. "She'll be a natural," Geneva was saying. "She's so limber, and she loves music. You should see her dancing around the house whenever I play the Victrola."

I waited for a break in the conversation. "Benny made something for you, Mama, on the bus coming down."

Mama turned her attention from Geneva to me. "He did? What is it? Let's see."

"Benny," I called, "come and give Grandma the picture you drew on the bus. We'll see if she knows who it is."

Mama took the paper Benny held out to her, unfolded it, and spread it on her lap. "My. My. Now who could this be?"

"It's me." Benny spun away from the rocker, eager to join Katie again on the steps.

"Whoa. Wait a minute." Mama reached for his arm. "What a great job you did. I'll declare, it looks just like you. Let me give you a thank-you hug."

Benny stood stiffly, enduring the hug, before dashing back to the steps.

Mama passed the picture to Julia in the glider. "We're going to have an artist in the family. Lacey was always good at drawing, too, I remember."

"Writing his name, too," Julia exclaimed. "Look how good he made all his letters, and he hasn't even started school."

Geneva stood and flounced past me. "I'd better check on Sarah. If she sleeps any longer, she'll be up all night."

Once Geneva was inside, Mama laid her hand on mine. "Such a smart boy. I can't tell you how good it is to have you home again. All that worry..., but you're here now, and that's what matters. All grown up, with a beautiful child, and a job and a life of your own."

"I'm sorry I made you worry, Mama. I didn't mean to, but I didn't know what Daddy would do. It took me the longest time to get up the courage, even, to write to Grace."

"And you don't know what a relief it was for me to get that

first letter." Mama squeezed my hand. "It was a Sunday, and Grace and Pete and the girls drove over from Tallahassee like they always did, but that day I could tell something was up the minute they got here. Grace was grinning like a Cheshire cat."

Grace laughed heartily. "We'd planned it all out in the car on the way over. Pete would get Daddy off first thing to look at the tobacco crop so I could slip Mama the letter."

"No sooner had they got out of the car good but Pete was dragging your daddy off to the field," Mama continued. "Then Grace pulled out your letter and I nearbout had a heart attack. I was flustered the rest of the day. I couldn't keep my mind on anything but you—a healthy baby boy and a job in New York City!"

"Did you tell Daddy?"

"Not right off. But I did tell him a day or two later, when I couldn't keep it to myself no longer. I felt like I'd bust if I didn't tell somebody."

"What did he say?"

"Oh, he didn't say a word. Acted like he hadn't even heard me. But I could tell he was glad to know you were all right, and glad too that you hadn't throwed the money away on that sailor. That was what bothered him the most when he first discovered the money missing."

"He still hasn't forgiven me, has he?"

"He ain't ever got over what happened, if that's what you mean. Maybe now that you're home, the two of you, face to face... Well, here's my little angel." Mama held out her arms as Sarah ran onto the porch, her face splotchy from the heat. "Come here, precious, and give Grandma some sugar."

Sarah climbed into Mama's lap, and I fell silent. Benny's drawing, which Julia had handed back to Mama, fluttered unnoticed to the floor.

❋ ❋ ❋

After the men returned and we'd all had supper and cleaned up the kitchen once again, Julia sank into a living room chair, one hand on her stomach.

"You been quiet all day," Roy said. "You tired? Ready to go home?"

Julia nodded, her lips set in a tight line.

Roy looked at me. "Sis, you staying with us again?"

"Sure, I guess. Anywhere is fine with me."

"We can make room for you here," Mama said. "I don't want to put Julia to no trouble."

"Um, I think Lacey better go with us." Julia blew out a deep, cleansing breath. "Looks like I'll be making a trip to the hospital tonight."

Chapter 4

Sunday, July 13, 1952

I woke early the next morning to a light tapping coming from somewhere outside, like someone knocking on a door or wall. As I opened my eyes and listened, trying to pinpoint the source of the noise, the tapping stopped. A quick check of the other side of the bed told me that Benny was still beside me, still sound asleep. Out the window, a faint gray light showed through the sheer curtains, but there was no sign of the sun. It couldn't be morning already. After Roy dropped the children and me off last night before speeding Julia on to the hospital, I had no sooner gotten Roy, Jr. and Benny into the bathtub and then into their pajamas than I had collapsed onto the bed myself, leaving Katie stretched out on the living room sofa. Then, sometime during the night, I'd been wakened by voices in the living room and had groggily felt my way in darkness down the hall.

"It's a boy," Roy was whispering to Katie. "Eight pounds, four ounces. Born right after midnight, a Sunday baby."

I could see Roy's outline from the moonlight shining through the window. "How's Julia?"

"Lacey? Sorry, I didn't mean to wake you. She's fine. Tired, but fine. Everything happened real fast. It's a boy."

"I heard. What are you going to name him?"

"Isaac David, for both his grandpas. Zach for short. That was Katie Did's idea." Roy had tweaked Katie's hair, and she had giggled and flopped over onto her stomach.

"Zach. I like that," I'd said. "I can't wait to see him."

"He's a McCormick, all right. Got red hair and a temper. I could hear him way down the hall."

Katie had burrowed her face in her pillow and I'd put one hand over my mouth to stifle a yawn.

"I'll let you two get back to sleep. Sorry to wake you. I just figured Katie Diddle Dumpling would want to know."

Katie, already asleep again, hadn't responded, and I had fallen back to sleep within a few minutes of returning to bed.

I closed my eyes and turned onto my side. The tapping came again. A woodpecker? I heard a faint creak—like a door being slowly pushed open. One of the children going outside this early? I swung out of bed and pulled on my robe. Katie was still sleeping soundly on the sofa. Maybe Roy, Jr.? I walked into the kitchen. A man was standing on the back porch, his hand on the knob of the half-open door. I jumped back and put one hand to my pounding chest.

"Oops, sorry," the man whispered. "Didn't mean to scare you." He pushed the door open wider. "Hey, Lacey. Roy said you were coming home."

I lowered my hand. "Neil?"

"Yep. How long's it been?" He took off his cap and grinned at me.

"Gosh, I don't know. You look different." With his cap off, I could see that his sandy hair was thinning on top already, making him appear older than I knew him to be.

"You can say it." He stepped inside and ran one hand through his hair. "Getting to be an old man already."

"No, you look great." The thinning hair brought out some maternal instinct in me. He was heavier, though, more muscular than I remembered.

"You, too. You were just a little squirt last time I saw you."

"It hasn't been *that* long."

"Want to bet? I joined the Army in January of '42, right after Pearl Harbor. You were what, about twelve? Thirteen? When I got back from overseas, you were gone."

"In 1942 I was fifteen, for your information. Turned fifteen that May, anyway."

"Couldn't have proved it by me," Neil said. "A skinny little beanpole."

I pulled my robe tighter and crossed my arms, aware of his eyes studying me as if trying to determine if my figure had improved any since then.

"Sorry I woke you. I came to see if Roy needed any help over on his daddy's place. Feeding the stock and everything. How is Mr. McCormick? Any better?"

"About the same, I guess. I saw him yesterday for just a minute. Mama said he seemed better to her. Roy's sleeping."

"Sleeping? This time of day?"

"Julia had her baby last night, this morning rather. Roy didn't get back from the hospital till a little while ago."

"Boy or girl?"

"Boy. Eight pounds. They're calling him Zach."

"Another boy, huh? I know Roy's excited. You got a boy too, so I hear."

"Yes, Benny. He's six now. What about you?"

"Nope." Neil held out his hands. "Nobody's roped me yet."

"Why not?"

"You sound like Julia. Where's the law that says everybody's gotta get married? Anyway, by the time I got back from the war, all the good ones were taken. Nobody left but silly little high school girls. You weren't even around for me to pick on. But, hey, let me get moving so you can go back to bed." Neil was still standing by the back door, and he put one hand on the screen latch.

"Oh, no, you didn't wake me. I was about to start some coffee. Stay and have a cup."

"Thanks, but I'll mosey on over to your mama's and see what needs doing."

I crossed the room to the sink. "It's Sunday, and there's a crowd of people there. Come on, stay for coffee at least. If I can figure out where Julia keeps everything."

Neil picked up the coffee pot and started filling it with water. "The coffee's in that canister right over there."

I handed it to him. "You seem to know your way around in here pretty well."

"I've shared a few cups of coffee with Roy in this kitchen. His always seems to taste better than what I make at home."

"You live by yourself then?"

"Yep, I guess you could say so. I got a trailer parked across the road from my folks. Gives me and them a little breathing room. I still stick my feet under Mama's table for most of my meals, though. I'm not much of a cook. Can't even make a good pot of coffee."

I laughed. "Not much you can do to coffee, one way or the other."

"It would seem so, wouldn't it?" Neil measured out the coffee, then set the pot on the stove and turned on the burner. "I never have been able to figure out why Julia's tastes so much better. We both use the same brand. Maybe it's the atmosphere."

"Maybe it's just your imagination."

"Could be. We'll see how this turns out."

"That means you're staying, then?"

Neil laughed. "Yeah, I guess so." He pulled out a kitchen chair, straddled it backwards, and propped his arms on its back. "So tell me what you've been up to for the last ten years."

"Okay," I answered, "but first, if you'll excuse me a minute, I'll go make myself decent." I hurried to the bathroom where I splashed cold water on my face and ran a brush through my hair. Compared to everybody down here, my skin looked pale and pasty—a city complexion. I rubbed my palms briskly against my cheeks to add some color and then ran my tongue over my lips to moisten them. When I went to the bedroom for some clothes, Benny stirred and turned over, but didn't wake up. I quickly changed into a light summer dress and slipped on my sandals before heading back to the kitchen.

"Um-m, the coffee smells good," I called from the doorway.

"Do I look any more—" I stopped in mid-sentence. Katie was sitting at the table across from Neil.

"Any more what?" Neil asked.

"Never mind." I could feel myself blushing, the heat rising to my face. "Coffee ready?"

"Almost. Katie's been telling me about the baby."

I began to open cabinets. "I guess you know where Julia keeps her cups, too."

Neil stood, reached over my shoulder, and took down two cups. "None for you, Miss Katie Diddle. Don't want to stunt your growth."

Katie giggled. "I'll gather the eggs." She picked up a basket by the back door and headed outside.

Neil poured the coffee and waited for me to take a sip. "What's the verdict?"

"Perfect." It was strong and black, just what I needed to wake myself up.

"You're not just saying that to boost my ego, are you?"

"No, it's really good." I took another sip. "Maybe it is the atmosphere. Mine never tastes this good at home, either."

"You live alone, too? With your boy, I mean? You never married again?"

Surprised at his use of the word "again," I didn't know how to answer. Had Mama and Daddy told everyone I was married? Surely Neil, Roy's best friend and my parents' closest neighbor, would have known the truth if anybody had. And what story had they told about my husband? Was I supposed to be a war widow? They wouldn't have passed me off as a divorcee, would they? I made a mental note to ask Mama later.

"No, it's just me and Benny."

"Roy says you're living in New York. That's a long way from home."

"Roy's been teasing Benny about being a Yankee since we got here. New York's okay. We like it there."

"All them people and buildings—no trees, no open country. I'd go crazy."

I laughed. "It has its own attractions. Haven't you ever wanted to travel, see something of the rest of the world?"

"I saw enough during the war. After that, home looked mighty good to me."

We continued talking and sipping our coffee until Katie returned with a basket of eggs. I set down my coffee cup and took the eggs to the sink to wash. "I guess everybody will be up soon and wanting breakfast." I turned to Katie. "What do you usually have? Besides eggs?"

"Mama makes grits, scrambled eggs, and biscuits."

"Uh-oh. I haven't made biscuits in years. Grits and eggs I can handle. You got any store-bought bread? Maybe we could make some toast."

Katie opened the pantry door and took out a loaf of bread. "Daddy's gonna want hot biscuits."

"Too bad. We're having toast."

Neil laughed. "Some Southern cook you are. Can't even make biscuits. You better go back to New York and stay there."

I made a face at him. "Oh, yeah? How about you making the biscuits then?"

Neil lifted one hand in protest. "Hey, I already told you I'm no cook. That's woman's work, anyway. I gotta go. I got my own chores to tend to."

"Woman's work, nothing. You eat, don't you? Why don't you stay for breakfast? I happen to be pretty good with grits and eggs, even if I don't make biscuits."

"Thanks, but I really gotta get moving. I'll just finish my coffee."

As I put the grits on to cook, Roy, Jr. came into the kitchen, rubbing his eyes.

"Hey, sport," Neil said. "You got any stronger since yesterday?" He reached out and took hold of Roy, Jr.'s arm. "I don't feel no muscle there yet."

Roy, Jr. clenched his fist and tightened his arm. "See?"

Neil felt his arm again. "Hey, I do feel a little something there. You gonna beat me up one of these days." Neil pushed up his sleeve, held out his own arm and tightened his fist. I could see the muscle of his upper arm ripple. He stood and stretched.

"Tell Roy I came by, okay? Good seeing you again, Lacey. You gonna be here a while?"

"Sure. A few days, anyway. It all depends."

"Then I'll be seeing you again. I'll let myself out."

❋   ❋   ❋

By the time I got breakfast on the table, Benny was also up, and after we all ate, the boys went outside while Katie helped me with the dishes. Roy was still sleeping.

"How soon can Mama come home?" Katie asked.

"Probably four or five days. She needs her rest now."

"Grandpa's at the hospital, too. Daddy said he's real sick. He can't talk or move."

"I know. I saw him yesterday. He had a stroke, and that affects the brain. It's like when you sprain a muscle in your arm or leg. It's sore and you can't use it for a while. But then it gets better and you can move it again. His brain needs time to heal."

"I don't want him to die."

"I don't think you need to worry about that," I said. "He's getting stronger already. Everybody says so. You can ask Grandma."

"You came back." Katie's voice was hesitant.

"Yes. Grandma sent me a telegram. She asked me to come."

Katie hung up her dishtowel. "Can I go out now?"

"Sure, honey. Sure you can. What did you mean, I came back?"

"Daddy said ..." She paused.

"Said what?"

Katie didn't answer.

"What did he say?"

Katie's voice was barely audible. "He said the only way you'd ever come home again was over Grandpa's dead body."

I scrubbed fiercely at the frying pan. Why on earth would Roy say something like that in front of a child? "That's not true.

I came as soon as I heard he was sick. You run on out and play with the boys. And don't worry about Grandpa." Roy didn't know half of what had happened. He hadn't been there when Daddy had called down the wrath of God on my head, had practically ordered me out of the house. And now he wanted to make *me* out to be the villain?

I had finished with the dishes and was reading the Sunday newspaper when Roy came out of the bedroom, stretching his arms above his head.

"What time is it? The kids all up?"

"They're outside." I rattled the newspaper and went back to my reading.

"What's eating you? You look like you ate a green persimmon."

"Katie seems to have the impression that Daddy is going to die. You need to talk to her, reassure her. Okay?"

"Okay. I'll talk to her. Just let me get a cup of coffee first."

"You know why she thinks that?" I glared at him over the top of the newspaper. "Because she heard you say the only way I'd ever come home was over Daddy's dead body."

"Well, that is why you come, ain't it? To kick dirt on his grave." Roy got a cup from the cupboard and poured himself some coffee. "I don't recall seeing anything of you up until you got word he was dying."

I laid down the newspaper. "Do you have any idea how hard it was for me to come back here? You weren't there when Daddy called me all those horrible names, when he practically threw me out of his house." I stood and slammed the iron skillet onto the stove. "How many eggs you want?"

"Two? Three? I don't care." Roy sat at the table with his cup of coffee. "You know you could have come to me or gone to Grace in Tallahassee. We would have helped if we'd known. You didn't have to forge his name and steal the money."

"And what could you have done? Or Grace, for that matter? Dwayne wouldn't even answer my letters. It was like he fell off the edge of the world." I put a spoonful of lard into the skillet and turned on the burner. "I felt so scared and humiliated. You have no idea."

"You could have told us the truth. Grace offered to let you live with her until the baby was born. Then nobody outside the family would have ever had to know."

"And give up Benny? You really think I could have done that? All any of the rest of you cared about was family honor, me besmirching the family name. You wanted me to lie? To pretend the whole thing never happened? Lying's one of the Ten Commandments too, you know." My voice rose to a high treble.

Roy raised both hands. "Okay, Sis, forget it, okay? It's all behind us. You see only your side, but remember the rest of us believed that cockamamie story you told about going to meet that sailor in Jacksonville. Then, when Daddy discovered the five hundred dollars missing from his bank account, we all thought the two of you were using it to feather your nest. We all had to sit by with our hands tied, watching Mama go crazy worrying about you."

"You think I was having an easy time of it? Eighteen years old, nobody to turn to, no place to go? You think I had it easy?" I took out my anger on the eggs, cracking them sharply against the side of the skillet, dumping them into the melted lard, and whisking them fiercely with a fork.

"Yeah, but did we know that? You told everybody you were going off to get married, remember? It wasn't till Grace got that first letter from you that any of us knew the truth. And that was what, six months later? By then it was too late for us to help. If you'd just told the truth early on."

I sprinkled the eggs with salt and pepper. "I have my pride. I couldn't own up to Mama and Daddy what Dwayne was really like. But I've got Benny. Every time I look at him, I know I did the right thing." I turned to face Roy. "Remember when we were kids, and I wanted to try out for the basketball team? Daddy said no, that it wasn't proper for girls to run around in shorts? You stuck up for me."

"Didn't do much good, as I recall."

"No, but you tried. That's what was important. I guess I was hoping you'd be on my side again. And I didn't come home just to see Daddy die. I want to make things right between us. I would have come before if he'd made the slightest move to show I was welcome, if he'd given any sign of relenting."

"Sometimes you gotta make the first move."

"I did. I paid back the money. It was hard, but I did it, a few dollars at a time, all five hundred."

"You did?" Roy raised his eyebrows. "Mama didn't tell me about that, but I'm glad to hear it. Anyway, what I said, whatever Katie told you, I'm sorry. Let's let bygones be bygones, okay?"

I set his plate of grits and scrambled eggs on the table, plopping it down a little harder than necessary. "That's easy for you to say. I feel like I've got a millstone around my neck, and I'm fighting to keep my head above water while everybody else is trying to push me down again."

"Relax, Sis. We all got problems. Don't think you're the only one." Roy picked up his fork. "Where's the biscuits?"

Chapter 5

"No biscuits today," I snapped. "You want toast?"

"No biscuits? Julia always . . . Never mind. This is fine."

"You sound like Neil. You want biscuits, you make 'em."

"When did you see Neil?"

"He came by this morning, early. Wanted to know how he could help out with Daddy's livestock. I told him about the baby, and he said he'd go on over to Mama's and see what needed doing there."

"Whew, I gotta get up and tend to things here." Roy cleaned his plate and took a final gulp of coffee before pushing back from the table and reaching for his cap. "When I get finished, we'll go back over to Mama's for dinner, and then on to the hospital. Meanwhile, make yourself at home."

"Okay, thanks." I carried Roy's dirty dishes to the sink, and then, remembering that Julia had made a macaroni and cheese casserole yesterday to take with us, I decided to walk down to the garden and see what I could find to contribute.

The sun, already high in the sky, promised another hot, humid July day as I walked through the back yard. The rows of plants with their bright crayon colors—red tomatoes, yellow squash, deep green cucumbers and beans—brought back memories of childhood, the feel of damp, freshly plowed soil beneath my bare feet, the taste of plump, ripe blackberries straight from the bush, sensations I hadn't thought about for years. I filled my bucket with green beans and started toward the house. Dragonflies were using the backyard clothesline for takeoffs and landings, and I looked around for Benny, wanting to call his attention to them, but he and Roy, Jr. were on the other side of the yard, throwing sticks for the dog to chase.

After washing the beans, I sat at the kitchen table to snap them. Roy's suggestion that I should have given Benny up for adoption was inconceivable. I couldn't imagine my life without him. Raising a child alone hadn't seemed strange in New York; for the past six years we'd been living in a rooming house surrounded by women without men, victims of circumstances much like mine, and Benny had never had occasion to feel the lack of a father. I'd never talked to him about Dwayne, and he had never asked, but now, being around Roy's children and Geneva and Tom's little family, plus the mention of my own father being in the hospital, I knew I couldn't postpone the subject much longer. Over the past year I'd formulated plans to tell him about Dwayne, rehearsing what I'd say, knowing we needed to talk about it before he started school, but I'd kept procrastinating about having the discussion.

I didn't even have a photograph of Dwayne to show Benny what his daddy looked like. The one small snapshot Dwayne had given me, an old school picture from his wallet, I had finally torn up in anger and despair. Now I wished, for Benny's sake, that I'd kept it. As I snapped the beans, I tried to call up an image of Dwayne's face, but I could no longer remember clearly how he looked—the shape of his ears, for example, or his eyebrows. I could bring up small pieces of him—the smell of his after-shave, the curve of his lips when he smiled at me, the dark, coarse hairs on the backs of his wrists, the flecks of gold in his brown eyes—but I couldn't put all the pieces together into a whole person. Sometimes out of the corner of my eye, I'd catch a fleeting glimpse of Dwayne in Benny—a tilt of the head, a certain quizzical expression—but it was always gone before I could analyze just what it was I'd seen.

Telling Benny about his father wasn't going to be easy, for Benny was sure to have questions, and I had so few answers to give him. All I knew was that he had grown up in some little town in West Virginia, a town I'd once looked up on a map but now had forgotten the name of, that he'd been in the U.S. Navy when I met him in Jacksonville, that he'd sailed for the Pacific just two months later. I had no letters from him, no mementos, nothing to prove that he ever existed, except for Benny, the only thing he'd ever given me.

I'd considered telling Benny that his father had gone off to war on a big ship and had never come back. And that was the truth, after a fashion. I had no idea what had happened to him after the war ended. After Benny's birth, after I'd contacted Grace to let her know where I was, I'd wake up every morning thinking this was the day I'd find Dwayne outside my door, full of plausible explanations for why he hadn't answered my letters. And as I rocked Benny to sleep each night, I had imagined him appearing without warning, sweeping me up in his arms, and swinging me around—just like the newspaper photographs of soldiers coming home to wives and girlfriends. Surely, I thought, when he discovered he had a son, he would return, and we would all live happily ever after.

But when the months and then the years passed and there had been no word from him, I had begun to imagine him dead, in a coffin draped with an American flag, a hero of his country. It had been easier to picture him dead than to imagine him back in West Virginia with a wife and children, maybe a little boy who looked a lot like Benny.

I finished snapping the beans and put them on to cook, then stepped out the back door to check on the kids. Katie was sitting in the backyard swing, idly pushing herself back and forth with one foot, and Benny and Roy, Jr. had strapped on cowboy holsters and were across the lane in the small stand of pines beside the sharecropper's cabin, ducking behind trees, pointing toy pistols at one another and making "Bang, Bang" noises. I stood for a moment, watching the intensity of their play. What was it about men and their war games? Dwayne had been so eager to get into the war, to "zap some Japs," as he had put it. And he hadn't even gotten his wish; the war had ended only a few days after his ship sailed for the Pacific.

By June of 1945, when I'd met him in Jacksonville, the war in Europe had already ended, and everybody knew it was only a matter of time before Japan surrendered, too. I had turned eighteen on May 8, VE day, and my best friend Betty Ammons and I had plotted through those last daydreaming weeks of our senior year about how we'd escape the summer tobacco-tying jobs awaiting us on the farm for something more exciting and cosmopolitan. Betty's older married sister in Jacksonville had assured us that job opportunities awaited in the insurance office where she worked and had promised we could stay with her and her husband until we had saved enough money to rent a place of our own.

That was also the summer that Geneva was waiting eagerly for Tom to come home from the war so they could get married and start a new life together, far away from the farm. I had no intention of remaining stuck at home with Mama and Daddy, condemned to marrying some hick farmer and having four or five children before I turned thirty. I had some serious living to do.

There had been weeks of tearful arguments with Daddy and Mama pleading and ordering me not to go, but I was eighteen, and so, the week after graduation, I had defiantly packed my meager belongings and escaped with Betty on the Greyhound bus to Jacksonville. I'd met Dwayne that very first day of my new life, as if the stars had been aligned for everything to happen just the way it did.

❀　❀　❀

Betty and I step off the bus in downtown Jacksonville on a Saturday afternoon. I've never been to a city before, and I'm overwhelmed with the traffic and the noise and the busyness of the streets. For the last mile, we've seen nothing but buildings crammed up against one another—so many that they seem to go on forever, and some of them are so tall that I can't imagine how mere men could have built them. How did they possibly get steel girders and lumber and concrete and all those things so high up in the sky?

As we wait for our cheap cardboard valises to be unloaded from the baggage compartment, I study the crowd around us.

"Where's your sister?" I ask Betty. "I thought she was picking us up."

"I told her to come at five o'clock," Betty answers.

"That's two more hours!"

"Exactly!" Betty gives me a triumphant smile. "That gives us a chance to get acquainted with things on our own. Come on, let's go."

My stomach gives a little jolt of panic as I remember all the warnings Mama and Daddy pounded into me about the city, but Betty seems to know what she's doing. "Go where?"

"Anywhere!" Betty answers. "Look at all these stores!"

We walk for a while, window shopping, until our valises become heavy and then we duck into a Woolworth's for a rest and a cool drink.

"Hi, beautiful!" A dark-haired sailor in a white uniform swivels around on a stool at the lunch counter and looks straight into my eyes, and my suitcase flies out of my hand, landing with a thud on the hard tile floor.

The sailor rushes after it, returning my embarrassed thanks with a courtly bow. "My pleasure. Are you gorgeous girls coming or going? Would you like to join us for a Coca-Cola?"

Before either of us can answer, another sailor hops down from the next stool over and gestures toward a nearby empty booth. "Hello, ladies. Pleased to make your acquaintance."

Betty and I look at each other and break into nervous giggles.

"I'm Dwayne," the first sailor says. "My friend Charles." He bows again. "Please join us. Our treat." He waves me into one side of the booth, and I find myself sliding in as if hypnotized. Dwayne slides in after me, with Betty and Charles opposite us, and before we're aware of what has happened, we're sipping cold sodas and telling these two strangers our entire life stories.

After finishing our drinks, we all walk back to the bus station where Dwayne gallantly rents a locker for our suitcases, refusing any reimbursement. He and Charles then spend the next hour showing us the town, and when we pass the movie theater and Dwayne asks if we'd like to join the two of them for a movie later in the evening, I look over at Betty in wonderment, not sure if this is really happening or if it's all just a dream.

❋   ❋   ❋

"Here's the milk." Roy came in the back door, a pail in his hand. "I gotta feed the hogs. The kids are gonna ride in the back of the truck. Be back in a few minutes."

Benny riding in the back of the truck? I hurried after Roy.

"We're just going to the field." Roy waved off my worries. "Don't be so jumpy. I ain't lost a young'un yet."

"Sit down," I told Benny. "No standing while the truck is moving. And mind Uncle Roy." Roy had no understanding of how new all this was for Benny, how unprepared he was to deal with farm life. I found Julia's straining cloth and strained and refrigerated the milk, checked again on the beans, and then gathered up the dirty, smelly clothes that Benny and I had been wearing for the past two days, along with the towels we'd used, and carried everything to the washing machine.

In retrospect, I couldn't believe how naive and reckless Betty and I had been that afternoon, two country bumpkins fresh off the farm, intoxicated by the city, but at the time I had been caught up in the romantic notion that this was the way life was supposed to be, that finally I was experiencing the sorts of things city girls did every day. And when we introduced the two sailors to Betty's sister at the bus station later, the sister, only three years older than Betty and newly married herself, found the story of our meeting so sweetly romantic that she hadn't put up any objections to the date. That summer, with VE Day so recently behind us and victory in the Pacific only a heartbeat away, all of us were floating on a swell of national patriotism so strong that anyone in military uniform was a genuine American hero—someone to be totally trusted and looked up to.

❇   ❇   ❇

In the darkened movie theater, Dwayne takes my hand halfway through the feature, and I am too pleasantly surprised to object. More talkative than Charles, he has a wide, contagious smile and soft, gold-flecked brown eyes that make him seem innocent and little-boyish and totally safe, as if he's someone I've known for my whole life.

After the movie, we stop for milkshakes and then walk for blocks under a full moon. I'm wearing my white graduation dress, a bright red belt accentuating my narrow waist and calling attention to my wavy auburn hair. The night is magical, and although I have no idea what Betty is feeling, I know that I have never felt this way before about any boy back at home. It's as if I've been transported to a different world—swept up in the middle of something grand and stupendous and historic. I feel like the central character of a Hollywood love story being played out on a grand MGM stage—and the new, not quite real Lacey McCormick who is walking the streets of Jacksonville in the company of Dwayne Fortrell is not at all the same person as the naive girl who'd left farm life only a day before.

❇   ❇   ❇

I was hanging the last of the towels on the clothesline out back when Roy and the kids returned. "We're back, all safe and sound," Roy called. "I'm gonna get cleaned up some so the hospital won't throw me out."

"Okay. I'm ready when you are." The children jumped down from the truck and ran off toward the chicken yard, Katie and Roy, Jr. excited to be showing their city cousin around, answering his questions about all the new things he was seeing. Against their soft drawls, Benny's New York accent sounded harsh and clipped. Did my own voice sound like that? I remembered Neil teasing me earlier in the morning about not being Southern any more, and I wondered when I'd see him again. I wanted him to meet Benny, but would he tease Benny about being a Yankee, too? Benny wasn't at all accustomed to being around men and their joking banter.

As a matter of fact, I wasn't used to being around men either. I'd spent the last six years avoiding them. Since Dwayne, I'd fled from smiles on the street, frowned fiercely at winks and catcalls, turned away from any man who tried to start a conversation with me. And my friends at the boarding house all had stories similar to mine, all of us regarding men mostly as bad memories we were trying hard to erase.

Chapter 6

"Hey, Grandma!" Roy took the steps two at a time. "It's a boy!"

Mama came out onto the porch. "I knew it'd be a boy. How's Julia?"

"Fine and dandy. You gotta see Zach, Ma. Eight pounds, four ounces."

While Roy filled Mama in on the baby, I carried the bowl of beans into the house. Grace was stirring something on the stove, but the rest of the house was quiet.

"Where is everybody?"

"Church," Grace answered. "Neva and Tom went over to visit with his mother this morning, and they were planning on going to church with her. Neva didn't want the kids to miss Sunday school. Mama told them to come here for dinner, though, and bring Mrs. Baker with them, so they'll be back after a while."

I set the bowl on the kitchen counter. Taped to the refrigerator door was Benny's crayon drawing. And beside it was another stick figure boy with a scribble of bright yellow hair and round blue eyes. Beneath it "Tommy" was printed in big block letters.

"Tommy made that one this morning," Mama said as she came into the kitchen. "It looks like him too, don't you think? Look how good he wrote his name."

"Very nice," I muttered. To Neva, everything was a competition that she had to win.

Tom and Geneva arrived a little after noon with Tom's mother, and after another huge Sunday dinner the kids headed for the tire swing. I shooed Mama and Grace off to the front porch. "Go on and visit with Mrs. Baker. I'll clean up in here."

"Yes," Geneva echoed, bustling about to clear the table and stack the dirty dishes. "Lacey and I will take care of things in here." She tied one of Mama's aprons over her Sunday dress and ran water into the dishpan. "I'll wash, and you can dry."

"Okay." I shook out the folds of a clean dishtowel, a little uncomfortable at being alone with Geneva in the kitchen. After six-and-a-half years of silence, it was hard to know where things stood between us any more. Besides Mama and Daddy, Geneva had been the only witness to my humiliation when I'd come home from Jacksonville only a few months after my defiant leave-taking. As the self-righteous older sister who'd always followed the rules and had taken it upon herself to make me do the same, her shocked "How could you?" and her prying questions had been even more hurtful than Mama's tears or Daddy's name calling and fierce pounding of the Bible. I'd had no ally I could turn to, nobody to offer sympathy or understanding.

After I'd re-established contact with Mama and Grace, I'd tried writing to her, too, extending an olive branch of reconciliation, but she'd never answered, not even so much as a Christmas card.

"Your boy is so quiet," she said as she handed me the first glass to rinse. "Not rambunctious like my Tommy. He's not at all like I imagined."

"Oh?" My eyes went automatically to the two drawings on the refrigerator. Was this another case of one-upmanship? I'd already noticed that Neva hadn't once used Benny's name since we'd been here. "And what did you think he'd be like?"

"More like you, I guess. Of course, not knowing anything about his father... Does he take after him?"

"I hope not." I rinsed another glass and turned it upside down on the dishtowel beside the drain.

"Tom's mother says Tommy reminds her of Tom at that age, full of curiosity about everything. Tom was quieter, though, she says, not as full of energy as Tommy."

"Benny is his own person. He doesn't have to take after anybody."

"He must resemble his father in looks," Neva persisted. "Nobody in our family has brown eyes. Or such dark hair."

Determined not to give Neva the satisfaction of revealing anything about Dwayne, I concentrated on drying a plate. Benny's hereditary characteristics were not anything I wanted to discuss.

But my silence didn't deter her. She just tried another angle. "It must be hard, raising a child alone. A boy, especially."

"We're handling things just fine."

"Well, look who's touchy today," Geneva huffed. "I didn't say you weren't. I just meant, considering the circumstances...." She didn't finish her sentence. "Anyway, Mama's excited about you being here. She was saying this morning how she hoped you'd stay for a nice, long visit."

"I can't stay too long. There's my job to get back to."

"But you'll be here through the week at least, won't you? We have to leave this afternoon. Tom has to be back at work tomorrow morning, you know, and Grace will have to go home, too, back to Pete and the girls. That means Mama will need someone to drive her back and forth into town to the hospital or the grocery."

"Roy's right down the road."

"Yes, but he has his hands full with the crops and now the new baby."

"So?" I waited for Geneva's answer, wondering what she was building up to.

"Tom thinks I should stay for the week, to be here to get Mama back and forth to the hospital, talk to the doctors, take care of finances, and all that. Mama never handled any money matters."

"That sounds like a good idea. I know Mama would appreciate it." If Geneva stayed for the week, then Benny and I could return home sooner than I'd planned. And considering how Daddy had reacted yesterday to my visit, the sooner the better as far as I was concerned. I'd followed Mama's directive and come home, and so far it had gotten me nothing but Roy's angry scolding for how I'd hurt Mama, Geneva's cutting barbs about Benny, and Daddy's refusal to acknowledge my even being here.

"I'd love to stay and help out," Geneva continued, "but I have so many responsibilities at home. Did I tell you we just moved into a new house? With getting settled in and decorating and with the children's activities—Tommy's swimming lessons, you know, and I'm about to enroll Sarah in a Thursday morning dance class—I don't see how I can stay for a whole week. Sarah gets off her nap schedule up here, and then she's tired and cranky all day. And Tommy's energy would drive Mama crazy. I know it would. Tom's mother says she doesn't know how I stand it." Geneva laughed as she added more hot water to the dishpan. "Not that he's not a great kid. He is, but he just has to be going, going, going all the time. He's so interested in everything. He's a handful, even for me."

I could imagine how exhausting it would be for Mama to be around Tommy for a whole week. Even the short time I'd spent around him had tired me out.

"So," Geneva didn't pause for an answer, "I was telling Tom last night, what with you coming such a long way, you were most likely staying for the rest of this week, at least, if not longer, and you could help Mama. It's not like you have to get back right away. And your little boy is so quiet that Mama would hardly know he was here."

"His name is Benny." All the old resentments of childhood bubbled to the surface. I'd already told Dorothy that I'd be gone for a week, at least, but I wasn't about to reveal that little fact to Geneva.

"Of course. Benny. And he's just as precious as he can be. You are planning to stay through the week, aren't you?"

At least I'd gotten Neva to say his name, much as that might have offended her Baptist sensibilities. "I have responsibilities, too. There's my job, for one."

"But you're entitled to a vacation, aren't you? After all, it's summertime."

"A vacation is not a luxury I can afford right now." Geneva had no idea of the struggle it had been to take care of Benny and myself on my meager salary. Every penny counted, and a week's worth of no pay would mean we'd be eating canned beans and soda crackers for the rest of the month. I'd been trying to put aside a few dollars to equip Benny for starting school, but this unexpected trip to Florida and back would likely use up every penny I'd saved.

Geneva handed me a platter to be rinsed. "But you've come so far. And Mama is so thrilled to have you here. She was saying this morning what a smart, sweet boy you have."

I rinsed the platter and took my time drying it, carefully running the towel around its scalloped edge, decorated with a delicate pink rose pattern. Mama had had this platter for as long as I could remember. *You nearly killed her*, Roy had said on Friday night when he picked me up.

"I'll stay through the week," I told Geneva, "but beyond that, I don't know."

"I knew you would. I told Tom—"

"Don't think I'm doing any favors for *you*. Mama and Grace are the only ones who kept in touch with me, who even acknowledged Benny's existence. You never answered my letters. Not even a Christmas card."

Geneva busied herself with scrubbing a pot. "I meant to write, I really did. But Tommy was such a handful as a baby, and then I got pregnant with Sarah, and you know how it goes. Anyway, I didn't know what to say to you. Our lives were so different. I was buried in housework and children—and there you were up in glamorous New York City, doing all these exciting things. I didn't figure you wanted to hear about my little old humdrum life."

"Glamorous? Exciting?" I laughed bitterly. "Aren't you forgetting one little thing? For the last six years, I've had the full responsibility of raising a child all by myself. Where did you think Benny was while I was living this exciting, glamorous life? Tell me that."

"Well, it must be exhilarating, anyway, just being there." Geneva lifted her apron to wipe her sweaty face before reaching for the heavy iron skillet on the stove. "I know about New York. I read the newspapers and magazines. It's got everything—museums, Broadway shows, Macy's, Times Square, the Empire State Building. Imagine living in the middle of all that."

"Broadway shows? Macy's? Times Square? I wouldn't know a thing about any of that. All I do is go downstairs to work every day."

"You've never been to Macy's? Or Times Square?" Geneva shook her head in disbelief. "I keep telling Tom that one of these days we need to go to New York so I can see for myself what all the fuss is about." She handed me the skillet and tipped the dishpan into the sink to empty it. "Anyway, Mama's going to be so happy you're planning to stay a while. And it'll take such a load off my mind, too. Now, you know that if anything happens during the week, if Daddy takes a turn for the worse, you can call me. Mama has my phone number. I'll come back the minute Mama or Daddy needs me, I promise." She rinsed and dried her hands and then ran off to tell Tom the good news.

By the time I wiped down the counters, hung up my wet dishtowels, and joined the others on the porch, everyone was making plans for going into town to the hospital. Now there was not just Daddy to check on, but Julia and Zach, too, everyone excited to see the newest addition to the McCormick clan. Tom and Geneva were discussing the logistics of packing their car and then dropping Tom's mother off at her house on the way to the hospital. "I'll let Geneva visit with everybody at the hospital while I keep the kids outside," Tom said, "and then we need to get on the road for Orlando."

"I'll stay here with the other kids," I volunteered. "Grace, you go on with Roy and Mama and take your time visiting with everybody. I'll be here all week, so I can see them later."

As everyone drove away, I headed for the front porch swing, hugely relieved at the reprieve of not having to face Daddy's disapproving glare for another day. Katie, Roy, Jr. and Benny were taking turns pushing one another on the tire. I leaned back and closed my eyes, the steady creak of the chain and the slight motion of the swing taking me back to a time before Dwayne and before Benny and before life got so complicated, back to those years after Roy got married and Simon left for the army, and only Geneva and I were at home.

After her high school graduation, Geneva had taken a job at the paper mill making cardboard boxes for overseas shipments—her contribution to the war effort—and for the next two years, every day after school and on weekends, I had become Daddy's right-hand helper, his "third boy," as he called me, doing all the dirty jobs that Geneva would never have soiled her hands with. I'd mended fences, slopped the hogs, picked hornworms off the tobacco plants, and even helped "fix" the young male calves. Daddy and I been a team, and I had been proud to be his helper.

Then Betty had talked me into running off with her to Jacksonville after graduation, and I'd met Dwayne. I'd gone from being Daddy's pride and joy to being his everlasting shame, to the point that he had practically disowned me, refusing now to speak to me or to acknowledge Benny as his grandson. I squeezed my eyes shut to stop the tears from coming. Certainly, I had made mistakes, out of youth and naiveté, but I couldn't regret having Benny. I could never consider Benny a mistake.

Ruth Rodgers

Chapter 7

Mama, Grace and Roy returned from the hospital filled with glowing news of Zach's perfection and of Daddy's continued improvement. Julia's parents had been there, too, to visit with Julia and see Zach, and the minister from Four Corners Baptist Church had stopped by to see Daddy, so there was lots of news to relate before Grace also said goodbye and headed home to Tallahassee. "I'll be back next Saturday," she told me, "so don't you go off anywhere before then." She gave bear hugs all around, including Benny, and I began to miss her already as she drove away, the July dust puffing up behind her.

Katie and Roy, Jr. led Benny off to throw some shelled corn to the chickens scratching in their fenced enclosure beneath the pecan trees, and Mama, Roy, and I continued to sit on the porch, using our cardboard fans to create a breeze. "Sure seems quiet with everybody gone," Mama said. "Roy, you all stay for supper now. When you go home, I'll be all by my lonesome, I guess."

"Aw, you ain't alone, Ma," Roy said. "I'm right down the road. And Lacey and Benny can move their stuff over here, now that everybody else has cleared out. I can manage my two till morning, and then they're staying with Julia's mama tomorrow. Lacey can come pack her things while I do the evening chores. I'll leave Katie here to keep you company till we get back."

At Roy's house, Benny trooped off with Roy, Jr. to help with the chores while I packed our few belongings. I was surprised at how well Benny was adapting to farm life, having never been exposed to it before. It was as if he had a natural affinity for it, and I was the one who was nervous, who didn't want to let Benny out of my sight. I wasn't accustomed to being away from him, and I kept making trips to the back door, following the progress of Roy's truck as he made the rounds from corn crib to hog pen to cow pasture. The packing didn't take long. I had brought only a few things: four changes of clothes for each of us, some of Benny's books and small trucks, his crayons and writing tablet, his stuffed dog with floppy ears that he'd had since he was three. Besides the few dollars and change in my purse, my total savings were stuffed in a sock in the bottom of my suitcase. Two ten-dollar bills, three fives, and three ones. Thirty-eight dollars. Barely enough for bus tickets back to New York.

And Benny was going to need new school clothes and shoes. Most of our clothes up to now I'd gotten from the Salvation Army thrift shop, but with Benny starting school in the fall, I wanted him to have some new things. I was sure that Neva had already shopped for Tommy's school clothes and supplies; he'd be going off in style, a new outfit for every day of the week, while Benny would have to make do with someone else's castoffs, just as I'd gone to school in Geneva's faded and worn-out hand-me-downs. And now here I was giving up a week's salary, maybe more, to stay with Mama while Neva got on with her comfortable country club life.

I sighed as I stuffed the money back into the sock and went outside to bring in the clothes and towels I'd washed earlier in the morning. It wasn't until I had repacked the suitcase with mine and Benny's clean clothes and was folding the towels on the kitchen table that I realized I'd done a load of laundry on Sunday. Mama, if she knew, would be aghast. When I was growing up, working on Sunday, other than the necessary cooking and feeding the livestock, had been strictly forbidden. When had I relaxed that rule?

When I'd gone with Betty to Jacksonville, I'd promised Mama and Daddy that I'd attend church faithfully every Sunday. And I had, for the first three Sundays, Betty and I tagging along with Betty's sister and her husband to the Baptist church closest to where they lived. But by the fourth weekend, after getting our first month's paycheck, Betty and I had moved into our own little furnished apartment above a dry-cleaning shop, and after another Saturday night date with Dwayne and Charles, followed by giggling girl talk afterwards about the evening, we'd both slept late on Sunday morning, not rolling out of bed until after ten. When questioned by her sister, Betty explained that we'd gone to another Baptist church closer to our apartment, and when a whole week passed with neither of us being struck by lightning or hit by a truck, missing church hadn't seemed such a grievous sin.

By that time, Betty and I had other things on our minds. We were both preoccupied with our own personal war effort, easing the loneliness of Dwayne and Charles, who were about to ship out any day now to give their lives, if it came to that, to defeat the Japs. Time was a thief, stealing the hours and days too quickly, and we had to wring the most out of every minute we could manage to spend together.

It's another steamy Saturday night, mid-July, and Dwayne and Charles pick us up at our apartment for our usual movie date. I've known Dwayne for a little over a month now, and time apart from him has become something to be endured until I can see him again, can hear his voice and feel his hand clasped around mine, his lips pressed against mine. Nothing else matters.

On our first few movie dates we had all sat together, watching the movie, but lately Dwayne has been looking for ways of breaking into twosomes, and tonight is no different. Once we have our tickets, Charles and Betty head for the middle section for a good view of the screen, but Dwayne steers me away to

*one side, to the very back corner against the wall. I practically
hold my breath waiting for the lights to dim and for Dwayne
to put his arm around my shoulder and pull me against him.
Each time I see him it's like the world has been created anew,
and we are the first two people who have ever felt this way
about each other.*

*As I rub my fingers against the thick, dark hairs on the
back of his wrist, I am the first person ever to touch him so
intimately, and he is the first person ever to see me as the
woman I am, not as the skinny tomboy everyone back at home
has always considered me. I pretend to concentrate on the
movie, but then Dwayne begins to kiss me and to rub his hand
up and down my arm, letting his fingers lightly brush against
my breast. Then he pulls my hand down against his leg, moves
it up toward the warmth of his crotch.*

❋   ❋   ❋

I carried the towels and washcloths to the bathroom closet,
shivering at the memory of the fever pitch emotions of that
summer. None of the boys around here—those I'd gone to school
with since first grade—had ever held that kind of attraction for
me, and Geneva had been so moony-eyed over Tom Baker, a
perfectly ordinary boy down the road, writing mushy love letters
to him every night, that I'd sworn off the whole idea of romance,
associating it with weakness, with Geneva's fussy primness
about feminine dress and decorum.

I'd been so adamant about stating to anyone who would listen
that I'd never go all ga-ga over a boy that the intensity of my
feelings for Dwayne had come as a complete surprise, leaving me
confused and shaken. At first, I had tried to resist the feelings
he aroused in me, but each time he was persistent and tender,
telling me over and over how much he loved me, reminding me
constantly that any day now he'd be gone, risking his life for
America. His memories with me would be all he'd have to sustain
him during those long, lonely months at sea.

❈ ❈ ❈

I find myself, even while pulling back in protest, wanting Dwayne to touch me again, waiting for his fingers to brush against my breast, positioning myself so that my breast will come in contact with his fingers. And when he pulls my hand toward the warm, pulsing bulge between his legs, I let myself touch him briefly, seemingly accidentally, before pulling away, curious about what is there beneath the smooth cloth of his white, neatly pressed pants.

Earlier in the evening as we were waiting for the boys to arrive, Betty had started in again with her warnings about not letting myself get too involved. Charles has told her that he has a girlfriend back home waiting for him. "He leveled with me right up front, and I respect that," she told me. "And he says Dwayne has a girlfriend back home, too. He's seen her picture. They're practically engaged, he says."

But I know that can't be true. Dwayne has told me that I'm the first girl he's ever felt this way about. He's constantly telling me how he thinks about me day and night, can't bear to be away from me, even for a minute.

❈ ❈ ❈

I walked to the back porch, looking for Roy and the two boys. Roy had loaded two metal drums into the bed of the truck and was filling them with water from the hose. Then he'd drive them out to the pasture and transfer the water by bucketfuls into the cows' watering tubs. Benny and Roy, Jr. were on opposite sides of the truck, apparently playing keep-away, scurrying from tailgate to front fender, peeking at one another and laughing, but each keeping to his own side. I watched for a minute before going back to the living room, where I settled into one corner of the sofa and closed my eyes.

The memories of that summer still brought a hot flush of embarrassment. How had I allowed myself to be so thoroughly tricked into letting down all my defenses? I had no good answer; when I was with Dwayne, all my logic, all the admonitions I've heard all my life, seemed to leave me. I became nothing more than a quivering set of nerve endings waiting for release.

❊   ❊   ❊

A few minutes after the movie starts, Dwayne tells me he doesn't feel well, he has an awful pain in his stomach, and he wants to go back to the apartment to lie down. I'm immediately sympathetic, but I want to let Betty and Charles know what's happening. Dwayne says there's no need to worry them—let them stay and watch the movie—and he stumbles out with me right behind him.

At the apartment he stretches out on our small sofa, his legs hanging over one arm, unbuckles his belt, and gives a huge groan. I hover over him, asking what I can do and where the pain is. Roy nearly died from a ruptured appendix when he was twelve, and Dwayne's mention of stomach pain takes me back to the terror of that experience. I keep asking where it hurts and how badly, fearful I'll have to get him to a hospital by myself. He groans again, unbuttons the waist of his pants and eases the zipper down so that he can reach the spot the pain seems to be coming from.

Then he asks me to massage it, guiding my hand below the waistband of his pants, pressing my fingers against a spot right where I imagine the appendix to be. "O-o-h, that's it," he says. "Over a little more this way, right there. That's where it hurts."

I kneel on the floor beside the sofa, wanting to be of help, and Dwayne suddenly pulls me down against him, shifting his position so that my fingers come in direct contact with the hot, pulsing bulge that he had kept pulling my hand toward in the theater. Embarrassed, I quickly jerk my hand away, but he groans again and pushes it back down. "Oh, sweet Lacey. Sweet, sweet Lacey. How am I ever going to survive without you?"

His tone is so pleading that I hardly recognize his voice. "Help me, Lacey, help me. Here's where the real pain is. You're so sweet, Lacey. I need you so much."

❄ ❄ ❄

I jumped up from the sofa and began to pace the floor, the guilt as hot and real as if it were happening right now, not seven years in the past. At eighteen, I'd been no match for Dwayne's conniving flattery. Seduction was not a word that had even been in my vocabulary. I picked up my suitcase and Benny's bag of toys and set both beside the front door, wishing Roy would hurry up and be done with his chores. I didn't want to think any more about that night, but its memory wouldn't leave me alone.

❄ ❄ ❄

By the time the movie ends we're back at the theater, meeting Betty and Charles outside and strolling down the street for our usual milkshakes as if nothing at all had happened. I know I can never tell Betty, and I know I can never let it happen again. Already the possible consequences are drenching me in a nervous puddle of sweat, and over and over I silently swear a solemn oath to God of future chastity until marriage.

But my oath lasts only until I see Dwayne again the following weekend, when he leads me to the same back corner of the theater, and soon we're both to the point that no excuse about sickness is needed for our early exit. Once again we meet Betty and Charles outside after the movie, with them none the wiser. After all her warnings to me about Dwayne's girlfriend back home, I know I can never confide in Betty, can never make her understand how helpless I've become in Dwayne's presence, how impossible it is to refuse those pleading eyes, those whispered endearments, those constant reminders of how each encounter may be the last time we'll be together. We've never discussed what will happen once the war ends, but Dwayne declares over and over that he loves me, and I tell him the same. And after what we've done, I am positive that whatever girl might have once been in Dwayne's past no longer matters—right now there is only me—and I am confident that the feelings we have for one another can lead to only one possible happily-ever-after, fairy-tale ending.

❊   ❊   ❊

The sound of Roy's truck coming back up the lane brought me out of my reverie and I pushed open the front screen door, one hand raised to call to Roy and tell him I was ready to go. But instead of heading for the house, Roy reached into the bed of the pickup for the bucket and walked toward the corncrib, both boys tagging along behind, heading off to another chore. I returned to the living room sofa.

How wrong I had been about a fairy-tale ending. By the end of July, Dwayne and Charles had disappeared from our lives as suddenly as they had appeared, and except for one short note to Betty from Charles, neither of us ever heard from either of them again.

❊   ❊   ❊

On the day after their departure, I spend the evening composing a long letter to Dwayne, pouring my heart out to him on paper. Betty scoffs at me for getting so emotional, but she writes a short note to Charles and sticks it into my envelope.

Then begins the torturous wait for a reply. Every day there is nothing. But it's too soon yet, I keep telling myself. They've been gone only a week when we hear at work that we have dropped an atomic bomb on Japan, on a city called Hiroshima. Rumors have been floating for weeks, but, nevertheless, everyone in the insurance office is rattled with shock as we listen on the radio to the reports of destruction. An entire city obliterated—everything gone in one horrible moment. I try not to think about what it must have been like for the victims. At least Dwayne and Charles are still at sea, safely away from the radiation that the radio announcer keeps referring to. Three days later, another bomb, and another Japanese city is destroyed. The bombs have the desired effect; less than a week later, on August 14, Japan surrenders, and the war is over.

When the news comes over the radio, waves of celebration sweep the city. At the insurance office, the radio stays on all day. In the street, automobile horns keep blaring, and by afternoon a crowd has gathered on the sidewalk outside the office, cheering and waving streamers. None of us can concentrate on our work; we all keep leaving our desks to look out the windows and share in the excitement. I am euphoric. Maybe this means the ship will turn around and come back to Jacksonville. Dwayne will return and there will be a proposal on bended knee.

Two more weeks pass with no word from Charles or Dwayne. But they are on board ship, I keep reminding myself, with no way to send or receive mail. I continue to mail off a letter to Dwayne every few days, repeating my declarations of love, telling him how much I miss him and how much I look forward to his return.

In early September, Betty receives a short note from Charles, a few lines about the terrible food aboard ship and how boring being at sea is, how disappointed everyone is that they missed their chance at war. Betty hands the letter to me and I read the few lines. There's a postscript after his signature, "Dwayne says tell Lacey hello." I read the letter over and over, looking for something more, and that night I cry myself to sleep.

Betty reminds me of Charles' warning about a girlfriend back home. "He's not worth moping over," she tells me. "There are lots more fish in the sea."

"You don't understand," I sob. "I love him. And he loves me." What I haven't dared tell Betty, haven't told Dwayne yet in my letters, is that I'm more than two weeks late for my monthly period. I pray every night for the welcome sight of blood, for a letter in the mailbox, for something to take away this panic that is consuming my every waking hour.

By the end of September I have missed another period, and there has been no further word from Charles or Dwayne. I'm nauseated every morning, barely able to drag myself to work.

I go into the bathroom at the insurance office and retch, then return to my duties. I'm getting behind with my files; my boss is beginning to watch me. I am paralyzed by fear, unable to take any action. I haven't seen a doctor yet, haven't confided in anyone, not even Betty. I don't want to know, for as long as I don't know, it isn't true. It simply can't be true.

By mid-October I can no longer concentrate on my work. I'm making stupid mistakes and spending longer periods in the bathroom. When my supervisor calls me into his office for a private talk, I burst into tears and find myself telling him, a middle-aged man, a virtual stranger, my most closely-guarded secret. He is kind and fatherly, patting my hand, telling me to go home to my parents until my sailor returns. I need support now, he tells me, someone to take care of me. Too bad the sailor and I aren't married, but we can fix that as soon as he gets back to the states. I'm not the first girl in this situation, and things will be all right, soon as my boyfriend returns and does the right thing.

But what I don't tell him is that Dwayne hasn't answered any of my letters, not even when finally, in desperation, I'd written that I was carrying his child.

"Of course you can't continue to work," the supervisor tells me kindly. "It's against our policy, and besides, it wouldn't set a good example for the other girls, you know. You just go on home to your mother and tell her what you've told me."

He makes it sound so simple. I want to believe him, want desperately to believe that everything will be all right. He tells me I'll be paid for the remainder of the week but I'm not to come in again after today; I'm to use that extra money to get back home.

When Betty sees me emerge from the office in tears, she follows me to the bathroom and insists on knowing what is going on. "Oh, Lacey, whatever will you do?" she asks when I tell her. "I told you what Charles said about Dwayne, about his girl back home."

I turn on her in anger and despair. "You're just jealous. He loves me. He told me so."

* * *

The banging of the back screen door interrupted my thoughts. "Mommy! Mommy! Guess what?" Benny ran inside, followed by Roy, Jr. "We took water to the cows. And I fed the hogs!"

"That's great!" I brushed his damp hair back from his forehead. "You look hot. Here, you'd better sit down and rest awhile. I'll bet you're both thirsty, aren't you?" I opened Julia's refrigerator and took out a pitcher of cherry Koolaid. I'd never tell Benny what a heel his father had been. I was going to raise him differently, to respect women.

Ruth Rodgers

Chapter 8

When we got back to Mama's, a green pickup was parked beside the house. "Who's here?" I asked Mama as I walked inside with my suitcase. Behind me, Benny was carrying his bag of toys.

"Neil stopped by to see what needed doing. Katie went with him to the pasture to drive the milk cow back to the barn."

I felt a shiver of anticipation. Neil had asked about my son this morning, and now I'd be able to introduce him to Benny.

"Benny can have Simon's old room if he wants," Mama told me. "That's where Tommy always sleeps when he's here. And you can have Roy's old room if you want to be near him. Or your and Geneva's room across the hall. Take your pick."

"Okay. We'll see." I carried the suitcase through what used to be Roy's room, now equipped with an unfamiliar new double bed and matching dresser, into what had once been Simon's room, really a small alcove off the bigger bedroom. The smaller room contained only a cot and a tall, narrow highboy, a lamp on top made from a varnished cypress knee, one of Simon's high school shop projects.

"Benny, you want to sleep in here?" I asked. "It's a lot like your room back at home, isn't it? Your own bed, and you can put your clothes right here." I pulled out one of the lower dresser drawers, which was empty.

Benny stood in the doorway, head down, holding his bag of

toys.

"I'll be right here if you want." I motioned to the bed behind us. This had been my room for those few weeks when I came home from Jacksonville, after Geneva, in my absence, had laid sole claim to the bedroom across the hall, the one we'd once shared. Roy was married by that time and Simon was still away in Europe, so I had moved my own single bed and belongings out of the shared room and over here, shutting the door to the rest of the family, hugging my secret within myself for as long as I could. The new double bed and dresser had to have come later, after we had all flown the nest and Mama had fixed it up as a guest room.

I reached for the bag that Benny was holding. "We'll put Dog on your pillow, just like at home. Or do you want to show him to Grandma?"

Benny let me take the bag out of his hands, but he grabbed the stuffed dog by one ear and held it tightly against his chest. "When are we going home?"

"Grandma wants us to stay and visit with her a while," I said. "Don't you want to spend some more time with Roy, Jr. and Katie?"

"Dorothy said hurry back 'cause she'd miss me every day."

I opened the suitcase and began to arrange Benny's clothes in the dresser drawer. "I know you miss Dorothy. And she misses you. But she has lots of other kids to keep her busy. Grandma wants to get to know you, and Grandpa, too, when he's better." As soon as the words were out of my mouth, I wished I could take them back. How could I be so foolish as to think that Daddy would ever accept Benny as his grandson?

Voices came from outside, and I stopped in the middle of my unpacking. "Sounds like they're back from the pasture. Come on, there's somebody else I want you to meet." I caught Benny's hand and walked to the porch just as Neil and Roy came around the corner of the house, Katie and Roy, Jr. running ahead of them.

"Come sit a spell," Roy said to Neil. "Rest up, for we're gonna have a big day cropping my tobacco tomorrow."

Neil followed Roy up the steps, and I raised one hand in greeting. "Hello again. I'd like you to meet my son, Benjamin. Everybody calls him Benny."

Neil took off his cap and wiped his brow with the back of his arm. "So this is your boy, huh? Hey, sport." He ruffled Benny's hair, and Benny turned his face into my skirt.

"He's a little tired of all the introductions. So many new people."

"That's okay," Neil answered. "You don't have to say 'Hey' to me, Benny. I remember when your mother wasn't no bigger than you. You believe that?"

Benny looked doubtful, peering up at him with one hand still clutching my skirt.

"That's the gospel truth. Ask her if you don't believe me. Me and her go back a long ways. What you got there?" Neil bent to examine Benny's stuffed dog, and Benny squeezed it tighter. "Hey now, I won't take him away. What's his name?"

"Dog."

"That's a good name. Makes a lot of sense. You take good care of him now. Don't go letting him bite nobody." Neil winked at me and straightened up.

"Uncle Neil, look at me!" Roy, Jr. was straddling the top of the tire swing.

"I see you." Neil bounded down the steps, pulled the tire back and let it go. "Hang on, cowboy."

When he returned to the porch, he and Roy began to talk about the tobacco crop. Katie gave Roy, Jr. another push on the tire swing. I tried to get Benny to join them, but this new change in sleeping arrangements and the presence of another new person seemed to have spooked him. He remained beside me at the door, the two of us ignored as Roy and Neil focused on the crops and weather.

"I guess I'll go help Mama with supper." I turned to go inside.

Neil looked up. "Good to see you again, Squirt. You got a fine boy there." He grinned at me and resumed his conversation with

79

Roy.

Mama was in the kitchen. "There's plenty of leftovers for supper. We'll eat early so you and Roy can go on to the hospital. Evening visiting hours are seven to nine."

"Tonight? Are you sure Roy's making another trip into town tonight?" I began to set the table. It had been a long day already, and I, for one, was exhausted. Tomorrow would be soon enough to see Zach and brace myself up for facing Daddy again.

Benny noticed the two pictures taped to the refrigerator, side by side. He spelled the name on Tommy's picture aloud—"T-O-M-M-Y. What's that say?"

"Sound it out," I say. "T-tuh, O-M--ohm, M-m-m, Y-ee."

Benny repeated the sounds after me. "Tommy," he pronounced, "that other kid. Where is he?"

"He went home already."

"Such a smart boy," Mama said. "I bet he'll do good in school."

"He's looking forward to it. Aren't you, Benbo?" I ruffled Benny's hair, a small thrill of pride running through me at Mama's compliment. "You think Neil might want to stay for supper?"

"You can ask him. He's sure been a big help these last few days. Been here every day wanting to know what he could do."

I walked back outside. "Neil, you want to stay and have supper with us? We're just about to eat."

Neil looked across the field at the sun, now low in the sky. "Suppertime already? I gotta be getting back. I always eat with the folks on Sundays." He stood and stretched, raising his arms above his head.

I could see the bulge of biceps in his upper arms. "I didn't mean to run you off. We have lots of food here. Mama says for you to stay."

"Thanks for the invite, but I really gotta go. Mama's probably holding supper on account of me now. I told her I'd be right back, and here I've been sitting around jawing the fat. Tell your mama thanks, anyway." Neil gave Roy, Jr. another hard, arcing push on the tire swing as he went by, then drove off without looking back.

❋   ❋   ❋

"Roy, you and Lacey go on to the hospital," Mama said after we finished eating. "I'll take care of the dishes. Lacey, you gotta see Zach's red hair. He's a McCormick, all right."

I carried my empty plate into the kitchen. I wasn't sure if I was ready to face Daddy again, especially not alone, without Grace there to stick up for me. "You look tired," I tell Mama. "I'll do the dishes, and Roy can go on by himself. I can wait till tomorrow."

"Hey, you already stayed home earlier today when the rest of us went," Roy called from the dining room. "Come on, you gotta see Zach and Julia. Benny will be fine with Mama and my two."

"I don't want to be gone too long," I told Roy as we walked to his pickup, letting him continue to think that leaving Benny was the main cause of my reluctance. "Benny isn't used to being away from me like this. He asked me today when we're going home."

"He *is* home." Roy got into the driver's side door while I slid into the passenger seat. "You, too. Living in New York City in a house full of Yankee strangers ain't no way to raise a young'un. Benny needs to be here among family, find out who he is."

"He knows who he is. I've got good friends there, and so does Benny. People care about us. That's more than I can say for family, some of 'em anyway."

"Just because we've had our squabbles don't make us any less family," Roy said. "Any one of your so-called friends could pick up and move tomorrow and you'd never see or hear from 'em again. You might not like it, but family is all you got and all Benny's got to fall back on."

"We have each other," I pointed out. "That's all the family we've had for the last six years, and we've been getting along just fine."

"So far. But he's growing up, and he's gonna have questions. Where's his daddy? His brothers and sisters? His grandma and grandpa? He don't even understand the concept of uncle and aunt and cousin."

"He's young yet. I'm trying to explain it all to him."

"You explained to him about his daddy?"

"That's my business." I crossed my arms and looked straight ahead.

"Only reason I asked is earlier today, Katie was asking me where Benny's daddy was, and I didn't know what to tell her. She said she asked Benny and Benny said he didn't have one, but Katie told him everybody had a daddy. So I was just wondering what you'd told him."

"I'll talk to him soon."

"You ain't told him nothing?"

"What's there to tell? I'll talk to him. You can tell your kids that Benny's daddy went off to war and didn't come back."

"You telling Benny he's dead?"

"No, not exactly. More like missing, I guess. Missing in action."

Roy shifted gears as we picked up speed. "You ever tried looking him up, letting him know he has a boy? He might be changed by now, glad to find out."

"I doubt it. Besides, I don't want him to know. Benny's mine." I searched for a way to change the subject. "That trailer we passed back there at the turn, was that Neil's?"

"Yep. Bought it last year when he turned thirty. Guess he decided thirty was too old to still be living at home."

"His truck wasn't there."

"Probably gone to church. From all accounts, he's been a pretty regular churchgoer lately since they got the new preacher."

"Oh, is he good?"

Roy chuckled. "Folks say he is. I wouldn't know since I go now to Shiloh Methodist with Julia. Anyway, that ain't why Neil goes. Way I understand it, the preacher's got a daughter home for the summer from one of them fancy colleges up North. Pretty good-looking, from what everybody says. Julia told Neil he ought to ask her out, but I don't know if he's even talked to her yet."

"So that's why he wouldn't stay for supper." I tried to picture the preacher's daughter in my mind—beautiful, young, dressed in the latest style. She probably had long blonde hair and manicured nails and a sweet, soprano singing voice. And, of course, she could play the piano beautifully. I glanced down at my own faded cotton dress and scuffed sandals and turned my attention to the road. In the long summer twilight, everything looked so exactly familiar that I could have traveled this road just last week on the school bus, giggling with my friends, or have jolted Daddy's old Ford into town to pick up something at the feed store or to take Mama grocery shopping. Even the dust was familiar, the sun-baked July soil stirred up beneath the tires and floating up to the open windows, carrying in it the unmistakable smell of summer. "Nothing's changed," I said to Roy as we bumped along the dirt road. "Everything's exactly the same."

Ruth Rodgers

Chapter 9

At the hospital, Roy led me first to the nursery window. Only two newborns were there, and I knew immediately which one was Zach by the light reddish fuzz of hair glinting from his fair scalp. The nurse wheeled his bassinet up to the window.

"Ain't he something?" Roy asked.

"He's perfect." Looking at him, swaddled tightly in his blanket, I felt a catch in my throat, and I remained at the window after Roy left, giving him some moments of privacy with Julia. Benny had been long and thin at birth, with a crown of fine dark hair and serious looking eyes that seemed to know me from our first meeting. He had cried when the nurse first handed him to me, but had quieted at the sound of my voice and looked up at me trustingly. From that moment everything else had dropped away—the homesickness, the fear, the anger—and I had known what the focus of my life would be. Was he missing me now? I'd have to hurry Roy along, remind him that he had to be up early tomorrow for his tobacco gathering day.

I walked down the hall in the direction I had seen Roy disappear. Julia was propped up in bed, pale but radiant. "He's beautiful," I said as I walked in.

"Thanks," Julia said. "How are the kids? I hope they're behaving themselves."

"They're fine. Katie's dying to see the baby." I remained standing, half my mind on Julia and our conversation, the other half on Benny and how he was getting along without me.

"I'll just peek in at Daddy before we go," I said after a few minutes. "He's probably asleep by now."

Telling myself to take deep, even breaths, I pushed open the heavy double doors that led to the critical care wing and made my way down the corridor. I hesitated at the doorway of his room, hoping he'd be asleep, but he must have heard or at least sensed that someone was there, for he opened his eyes and looked in my direction.

"Hi, Daddy." I stepped tentatively into the room. "It's me, Lacey. How are you feeling?"

His eyes, at first quizzical, seemed to harden. His mouth twitched, but no sound came out.

I took a few steps nearer to the bed. "You gave everybody quite a scare, you know. Mama sent me a wire and asked me to come home. How are you?"

Daddy continued to stare at me, his expression fierce and concentrated.

"Benny came with me. Two days and a night on the bus to get here. That wasn't easy with a six-year-old."

Daddy closed his eyes, his face going slack as if the effort of looking at me had exhausted him.

"Daddy?"

There was no response.

"I was hoping you'd get to meet him while we're here, see what a great kid he is."

Daddy's eyes remained closed.

"Okay. Be that way if you want." Hot, helpless anger coursed through me. "I don't know why I even bothered to come. I knew it would be like this."

Roy spoke behind me. "Hey, Pa. You awake?" He gave me a disapproving glare as he walked past me to the bed. "The doc says you're doing better. Gonna be up and out of here in no time."

I quietly eased out the open door and returned to the lobby.

"It won't do to get him all worked up," Roy said to me once we were back in the truck and on our way home. "He's a sick man, in case you hadn't noticed."

"I didn't say a thing to him except I'd come all the way from New York to see him, and I hoped he'd get to meet Benny while we were here. Then he closed his eyes like he could just erase us both out of existence." I tried to keep my voice calm and steady. "I don't know why I came back, how I could have expected him to have changed any. He was so furious at me before I left, slinging Bible verses in my face and calling me horrible names. He practically threw me out of the house." I blinked away angry tears.

"He warned you about what could happen if you ran off to Jacksonville, but you wouldn't listen."

"I know I made some bad decisions, and I've had to live with them. But you weren't around when I came home. You have no idea how bad it was. He went absolutely crazy, raving about hunting Dwayne down and making him marry me at the end of a shotgun. That's why I had to mail that letter to myself so I could say it came from Dwayne. I don't care any more about his disowning me. I can live with it. But he can't do this to Benny."

"Do what to Benny? What's he gonna do, laid up in that hospital bed?" Roy's voice was harsh and disapproving. "I hope you didn't come all this way just to give him another stroke. It won't do for you to go agitating him in his condition."

"I'm the one coming all this way to make amends, and he's the one refusing to accept them. So how is everything still my fault? Tell me that." I crossed my arms and stared straight ahead at the road in front of us.

Roy didn't answer, and we rode the rest of the way home in silence.

❊　❊　❊

The kids were on their stomachs on the living room floor when Roy and I returned, the Sunday comics spread out in front of them. Katie was pointing at each picture square as she read aloud. Benny looked up briefly as we walked in but then turned his attention back to the comics.

"Hey, Benbo, we're back." I reached for a foot waving in the air as I sat on the sofa just behind him and held on for a moment, torn between relief that he'd been okay in my absence and hurt that he hadn't missed me as much as I had missed him.

After Roy left with Katie and Roy, Jr., Benny moved onto the sofa beside me, leaning against my shoulder. I put one arm around him. "It's getting late," I told him. "Time for a bath and a story and then it's beddy-bye for you."

Mama yawned. "Bedtime for me, too. I'll see you in the morning."

"Goodnight, Mama."

After helping Benny with his bath, I tucked him into Simon's old bed and put Dog in his arms. "Benbo, we need to talk."

Benny's eyes widened at the seriousness of my tone.

"It's about your daddy. I know Katie and Roy, Jr. asked you."

"I told them I didn't have one, but Katie said everybody had to have a daddy. Is that true?"

"Well, sort of. You did have a daddy once, but he never even saw you. It was during the war, and he went off on a big ship before you were born, and I never saw him again."

"Did he get killed?" Benny asked.

"No, I don't think so. We just got separated and he never found us again after the war."

Benny propped himself up on one elbow. "We can find him."

"No, it's been too long a time." I adjusted Benny's pillow. "But we've got each other, and that's all that matters. If Katie or Roy, Jr. asks you again about your daddy, you just tell them he went off to the war before you were born."

"A soldier?" Benny asked, his eyes wide. "Was he big?"

"A sailor in a white uniform. He was in the United States Navy. Yes, he was big. Real strong and handsome, with dark curly hair, just like yours."

"Big as Roy, Jr.'s daddy?"

"Yes. Just as big."

Benny smiled. "I'm gonna tell Roy, Jr. tomorrow my daddy went off to fight, and he's big, and he's coming to find me when he's finished fighting."

I sighed. "I wouldn't count on it, Benbo. The war's been over a long time. Sometimes people just drift apart and they never find each other again."

"I'll go find him when I'm bigger. Roy, Jr. can help me. We'll look on all the boats."

"No, honey, you don't understand. Someday, when you're older, I'll tell you more." I bent and kissed his forehead. "You and Dog go to sleep now. And if you need anything during the night, I'll be right here." I pointed to the bed in the bigger room, visible through the open doorway.

I waited until Benny had turned onto his side and closed his eyes before turning off the light. Then, still too full of thoughts to sleep, in spite of the tiredness I felt, I returned to the living room and picked up the Sunday paper. The front page was covered mostly with news of what was happening in Korea. President Truman was still referring to it as a "conflict" rather than a "war," as if avoiding the term somehow made it more palatable to all of us who had lived through World War II.

If Dwayne still wanted a war, he could go fight this one. Save the world from Communism. I could understand Benny's desire for a big, strong father figure to brag about to the other boys, but I couldn't help cringing at his eagerness to go find him. How could I explain to a six-year-old that there was no way his father was ever going to re-enter our lives? In my early letters to Dwayne, I had begged for a response, promising undying love if he would only throw me a tiny morsel of hope—write only a paragraph, only a sentence—to say he loved me and would return, but now, after all the years of abandonment, there was no way I wanted him back into our lives, not even if he came crawling on hands and knees over broken glass.

Finally, I laid the paper aside and prepared for bed, but I could not relax into sleep. The hospital visit kept replaying in my mind—Daddy's cold, steely eyes, his face turning away when

I mentioned Benny's name. The advice from my supervisor at the insurance office in Jacksonville to go home to my parents had been kindly and well- intentioned, but if I had been able to foresee what was to follow, I knew now that I would have fled anywhere other than home.

※　※　※

I'd arrived home in mid-October. Although the war was over, Simon was still in Europe doing cleanup work, and would not return home for months yet. Grace and Roy were both married, with their own families, so that left only Geneva still at home with Mama and Daddy, and she was counting the days until Tom was to be released from his army post in the Pacific. Her job at the paper mill meant that she was gone every weekday, leaving early and coming home late, so for most of the time it was just me at home with Mama and Daddy. I didn't tell them much at first, only that the office was laying off girls now that the men were coming home and needing jobs. But I was half-dead with fatigue, and the morning nausea wouldn't go away.

※　※　※

"You have to go see Dr. Hastings," Mama keeps telling me. "You've got some sort of virus. All them city germs."

"I'm fine," I tell her. "There's nothing wrong with me." I've known Dr. Hastings my whole life: he tended all my childhood illnesses. But Mama won't let up, and by mid-November, I finally give in to her insistence.

"You're at least four months pregnant," Dr. Hastings tells me after a brief examination. "But you knew that already, didn't you?"

I nod, unable to meet his eyes.

"You'd better tell your mother. She's going to have to know."

I begin to cry right there on the examining table, and Dr. Hastings pats me on the shoulder. His tone is soothing and sympathetic. "You're not the first girl this has happened to, though I know it seems that way right now. Everything will work out all right. You just tell your parents, and they'll take care of everything. Of course, the best option is marriage, but if you don't want to do that, there are places you can go and have the baby quietly, with nobody knowing. The state adoption agency will find it a good home, and you can get on with your life. Right now you just concentrate on taking care of yourself and this baby." He smiles reassuringly. "You talk it over with your parents. We'll get you started on some prenatal vitamins and iron, and I want to see you again in a month. Okay? Your body is doing a wonderful thing here, you know, and you've got to do everything you can to help it along. No more tears now. Let me see a smile before you go."

I try to give him a smile, and on the way home I confess to Mama what Dr. Hastings has said, filling her in with part of the truth about Dwayne, about his being in the U.S. Navy and having sailed from Jacksonville in late July, but I don't tell her that he hasn't answered any of my letters. I assure her that Dwayne is coming back for me, that we will be getting married as soon as he returns.

❄ ❄ ❄

I turned over in bed, fluffed my pillow, got up to check on Benny, and made another trip to the bathroom, but sleep wouldn't come. The memory of those last few weeks at home wouldn't leave me alone. Mama had wrung her hands and cried at hearing the news, but all in all, she had taken it better than I expected, and strangely enough, unburdening myself to her had been liberating. For a few days I had actually let myself believe the story I'd told Mama, and I had experienced a new burst of optimism that I would hear from Dwayne and that things would turn out all right, after all. But as more weeks passed with no letters arriving in our mailbox, Mama had become more and more frantic. Daddy still hadn't been told, and I kept begging for more time. After all, Dwayne was in the middle of the ocean on a ship. Communication was slow. His letters had been lost. I wrote one last time to Dwayne, a long, hopeless, self-pitying letter telling him how scared and lonely I was, begging for an answer, any kind of answer at all. Every day I was the first one to the mailbox. Nothing.

❈   ❈   ❈

"I told Grace," Mama says to me the day after Thanksgiving. "She and Pete were getting ready to go home and I took her into the kitchen to pack up some of the leftovers to take with her. Nobody else was around. She says you can stay with them until the baby comes. There's an adoption place in Tallahassee, and nobody outside the family will ever have to know."

"No," I say. Lately, I've begun to feel the baby fluttering inside me, like something swimming. "I'm not giving it up. Dwayne is coming back for me."

"You're starting to show." Mama looks pointedly at my stomach. "We can't go on like this much longer. I have to tell your daddy. He'll make this sailor do the right thing by you."

❈   ❈   ❈

Even now, six-and-a-half years later, the fright I'd felt at Daddy's reaction came back as vividly as ever, and I drew my legs up into a fetal position and pulled up the sheet against a sudden chill that shook my body at the memory.

❈   ❈   ❈

Daddy bursts into my bedroom one morning without warning, his eyes glittering with religious authority, his voice hissing with condemnation.

"I never thought I'd be told my daughter was a harlot," he shouts. "After the way you were raised, and now you go off and do something like this? I warned you about running off to Jacksonville, didn't I? But you wouldn't listen." He stops to draw breath. "The first time you get out of our sight, you start flaunting yourself and let some man..." He sputters, unable to continue. As one of the deacons at Four Corners Baptist Church, he's an exemplar of Christian values, and my sin has

brought shame not just on me but on him and the entire family. I pull up the sheet and cower in my bed, helpless as a whipped dog as he gains new wind. "You think you're all grown up, do you? Well, you may be able to get out of my sight, but you never get out of God's sight. Did you ever stop to think about that?"

Over the following days, he brings out his Bible and reads me one passage after another—verses about the body being the temple of the Holy Ghost, about carnal lusts and perversions, about the sinfulness of fornication. In his eyes, I have already cast myself down into the pit, given up my inheritance to the Kingdom of God. I am no longer any daughter of his, for no daughter of his would do such a thing. He makes it clear that no bastard child will be allowed in his house and that nobody outside the family must ever learn about my pregnancy. I must be sent away to Grace until the baby is born, and then it must be given up for adoption. There are no other options.

Mama tries to intervene, but nothing will deter him from his single-minded sermon. "You did this just to spite me, didn't you?" he accuses. "You weren't satisfied to run off to Jacksonville against my orders just to prove you were all grown up. You had to take it one step further. Well, you proved yourself, all right. And look what it got you."

When I refuse to give the baby up and insist that Dwayne is coming for me, his fury becomes even more terrible. He says he'll contact the U.S Navy, have him sent home, force him to marry me; he won't have his family honor disgraced.

❈ ❈ ❈

After wrenching days of arguments and tears that left me unable to sleep, I would lie wide-awake in this very same room, my stomach knotted with fear, cradling with one hand the baby inside, its movements becoming more definite, the sudden flip-flops as it changed position, the stretching of an arm or a leg. I would close my eyes and see Dwayne, his brown eyes filled with that strange, almost scary look he had gotten that first time he pulled me down on top of him on the sofa, hear again his voice, low and husky with wanting, "Sweet, sweet Lacey." I couldn't believe that he wasn't coming back to rescue me from this nightmare.

In desperation, I'd concocted the plan to send myself a letter that would be from Dwayne, saying he had been given leave to come home and would meet me in Jacksonville where we would get married. After showing Mama and Daddy the airmail envelope and telling them the good news, I had arranged a ride to the bus station with Roy, where he stood at my elbow while I bought my ticket to Jacksonville with the last money I'd saved from my job.

※ ※ ※

"The bus won't leave for another hour," I tell Roy. "You don't need to wait. Go on. I'll be fine."

Roy looks at the bus schedule and back at the clock. "You sure Dwayne's meeting you in Jacksonville?"

"Positive." I force a confident smile. "You go on. I know you have work to do."

"You write and let us know where you are soon as you have an address. Mama's going to be worrying."

"I will. I'll bring Dwayne home soon to meet everybody." I shoo him away.

As soon as he is gone, I hurry down the street to the bank, the forged check for five hundred dollars burning in my hand.

"I'm getting married," I say to the teller. "In Jacksonville." I hand over the check. "My wedding present from my parents. My fiancé is coming home from the Pacific. He was at Okinawa." I chatter on nervously, while the teller cheerfully counts out the bills and congratulates me.

Back at the station I board the bus for Jacksonville in case anyone should decide to check, but once I arrive there I buy a ticket for the next northbound bus. I have no idea where I'm going or how I'm going to manage on my own, but I know I have to protect my baby.

Chapter 10

Monday, July 14, 1952

When I walked into the kitchen the next morning Mama had already made coffee and was kneading biscuit dough. "You're up early," she said.

"I heard noises out here. Sounded like somebody talking."

"Oh, that was just Neil. He came over and milked the cow before heading to Roy's."

"Already?" I reached into the cabinet for a coffee cup. I'd have to get used to these early morning hours again.

Mama pinched off a handful of dough and rolled it in her hand to shape a biscuit. "Benny still sleeping?"

"Yes. He stayed up past his bedtime last night." I poured myself a cup of coffee, lowering my nose to breathe in its aroma, feeling the warm steam bathe me into wakefulness before taking a sip. "Um-m. Good." I watched as Mama shaped another biscuit. "Daddy seems to be improving."

Mama placed the biscuit on the pan. "When the doctor said to notify family, we didn't know if he'd pull through or not. Your being here is such a help, to him and me both. I know he's pleased as punch about you coming all this way to see him."

"Pleased? You're dreaming, Mama. Last night, when I told him Benny and I had spent two days and a night on the bus to get here, he wouldn't even look at me. He shut me out like I wasn't even there. He'll never forgive me, will he?"

"These last few years have been hard on him. Hard on both of us." Mama continued patting out biscuits, not looking at me. "You were so set on going off to Jacksonville, so determined to go against our wishes. He looked at it as defiance, pure and simple. He thinks you got pregnant to spite him."

"To spite him?" My hand jerked, sloshing coffee onto the oilcloth table cover. "I got pregnant to spite him?"

"He's a good man, Lacey. He tried, both of us tried, to raise all you children with Christian morals. And he's never asked anything of any of you that he didn't live up to himself. You know that."

"He wanted—all of you wanted—me to give away my baby. I was so scared, but I knew I wasn't giving my baby away to strangers. Roy thinks it was the money he still holds against me." My hand shook as I lifted the coffee cup to my mouth. "I thought returning it would make things better. But he's still the same."

"It wasn't so much that he begrudged you the money itself, but it was the way you did it. Wait a minute." Mama put the pan of biscuits in the oven and wiped her hands on her apron. Then she left the kitchen, returning with a wooden cigar box, a rubber band holding it shut. "Here. Open it."

I took off the rubber band and raised the lid. The box was full of money, a jumble of one and five dollar bills, a few tens. "What's this?"

"It's all there," Mama said. "All five hundred. He wouldn't take it. Said he didn't want no tainted money. I saved it all for you."

"Tainted?" What did he think I'd done for those dollar bills? I'd gone without meals to pay that money back. Emptied wastebaskets, cleaned toilets, scrubbed floors on my hands and knees. "It's his money." I pushed the box away. "I paid him back, every penny. I don't want it."

Mama put her hand on my shoulder. "You need it more than we do. Take it for Benny's sake."

Five hundred dollars. I could buy Benny new school clothes,

make a deposit on an apartment, buy myself a new outfit for job hunting. "No! He's not going to do this to me." I wrenched away from Mama's touch. "I went hungry to send him this money. He's going to accept it if I have to cram it down his throat."

Mama frowned. "Your father is a very sick man, Lacey. You're not going to upset him in his condition."

"Then why did you send me that telegram to come home? You knew what it would be like. When I mentioned Benny, he closed his eyes and turned his head away as if he didn't want to hear about him, as if by ignoring me he could pretend Benny didn't even exist."

"The doctor said ... I didn't know if you'd come or not. I was afraid—"

I looked at Mama's slumped shoulders, her gray-streaked hair. "It's all right, Mama. I'm glad I came. I've wanted to come for the longest time. I wanted everybody to meet Benny."

Mama stirred the grits on the stove. "You don't know what it means to me, having you home again. And seeing what a great job you've done with Benny. Roy is tickled pink. He's hoping you'll stay, get a job here."

"Yeah, he thinks Benny and I should move back here, be one big happy family again. What a joke. I should pack my bags and get me and Benny out of here fast while we're still in one piece." I closed the cigar box, snapped the rubber band around it, and pushed it across the table. "Here. It's his money. Make him take it."

Mama reached for the box. "If you ever change your mind, it'll be waiting for you. On the top shelf of the wardrobe in your and Geneva's old room."

❊　❊　❊

After breakfast, I reached for the car keys on the nail beside the back door. "I promised Julia last night I'd do her laundry today while Katie and Roy, Jr. are over at her mother's. Benny can go with me, and you can get some peace and quiet after all that houseful of company. Is it okay if I take the car?"

"Sure. There's nobody else here to use it. Tell Roy to come eat dinner with us. With Julia in the hospital, there's nobody there to cook for him."

"Okay, I'll tell him if I see him."

Daddy's new car was a long, low '51 Chevy with wide, round fenders, quite a change from the old, boxy buggy of a Ford I had learned to drive. It jerked backward as I let out the clutch too fast after shifting into reverse, then jumped again as I started forward. Benny's eyes grew wide, but I smiled reassuringly. "I'm a little rusty, I guess. I'll get the hang of it in a minute." It had been a long time since I'd driven a car; in New York we had walked everywhere or taken the subway.

Benny sat very still and straight, looking out the windshield as I maneuvered the car into the road. "Can you drive us back home?" he asked.

"Well, I guess I could, but this isn't my car. We're just borrowing it to go over to Uncle Roy's for a while."

Benny settled back. "I'm gonna tell Roy, Jr. about my daddy and see if he wants to help me look for him. I bet we can find him."

"Don't count on it, Benbo. Like I told you last night, it's been too long a time. And Roy, Jr. won't be there, anyway. He and Katie are spending the day with their other grandma."

"Other grandma?" Benny looked confused.

"Aunt Julia's mother," I explained. "Don't worry. You have only one grandma. And one grandpa, so you don't have to worry about any other ones."

Benny was quiet for a moment. "I want to go home," he said finally.

"I know you miss everybody," I said. "We'll go soon, I promise. We can go into town later and give Dorothy a call, tell her we'll be staying through the week. You can tell her about your cousins and the tire swing and everything."

Benny's eyes brightened. "I'll ask her if my daddy's been there, looking for us. We have to get back, in case he comes."

I tousled Benny's hair, so coarse and curly like his father's.

"Honey, it's been six years. Your daddy never even saw you, never got to know what a super kid you are. It's just you and me, Benbo, always was and always will be. No matter where we are, it's you and me. Understand?"

Benny nodded, but I knew he didn't.

※　※　※

By eleven-thirty I was hanging the last load of clothes on Julia's clothes line. All morning I'd been listening to the steady rumble of the tractor in the field as it pulled the sled up and down the rows of tobacco. Roy and Neil were out there, bent over in the blazing July sun, picking the ripening leaves off the tobacco plants and loading them onto the sled to be hauled up to the tobacco barn. A few years ago I'd have been among the girls and women at the barn, waiting for the load of tobacco to come in from the field, to be tied onto sticks and hung in the barn for curing, my hands and arms getting covered with the sticky black tar that was almost impossible to remove. At least I had left all that behind me.

I was pinning a pair of Roy's work pants on the line when I heard the tractor coming toward the house. Roy was driving, and Neil was standing beside him on one running board while a young Negro man stood on the other. Roy stopped in the lane, and the young Negro man jumped down and started toward the little frame house I had noticed the day before. Soon he was joined by a woman and several small children who emerged from the shadows of the shed roof attached to the tobacco barn and all of them disappeared into the house.

Roy and Neil dismounted and walked toward me. Both wore caps and long-sleeved shirts that were coated with black tar. Their hands were black, and there were black streaks across their foreheads where they had wiped the sweat off with their hands.

"Hey, Lacey," Roy called, "thanks for doing the wash."

"Nothing to it," I called back. "Hey, you must be quite the squire these days, having a full-time sharecropper living on the

99

premises."

Roy grinned. "I'm doing okay. Seeing as how I'm farming most of Daddy's land now as well as mine, I needed some help. Silas is a good worker. I can say that for him."

Roy's words brought back Daddy's face in the hospital bed, the frailness that had crept up on him over the past six years, and I was silent as I watched Roy take down a bar of soap from above the pump house door. He and Neil passed it back and forth as they both scrubbed the tobacco tar from their hands and faces at the outside spigot.

"You got us some chicken fried up, too?" Roy asked when they were both clean. "I'm starved."

"Me too," Neil added. "We gonna get some of your good New York cooking?"

"Afraid not." I looked at Roy, avoiding Neil's teasing grin. "Mama said for you to come to her house for dinner. You too, Neil. She's fixing plenty."

"Thanks," Neil answered, "but I already told Ma I'd eat with her today—Julia being in the hospital and all. Wouldn't want to disappoint her." He flashed me a smile. "I'll take a rain check, though, for after you relearn how to make biscuits."

"You might have to wait a while for that." I untied the bag of clothes pins from around my waist and placed it in the empty basket, and by the time I straightened, Neil was already in his pickup, spinning off in a cloud of dust.

❄   ❄   ❄

Over dinner, Roy asked if I'd take Mama to the hospital to see Daddy, explaining that he had to get back to work. "Tell Julia I'll see her tonight. Daddy, too."

"What about Benny?" I asked. "He can't go to the hospital, can he?"

"He can go in the lobby, all right," Roy answered. "Just not into any of the rooms. You and Mama will have to take turns visiting, that's all."

"Okay, then, sure." While Mama visited, I could call Dorothy from the pay phone in the lobby and let her know how things were going and when I'd be back.

After the dishes were done, I went to the bedroom and riffled through the few clean clothes I'd unpacked from my suitcase. Everything was old and faded. When I'd last left home, telling Mama and Daddy I was meeting Dwayne to get married, the only clothes I could still fit into were one elastic-waist skirt and a few loose-fitting blouses, so all my clothes from high school, plus the three or four stylish career outfits I'd bought with such promise in Jacksonville, had been left behind in the cedar wardrobe in my old bedroom, relics of a life buried almost as soon as it had begun. Maybe they'd still be there. They'd all be hopelessly out of style now, but maybe I could refashion them and make them work.

I crossed the hall and opened the door of the wardrobe. Sure enough, here was the red linen with the white sailor-style collar, and the tight black skirt with the sexy kick pleat, like Katherine Hepburn's in the movies, even my white graduation dress, yellowing slightly with age. Would they still fit? I finally pulled out a blue and white dotted Swiss with a square neckline and a swingy gored skirt, my senior Home Economics sewing project. A row of tiny white buttons ran down the front from its neckline to its mid-calf hem. The length was outdated; everybody was wearing skirts just below the knee now, but when I tried it on, it still fit perfectly. I applied some bright red lipstick and then wiped most of it off, remembering Daddy's admonitions, and brushed my hair. I still looked pretty good, I told myself as I twirled in front of the mirror. If Neil thought I was still the little pest who used to follow him and Roy around, he should see me now. I wondered again what the preacher's daughter looked like.

❋   ❋   ❋

On the way to the hospital, Mama directed me to Simon's little walk-up apartment one street over from downtown to see if he had returned from his trucking run, but there was no sign of him there. "I guess he's not back yet," Mama said. "Sometimes he's gone for a week or more at a time. I'll ask Roy to check tonight."

"I hope he gets back soon," I said. "I'd hate to come all this way and not even see him while I'm here."

At the hospital I sent Mama off to see Julia and Daddy and then headed for the pay phone.

Dorothy's familiar voice was comforting. "Lacey, hello. It's Lacey," she called to someone. "How's your father? Is he better?"

I explained the situation. "I may need to stay a little longer than I first planned, but I'll let you know. Benny wants to say hello." I handed the phone to Benny. "Make it quick. I don't have much change."

"Hi," Benny said, and listened for a few seconds. "Okay. I love you, too." He handed the phone back to me but then tugged on my arm as I said goodbye.

"Wait, Mommy. I forgot to ask if my daddy had come looking for us."

I led Benny to the sofa and pulled him close beside me. Nobody else was in the lobby. "Benbo, I don't want you to get your hopes up about your daddy. All this time, since you were a little tiny baby—all the summers in the park, all the winters playing in the snow, all the Christmases, birthdays, all the days playing with the other kids—a long, long time. Remember how long a time it's been? Six whole years." I counted off six slowly on my fingers. "Your daddy never even saw you. He left ages and ages ago, before you were born. It's just you and me. Always was and always will be. We don't need anybody else. Okay?"

Benny nodded, but I knew that I had opened a door that could never be closed again.

When Mama returned to stay with Benny, I walked first to the critical care wing, every step feeling as if I were wading waist-deep against a strong current. I'd peek in at Daddy only for a minute, just long enough to tell Mama I'd seen him, before going on to visit with Julia. No confrontation, no "agitating," as Roy had put it. I'd simply say hello and then leave.

Daddy's eyes turned toward the door as I entered. Of course,

Mama would have told him I'd be coming. "Hi, Daddy." I kept my voice upbeat, optimistic. "Mama said you were looking stronger. Are you feeling better?"

Daddy's eyes focused on me, but his face remained expressionless.

"Benny's in the lobby right now. I can only stay a minute." I took a few steps closer to the bed, remembering my conversation with Mama earlier in the morning, the cigar box full of money that he wouldn't accept. "I'm sorry about taking the money. I really am. But I had no choice. I had nowhere to go, nobody to turn to. I paid it all back, every penny. Why wouldn't you take it?"

Daddy's eyes blinked shut and then opened again. He waved his right hand and grunted as if trying to say something, but then finding it too much of an effort, fell silent again With one side of his mouth drawn down, his expression wasn't exactly a frown but something more like sadness or resignation. Looking at the heavily lined contours of his face, the thinning white hair, all the anger I'd been storing up over the years—all the unfairness of his continued rejection of me and of Benny—shriveled into a hard, helpless knot in the pit of my stomach.

His hands, which I remembered as strong and tanned and rough with calluses, were freckled with age spots, their dark blue veins twisted and mottled just beneath the skin. He'd always seemed old to me, from the time I was a child, but it had been a vigorous, ageless old, not anything associated with illness or death. *I'm farming most of Daddy's land now as well as my own*, Roy had said this morning, and standing there, with my hand on the hospital bed railing, it hit me, like a blow to the chest, that his mortality was a sure fact, not an abstraction.

"Never mind," I said, my voice growing shaky. "I'll go now and let you rest. But I want you to know that when Mama asked me to come home, I did it. I didn't think twice." I touched the back of his hand lightly with my fingertips, then turned and fled before the tears that had sprung to my eyes had time to fall.

In the hallway I shook my head to clear my mind before walking to the nursery window. Why had I let myself get so emotional? After all the names he had called me—all the accusations he had flung at me—why did I still care? It wasn't for me, I told myself, but for Benny that I coveted his good opinion, his acceptance.

Behind the nursery window, Zach was sleeping, his hands curled into tiny fists. I brushed at my wet eyes, remembering uncurling Benny's infant hand and sticking my finger into his palm, the surprisingly strong grip of his fingers around mine. This tiny baby had to do absolutely nothing to earn Daddy's love and acceptance as a McCormick while Benny would likely never get it. It wasn't fair. Anger rose again, but I tamped it back and crossed the hall.

Julia was in bed, head elevated against her pillow, eager for news of the kids.

"Katie and Roy, Jr. are spending today at your mother's. Roy ate dinner with us, and he said to tell you he'd see you tonight. By the way, you're looking great. And Zach is precious."

"Thanks. I'm so glad he's finally here." She patted her rounded stomach. "However do you keep such a trim figure? I'm envious."

I put my hands around my waist, spreading my fingers across my flat stomach. "Just luck, I guess. This is one of my old dresses from high school. It's years out of style by now."

"It's very attractive. It brings out the blue of your eyes." Julia shifted to a more upright position. "You've got the life. A single girl in New York City."

I grimaced. "You sound like Neva. I'm the mother of a six-year-old, remember?"

"I know, but even so, it must be exciting. You're young, attractive—you must meet loads of men in the city."

"Not me. I washed my hands of men a long time ago. Who needs 'em?"

"There are a few things they're good for. I guess that could be good or bad, depending on how you look at it." Julia's mischievous smile made me laugh in spite of myself.

"All the menfolks going off to war sure changed things for our generation," she continued. "It's a new age for us, I guess, being able to support ourselves and not have to have a man take care of us. Of course, Roy didn't go off to fight, so I missed out on that. I just got to stay home and have babies."

"I don't have much of a career yet," I admitted. "Maybe someday, when Benny's older."

As I drove Mama home I kept thinking about what Julia had said about it being a new age for women. Maybe she and Neva were right—I hadn't been taking advantage of the opportunities that were available to me in New York. I had just been letting myself drift along for the last six years, letting time flow past me like a river while I stood on the bank without casting in my line. But things would be different in the fall when Benny started school. I had big plans for the future.

Right now, though, Julia's words kept getting mixed up with Daddy's frail, old-man gauntness. Maybe I'd take him a present from Benny tomorrow, a drawing. To Grandpa. From Benny. He'd have to accept a gift.

Ruth Rodgers

Chapter 11

Back at home, I sat in the porch swing, still wearing the dress that, according to Julia, looked so attractive on me. Maybe I'd just keep it on for a while. It had been a long time since I'd given any thought to my looks or figure. At my job in the rooming house, working around kids all day, it hadn't seemed important.

Mama went inside and brought out two cardboard fans, handing one to me before taking a seat in one of the rockers. "Whew, it's hot."

Benny wandered around the corner of the house. "Don't go too far," I cautioned him. "Stay where I can see you."

"Oh, let him explore," Mama said. "There's nothing around there except the clothes line and my flowers. He can't hurt nothing."

"He's not used to wide-open spaces like this. It's different in the city." I watched as Benny picked up a stick and dragged it behind him. When I was his age, I'd played outdoors all day long—climbing trees, watching the frogs and turtles at the pond, exploring for treasure. I was always discovering things: a tiny bit of leather, a broken piece of china, an especially smooth stone—certain that these were items left behind by Indians who once lived in this very spot. Roy, five years older, had grown up too soon, already doing a man's work by the time he was ten, and Neva was more of the indoor type, her nose stuck in a book or in the kitchen with Mama, perfecting her domestic skills, so as the baby of the family, I was left alone to be a child in what seemed to me a houseful of adults. Grace and Simon, both teenagers by then, had seemed almost as grownup as Mama and Daddy.

"What's it like living in New York?" Mama asked.

"It's big. Lots of people. Lots of stores, teeny little places with strange names, Italian and Irish and Jewish and German and Chinese. Not many trees, except a few in the parks. You'd think the building I live in is really huge. It's four stories tall, plus a basement, but that's short compared to most of the buildings uptown—so many skyscrapers there you'd think they'd block out the sun. And there's always something going on."

"I always heard Yankees were stand-offish. Wouldn't give you the time of day."

"People who say that are the ones who've never been there. Once you get to know them, they're like people anywhere. I have lots of good friends. We sit out on the stoop at night and listen to the radio and watch the kids play stickball in the alley."

"Stoop? What's that?"

"That's what New Yorkers call porches. They're not big like this porch, but they serve the same purpose. People are pretty much the same up there as down here."

"I wouldn't know." Mama waved her cardboard fan faster. "The farthest north I ever been was to Macon, Georgia, when Grace took me up there to visit my cousin Ophelia. Grace wanted us to drive on up to Atlanta and see that Stone Mountain, but Macon was far enough from home for me. I figure if God had wanted me to see mountains, he'd have put some down here in Florida."

I laughed. "You know how I ended up in New York City? In Pine Lake I bought a ticket to Jacksonville, in case anybody checked, you know, but nobody was waiting for me there, of course, so I went up to the counter and bought another ticket. The man asked me where I was going and my mind went blank. The only place I could think of was New York City. When I got off there, I figured I'd reached the end of the line."

"However did you manage, all alone like that? I'd have plumb died of fright."

"Well, it was a long trip, so I did a lot of thinking on the bus. I figured first I'd get a cheap hotel room for a few nights while I spent my days looking for a job. I just started knocking on doors and asking for work. My first job was cleaning offices at night. Later I met Dorothy and moved into her rooming house and got the job I have now. The rest you know from my letters."

"God was surely watching out for you. I prayed every night for you to be safe."

"Thanks, Mama. I know you did. You look tired. Why don't you go rest a while?"

"Maybe I'll go in and put my feet up and turn on the electric fan. You coming?"

"I'll stay out here and keep an eye on Benny."

After Mama went inside, I leaned back in the swing. I didn't want her to know how terrified I'd been when I first arrived in New York, but that was a day I'd never forget.

❋   ❋   ❋

It's dusk when the bus stops, and I collect my suitcase and step out into this strange, teeming city, ready to tackle whatever I have to for the sake of the baby inside me, but the freezing air immediately turns my lungs to ice and makes me shiver all over. I'm wearing only a cotton skirt and blouse and a light sweater, for it hadn't been cold at home when I left. I lift my suitcase in front of me to ward off some of the wind and start reading signs, looking for a room for the night, but I see nothing except storefronts and offices. Afraid to wander too far from the bus station, my only touchstone in this humongous, frightening place, and frozen to the bone, I huddle in a doorway alcove and wait for someone who looks trustworthy to pass by so that I can ask for directions.

When a young, ruddy-cheeked policeman walks by on his beat, I drum up the courage to speak to him, but when I tell him I need a place to stay the night, he insists upon hailing a taxi for me and directing the driver to take me to the nearest Salvation Army shelter, despite my protests that I have money.

Accepting charity is an embarrassment that goes against all my upbringing, but he won't take no for an answer. "Just for tonight," he says. "They'll feed you and give you some warmer clothes, at least. Then you can leave in the morning."

At the shelter, I reluctantly accept the offer of some hot soup and a cot, planning to leave at daybreak, but the morning air is even more frigid than the night before and white flakes of snow are falling—something I've never seen before—so I'm still working up my courage to brave the weather when a matronly, silver-haired counselor comes over and takes me into a private office where she enthusiastically describes the Florence Crittenton Home for Unwed Mothers only a few blocks away.

"No, you don't understand," I insist. "My husband is in the Navy and will be coming home soon. I just need a room for a few days, that's all. I have money." As I pull out my wallet to show her the folded twenty dollar bills from the bank, I notice that her eyes are focused on my left hand, conspicuously devoid of a wedding band.

I cover my left hand with my right one. "He's coming home from the Pacific, from the war. We didn't have a chance to have a real wedding yet, in a church with an organist and flowers and cake. But we're planning one, just as soon as he gets home."

❄ ❄ ❄

Benny had walked out of my sight line. I stood, crossed the porch, and started down the steps. "Benny, where are you?" Then I saw him, headed toward the old wooden wagon beside the corn crib. "Don't go beyond the wagon," I called. "Stay in sight." I went inside and got a Coca-Cola from the refrigerator, left over from the ones Geneva had bought on Saturday, then returned to the swing and rubbed the cold glass bottle against my face. I couldn't believe how easily lying had come to me on that first freezing morning in New York. Maybe it was because it hadn't seemed like lying at the time; I was still in naïve denial then—all my daydreams and nighttime fantasies had been of Dwayne's return, of the storybook wedding and the happily-ever-after ending.

❅   ❅   ❅

I leave the shelter with a heavy winter coat, along with a pair of warm gloves and wool knee-high socks and heavy black boots, all selected from their thrift shop, and all of which I insist on paying for. I put on the socks on top of my own thin white ones and stick my saddle oxfords into my suitcase, carrying it with me as I walk back out into another frigid December day.

After buying a newspaper from a corner stand, I duck into a tiny café to study the help-wanted ads over a cup of coffee, but the sheer quantity of them is overwhelming. The addresses mean nothing to me, and the telephone numbers are useless, since I have no way of telephoning except from a pay phone booth. Since there are so many, I decide a better approach would be to just start walking and ask for work at every office and store I come to.

But as soon as potential employers glance down at the growing bulge of my stomach, they gently shake their heads. No, they have no vacant positions, certainly nothing suitable for someone in my delicate condition. All day long I keep getting recommendations for the Florence Crittenton Home, and all day long I keep repeating the same story about a husband in the Navy who'll be home soon.

I make no headway in finding a job, but I do spot a "Rooms for Rent" sign on an aging brick building squeezed into a row of similar buildings. When I walk inside around dusk, a group of men are milling about the small first floor lobby area, coat collars turned up, cigarettes dangling from thin lips. I nearly turn around and leave, but the cold outside makes me turn back toward the light and warmth offered by the building. There's no sign of a check-in counter, but upon my timid query to one of the men, a tall, spare woman, brown hair pulled tightly into a bun, appears from a dim back room. She has one vacant room on the top floor that I can have for twelve dollars a week. I pay in advance without even seeing the room and then hurry up the three flights of stairs, slide the bolt across the door, and sink immediately onto the bed, pulling the coat over me for warmth.

Benny, inside me, is the only thing keeping me strong, pushing me on to make it in this strange, terrifying place. I talk soothingly to him, assuring him that everything is going to be okay. I have already named him Benjamin. It's a name I like the sound of, strong and solid, and it's from the Bible—Benjamin, the younger brother of Joseph. I'd never liked Joseph's arrogance toward his brothers, but I'd loved Benjamin and I'd felt such sympathy for him when Joseph had tricked him by hiding a silver cup in his bags of grain and then accusing him of stealing it. I've considered a few girls' names—Abigail, Diana, Rachel—but I'm positive he's a boy. Over the last few days he has become more active, and he seems to react to my moods, twisting and turning whenever I let myself give in to hopeless anxiety, calming when I talk to him soothingly, reassuringly, as I do now.

After several more days of job-searching, with Christmas approaching and desperation rising like a sour taste in my throat, I find a job cleaning offices at night. The office building is six blocks north, and then I have to walk up and down several flights of stairs, carrying brooms, mops, and cleaning supplies. I keep the job for nearly four months, until I can no longer climb the stairs, until my back and legs burn with a constant ache and Benny's kicks make me weep with fatigue and fear. As my delivery date draws nearer, I have seen no doctor in New York, and I have no idea what I will do when I go into labor. Several times I page through the phone book in one of the offices for the number of the Florence Crittendon Home for Unwed Mothers, but I don't make the call. I have no intention of giving up my baby. Somehow we'll manage. How, I don't know, but I won't let myself think about that. Right now

I'm getting by one day at a time. January passes into February and then into March, and I still haven't contacted anyone in the family, having nothing newsworthy to tell them.

❄ ❄ ❄

I finished my soda, set the bottle on the floor, and walked into the yard. Benny was playing in the wagon, climbing in and jumping out. I stood for a moment watching him, relishing the quietness—no traffic, no horns or sirens blaring, no radios blasting. A breeze rustled the leaves of the pecan trees, and I lifted my face to catch its momentary coolness. White clouds floated against blue sky. I had missed this space and quiet that allowed me to wander and think, missed the feel of the sun-warmed soil against bare feet, that intimate connection to the earth that had been a daily part of my childhood.

A pickup came down the road from the direction of Roy's house. Dark green. It pulled up beside the house and stopped. I waved. "Neil! Hi."

Neil stepped from the truck and walked over. "Hey, Lacey. We just finished over at Roy's place, so I figured I'd see what needed doing here before I go on home. You're all dressed up."

"Oh, this old thing?" I had forgotten that I was still wearing the dress I'd put on for going to the hospital. "We went into town earlier to visit with Daddy and Julia. This was one of my old high school dresses. I can't believe it still fits." I twirled a little for Neil's benefit.

"Skinny as ever, huh?" Neil grinned and adjusted his cap. "How's Mr. McCormick doing?"

"A little better, I guess. Mama thinks so, anyway."

"Well, I guess I'll go on and drive the milk cow up to the barn for you. Wouldn't want you messing up that fancy dress, now."

I felt myself blushing. "You don't need to do that. I know you're tired from cropping tobacco all day. Benny and I can take care of the evening chores."

"I don't know about that. You sure you ain't gone and got citified on me, Lacey Lu?" He nudged my arm with his elbow.

"You're the only person who ever called me that. I'd forgotten." I was acutely conscious of Neil's nearness, his teasing elbow nudge still warm against my arm. I stepped away, confused, remembering the last time I'd let a smile and a touch weaken me. "Benny and I can get the cow to the barn. I haven't forgotten that much." I looked toward the wagon. "Hey, Benny, come say hello to Mr. Hardister. You remember him from yesterday."

Benny peeked at Neil over the side of the wagon.

"He's a cute kid," Neil said. "Reminds me of you at that age."

"You think so?" I smiled with pleasure. "I can't see any resemblance."

"It's not looks so much. Something else. Mannerisms, that way of ducking his head and taking everything in when nobody knows he's even listening. That's you, exactly."

"He's like a sponge. Absorbs everything. Sometimes I wish he would let things go. When he gets his mind set on one thing, it's like—"

"Just like his mother." Neil laughed. "Admit it, Lacey Lu."

"Okay," I said. "How could he help being like me? He's my life, Neil. Without him—"

Benny jumped down from the wagon, and I went over and caught his hand. "Come say hello to Mr. Hardister."

"Hey, sport. How's Dog doing? You can call me Uncle Neil if you want." He looked over at me. "Roy's kids do."

"Thanks, Neil. That's really sweet. Benny, can you say hello?"

"Hi." Benny ducked his head and kicked at the ground.

"See what I mean?" Neil smiled at me. "You sure you've got things covered here?"

"Positive. But thanks for the offer."

"What's an uncle?" Benny asked after Neil drove away.

"Well, they're family," I explained. "My brothers are your uncles. Uncle Roy and Uncle Simon, but you didn't meet him yet. And my sisters' husbands; they're your uncles, too. Like Uncle Tom."

"Was that man in the truck my uncle?"

"Neil? No, he's just a good friend. I've known him since I was a little girl, so he's almost like family. But you can call him Uncle if you want. Katie and Roy, Jr. do. You want to?"

Benny shrugged. "Not if he's not my uncle, I don't. I'm hungry."

"Me, too. Let's go to the pasture and drive the cow up to the pen, and then we'll see if we can help Grandma get supper on the table."

It was kind of Neil to offer, but I agreed with Benny. Maybe Neil thought of me as a kid sister, but I wasn't a kid any more, and my confused reaction to his earlier elbow jab didn't feel sisterly at all. I had better be careful. I had, I reminded myself, washed my hands of men a long time ago, put all such thoughts behind me.

Ruth Rodgers

Chapter 12

After supper, Benny went out to play on the tire swing while Mama and I did the dishes. "I hope Roy remembers to check Simon's place when he goes into town tonight," she told me. "I hate it that he don't even know about Daddy's stroke."

"He'll be back soon, I'm sure. We can check again tomorrow."

"Roy says he's drinking again."

"Who's drinking? You mean Simon?"

Mama handed me a plate. "I'm afraid he'll have an accident on the road somewheres. Roy says there's always a couple of empty liquor bottles in his cab."

This was the first I'd heard of Simon's drinking. Mama had never written much about Simon in her letters to me, just that he was driving a truck and was on the road most of the time. "When did this start? After he came home from the war?"

"He was like a different person when he came back." Mama's hands stayed busy in the sink. "His unit stayed in Europe quite a while after the war ended, cleaning up them concentration camps and whatnot, before he got discharged. When he first got home, he didn't know what to do with himself. Seemed like he couldn't keep his mind on anything. He'd go off to the field to plow and forget to take the mule, or he'd take corn to the hogs and not come back for hours."

"That doesn't sound like Simon like all."

"That's what we thought, too. It scared me, the way he was

acting. I tried to get him to see the doctor, but he wouldn't go. Then he started screaming out in his sleep, and we'd find him mornings sitting straight up in a chair in the dark with his back against the wall and his gun in his lap. But it was when I started finding whiskey bottles under his bed that Daddy put his foot down. Told Simon there'd be no drinking under his roof."

"So Daddy kicked him out?"

"Simon had money saved up from his army pay, so he got that apartment in town and found a steady job hauling logs for the pulp mill. That was before he got his own rig."

"Weren't you worried about him being all by himself?"

"Of course I worried. Who wouldn't? But we figured he just needed to pull himself together and stop dwelling on the war. Other boys came home about the same time, and they were doing all right. The pulp mill was steady work; we figured it would take his mind off things. And he did seem better, right up until lately."

"Why didn't you write me anything about this?"

Mama shrugged. "I figured you had enough of your own worries without me adding more. Besides, this was mostly when he first got home, before we heard anything from you. I didn't know where you were or how to get in touch in you. Between you and Simon, I thought I'd go crazy myself there for a while."

"I'm sorry, Mama. I didn't mean to worry you. I was afraid to write and let you know where I was, afraid Daddy would send the law after me for stealing that money."

"That was all just bluster. He would never have done it." Mama handed me another dish. "Now with him in the hospital. . . I don't know what I'll do if I lose him. I've never been by myself before. When I married him, I was nineteen years old. And your daddy was thirty-four, an old man, I thought then." Mama laughed.

I was curious. Mama had never talked before about how she and Daddy had met. "Did you know him, before his first wife died? Did you know her?"

"Oh, yes, I knew them both, but they were lots older, so I thought of them as adults, and me as just a child. I taught the

Sunday school class Grace was in. She was such a happy little girl."

"And Elizabeth, she died in childbirth?"

"She started hemorrhaging, and they couldn't stop the bleeding."

"The baby—was it stillborn?"

"It was a breech birth, with the cord wrapped around his neck. Never even took a breath."

"That's so sad." I had never given any thought before to Daddy's first marriage—to how terrible it must have been for Daddy to lose his wife and baby that way, to have them both gone so early and so tragically. How had he managed to cope with such a loss?

"The saddest part was them two little children left motherless," Mama said. "Simon was three, just a baby. And Grace not much older. Isaac walked around in a daze, paying no mind to them, not knowing how to do for them."

"So what happened then? How did you fall in love?"

"He needed a wife. And them two children needed a mother. That was obvious to everyone. So folks looked around and settled on me."

"Other people picked you to marry him? And he agreed?" I couldn't believe what I was hearing. "Did you love him?"

"He was a good man, a good, churchgoing man, and I wasn't spoken for. And I felt so bad for Grace and Simon. Grace took her mother's death hard. Both of them did."

"So you married him because you felt sorry for Grace and Simon?"

"It's been thirty-two years now, and he's provided me with a good life."

"It doesn't sound very romantic."

"Romance, that's all young folks think about nowadays," Mama said. "And look where it gets them. Look where it got you. We've had a good marriage, and I just hope and pray someday you'll find a man as good as your father."

"How can you keep defending him, Mama? He practically

threw me out of the house, called me terrible names. And now you tell me he kicked Simon out, too."

"Simon was twenty-eight years old. He needed a push out of the nest. And Daddy didn't throw you out. You left on your own accord, waving that letter around, telling us you were getting married. Remember?"

"But he called me a harlot, Mama. And worse. You heard him. And he was going to send me away and make me give up Benny. I couldn't do that."

"He had a right to be angry after what you did—running off to Jacksonville like that, thinking you were all grown up and didn't need to listen to him any more. You think it didn't tear him apart when he found out what you'd done? And me, too?" Mama's voice cracked, and she turned away from me.

"He was more concerned about what the church and the community would think than about me and what I wanted. Both of you were." I dried the last dish, hung up my wet dishtowel, and walked out of the kitchen. I wanted to see Simon. He'd understand what I'd been through. I'd been so proud of my big soldier brother when I was in junior high. He, the quiet, withdrawn stranger at home, had written the family long, descriptive letters from all the exotic places he was stationed, first from North Africa and then Europe, vivid details about the countryside and quaint little villages and farms. Fighting was hardly ever mentioned; the soldiers, according to Simon's letters, seemed to spend most of their time thinking up practical jokes to play on one another, when they weren't talking about home and what they'd left behind. Simon seemed to know the life story of every man in his unit, and through his letters, I came to know them too. It was then, when Simon was farthest away from home, that I felt closest to him. He brought the war to us—all its high drama, low comedy, and personal pathos—as if it were a grand movie played out in living Technicolor.

But it had been a strangely bloodless war, I realized now, with death mentioned only in the briefest of asides. One of the boys he'd been closest to, Clancy from Tennessee, whose life story

Simon had relayed in detail, rated only a sentence. "Our unit took some fatalities yesterday, Clancy among them."

I had cried upon learning of Clancy's death, but I'd never considered the toll the war must have taken on Simon. How much had he held inside? What horrors had he seen that he couldn't commit to paper? And how could Mama and Daddy have abandoned him like that? As if all he had to do was snap out of it, forget all he'd seen and experienced? I wanted to tell him what his letters had meant to me, how I'd cried myself to sleep over Clancy's death.

And now, Mama's revelation that Daddy had banished him from the house, too, gave us something in common, a new bond.

Ruth Rodgers

Chapter 13

Tuesday, July 15, 1952

By nine o'clock the next morning the air was growing thick and clammy, the sky becoming a damp, gray blanket. As I sat on the front porch shelling butterbeans that I'd picked from the garden, I had to stop every few moments to wipe away the sweat that kept trickling down my forehead. Benny was off with Katie and Roy, Jr., playing tag in the shade of the pecan trees, Benny excited to have company again after a whole day of playing alone.

I'd still been in bed when Roy had dropped the two of them off at daybreak, his voice carrying through my open bedroom window, asking Mama if she wanted two young'uns for the day while he helped Neil with his tobacco.

As I threw a handful of butterbean hulls into the tub at my feet, I could hear one of the children counting for hide-and-seek, and I raised my head to listen, trying to distinguish whether it was Benny or one of Roy's children. At this distance they all sounded alike. Benny's words were already slowing down; his vowels were becoming more drawn out, and the "g's" were being dropped from word endings. A few more days, and nobody would know he hadn't always been a Southerner.

By eleven-thirty, the clouds were piling upon one another, growing darker and heavier, the air still and charged with expectancy. After calling the kids inside, I got out plates to set the table for lunch. "Going to let loose any minute now," I said to Mama, and as I spoke, a flash lit up the northern sky, followed by a distant rumble of thunder.

"Looks like a bad one," Mama agreed. "That means Roy will be here in a minute for dinner. Might as well get everything on the table."

As we began to carry platters and bowls from the kitchen to the dining room, the rain began suddenly and heavily, and Mama and I both ran to close windows throughout the house. By the time we'd finished, Roy was at the front door, his clothes dripping. He stepped inside, peeled off his wet shirt, and wiped his face with it.

"Food's all ready," Mama said.

"Smells good. Let me wash up a little first. Get some of this tar off."

"You want one of your daddy's shirts?" Mama asked.

"Sure," Roy answered, heading already for the bathroom. I finished putting out serving utensils and poured tea into glasses while Mama went off to fetch one of Daddy's old chambray work shirts.

Roy slipped it on, leaving it unbuttoned, while everyone took their seats around the table. It was too small for Roy, I noticed with surprise. It pulled across the shoulders and wouldn't have buttoned even if he had tried. Was Daddy that small? I'd always thought of him as huge, impossibly tall, with long, strong arms that could lift me high into the air and set me astride the old mule that pulled the plow.

Roy said grace, and I filled my plate with chicken and dumplings, a big helping of butter beans seasoned with salt pork, and fresh sliced tomatoes and cucumbers, urging small tastes of everything on Benny, who was still getting used to all the new foods he was encountering. The lightning strikes were getting closer, the thunder reverberating off the wooden walls; and rain was pounding the tin roof. I jumped at each thunder clap, and Benny, beside me, stared wide-eyed out the front window.

"Some storm, huh, Benny?" Roy asked. "Bet you don't see this in New York."

After dinner everyone sat inside, sweltering, waiting for the rain to subside, and when it slowed finally to a drizzle, Roy stood and changed into his own shirt. "Time to get back over to Neil's. Ma, if you want to go see Daddy tonight, be ready right after supper. I told Julia I'd come see her and Zach soon as I finished with work."

It was another fifteen minutes before the rain stopped entirely and the sun returned. Katie and Roy, Jr., restless from being indoors, wanted to go outside and play.

"Stay out of puddles," Mama told them sternly. "Your daddy's not gonna be happy if he comes back and finds you all wet and dirty."

"That goes for you, too," I told Benny. "Don't get your good shoes wet." I watched as Benny followed the other two down the porch steps. He was the only one wearing shoes.

"I think I'll go out, too," I told Mama. "I need to stretch my legs after all this sitting."

The air was fresh from the rain, and everywhere I looked, wet leaves glistened in the sunlight. To the west, long, straight rows of waist-high corn stalks stretched to the tree line in the distance. Beyond the corn field, just around the curve of the road, was the Hardister place—a rambling, white farmhouse set back on a hill. I couldn't see the house now because of the big oaks surrounding it, but in winter when the trees were bare, its chimney was visible across the field. As a child, I would watch their fireplace smoke curling into the sky and imagine myself sending and receiving smoke signals from Neil. I'd never gotten beyond "Hello" and "Come over" as ideas for messages, but the notion, nevertheless, had been exciting, my own special secret. Thinking of it now brought back my earlier feeling of confusion yesterday at the corncrib, a quickening of my heartbeat.

I walked in that direction as far as the bend in the road before hearing voices from the Hardisters' tobacco barn. They were still working. The tobacco leaves would be wet and heavy after the rain, drenching the fronts of everyone's clothes as they grouped the leaves into bundles of three and tied them onto sticks to be hung in the barn. I turned around and headed back to the house to check on the kids.

Later that evening, after Roy and Mama had left for the hospital, I sat in one of the porch rockers while the kids played on the tire swing. From the pond, a chorus of frogs began to croak, and soon crickets joined in from the surrounding trees. A whippoorwill called from somewhere in the distance, and an answering call sounded from another direction.

"Just listen," I said. "Sounds like those frogs are holding a regular convention."

"They always get loud when it rains," Katie said. "Daddy says they're celebrating."

As dusk began to settle, fireflies flickered in the brush line along the fence, and I pointed them out to Benny, who was fascinated with the blinking lights. Katie ran inside to get a Mason jar, and she and Roy, Jr. were soon leading Benny on a chase to catch some for closer inspection.

I remained in the rocker, savoring the quiet. Daddy was in the hospital and Mama was beside herself with worry over him and over Simon's drinking, but right now, for this particular moment, I felt like the writer of that poem I'd read in high school, "All's right with the world." I didn't remember the title or who wrote it, but I remembered the feeling the words gave me when I'd first read it, and how ever since then, whenever I'd felt that quiet swelling of joy at my surroundings, the joy was always associated with that poem. Simon would know it; he and Neva had been the literary ones of the family. Grace used to joke about how Simon carried a book to the field with him and read while he plowed and that's why his rows were always crooked.

I hoped I'd get to see Simon while I was here, but I wouldn't know what to say to him. As a child I'd always been a little bit in awe around him. The ten-year age difference had made him seem like an adult to me, someone mysterious in his silent reserve, someone to secretly worship from afar. I'd like to know him now as a real person, an ally who'd felt Daddy's wrath just as I had.

Nobody else, not even Mama, seemed to realize how Daddy had shut me out so completely. Maybe Simon would understand. I leaned back and closed my eyes.

"Hey. Yoo-hoo."

I jerked to attention, the chair coming down hard on the front curve of the rockers, my heart knocking in my chest. Neil was coming across the yard.

"Neil! You startled me. Where did you come from?"

Neil grinned and grabbed the tire swing, giving it a push as he passed it. "I cut across the field. I was out firing up my tobacco barn and decided to check on the corn. Mr. McCormick's crop is looking good."

"He'll be glad to hear that. Roy and Mama are in town right now visiting with him and Julia. I'm watching the kids."

Neil came up the steps and sat in the glider. "Some watcher you are. I don't see no kids."

I pointed. "Over there, catching lightning bugs. Benny's never seen any before."

Neil looked. "Poor, deprived kid. Guess you don't see many lightning bugs in New York, huh?"

"No. But there are other compensations."

"Yeah? I sure can't think of none." Neil leaned back and smiled at me. "Anyways, I figured I'd check and see if there was anything Miz McCormick needed doing before I turn in. I know Roy's got his hands full with the new baby and all."

"We got everything taken care of. The kids and I drove the cow back to the barn and gave her some hay. And we took some corn to the hogs."

"Putting you back to the old grind, huh? Bet you'll be glad to get home to New York."

"I can still put in a pretty good day's work. I spent the morning shelling butter beans." I held up my right thumb.

Neil leaned forward. "Oh, no. Poor Lacey Lu's got a sore thumb."

Embarrassed, I tucked my hand back into my lap and looked across the field, avoiding the glint of amusement in his eyes.

"Hey." Neil waited for me to look at him. "Just teasing. You look like city life's been agreeing with you. Must be those *compensations.*"

I blushed at the tone of his voice. "Benny keeps asking when we're going home."

"And what about you? Some *compensation* you're eager to get back to?"

I glanced at Neal and quickly looked away. "No, nothing special."

"No boyfriend waiting in the wings?"

"Afraid not." I walked to the edge of the porch and peered into the twilight. "I'd better call the kids back. It'll be dark soon."

Neil stood and took a step toward me. "A pretty little thing like you ain't out painting the town every night? For shame." He grinned and gave me a nudge with his elbow.

"I have a six-year-old, remember?" I kept my eyes on the kids, but I was acutely conscious of Neil's nearness. "What about you? Roy says you've got your eye on the new preacher's daughter."

Neil grinned bashfully. "He told you that? When?"

"Sunday night, when we were going into town to the hospital. Is she pretty?"

"She looks okay."

"Just okay? You asked her out yet?"

"Nah, not me. She's in college, one of them hoity-toity Northern girls' schools. She wouldn't go out with me."

"I bet she would. She'd probably like to go out and have some fun while she's here, meet some people, instead of sitting home with her parents."

"You telling me to ask her out?"

"That's up to you, I guess. I just meant don't sell yourself short. Any girl in her right mind would go out with you in a minute."

Neil smiled. "Thanks, Lacey Lu." He put one arm around my shoulder and gave me a friendly tug. "You mean that?"

"Sure I do." Pulled off balance, I stumbled against him and put one hand on his back to steady myself.

"You turned out okay yourself, considering." Neil squeezed

my shoulder and then moved toward the steps. "I gotta get home. Come over sometime and see the folks while you're here. Ma said yesterday she sure wanted to see you before you left."

"I'll do that. I'll come over tomorrow."

"They asked me how you looked and I told 'em as skinny and red-headed as ever."

"You didn't!" I pushed Neil playfully on the arm.

"Hey, watch it. I forgot dangerous." Neil put up both hands to defend himself. "It's good to have you back, Lacey Lu. Like old times. See you later." He crossed the road, climbed over the split rail fence, and turned to wave before striding off between two rows of corn.

❉   ❉   ❉

After slipping inside to get a cold drink, I returned to the porch just as a big tractor-trailer rig rounded the curve and pulled to a stop beside the house, spewing diesel fumes in its wake. For the second time that evening, I felt a quickening of my heartbeat. There was only one person it could be.

As he stepped down from the cab and came toward the porch, I studied his features. He was still slender, taller than Roy, and darker and wirier, taking more after Elizabeth, Daddy's first wife, in his hair and complexion, but he had Daddy's high forehead and piercing blue eyes.

"Simon! Hello." I lifted one hand in a wave. "You're back from your trip. You don't know how relieved Mama will be to find out—"

"Lacey?" Simon's eyes widened with alarm. "Is that you? What are you doing here? Did something happen?"

"Everything's okay." I smiled to reassure him. "Daddy had a stroke, and the doctors weren't sure how bad it was at first. Mama sent me a telegram to come home. But he's doing better now. Nobody knew how to reach you." I took a step forward as Simon came up the steps, unsure how to greet him. Simon wasn't a hugger. "It's good to see you. Mama's been so worried about you not knowing. We've been going by your apartment every day, looking for you."

Simon took off his cap as he sank onto the glider. "I've been gone all week. Just got back. So he's doing better now, you say?

I returned to the rocker. "Well, he can't move his left side, and he can't talk much, nothing that anybody can understand, anyway. But everybody says he's looking better every day. Roy and Mama are at the hospital now, and I'm watching the kids."

"You haven't seen him?" Simon laid his cap on the swing beside him and ran one hand through his hair.

"Oh, I've been a couple of times already. He's still disowning me, though. Looks right through me like I'm not even there. I don't know why I even came back."

Simon didn't answer, only pulled a packet of cigarette papers from his pocket and removed one of the thin paper strips. "I know Mama was happy to see you, anyway. How's she doing?"

"Okay. She's worried, as usual. She never saw him sick before, she says. Not even a cold."

"Looks like I missed all the excitement. How long have you been here?"

I told him about getting the telegram from Mama and the bus trip down from New York and then everything else that had happened in his absence, about Grace and Neva being up for the weekend to see Daddy, and about Julia going into labor on Saturday night.. "So Julia's in the hospital, too. It's a boy, born early Sunday morning. They named him Isaac, but they're calling him Zach. He's a McCormick, all right. Blue eyes and red hair."

"And Roy's proud as a peacock, I bet." Simon deftly curved the paper strip between two fingers and shook a line of tobacco down its center. "So, how's New York treating you? You doing all right?"

"Fine. It's strange, being back. I hadn't realized how much I'd missed everything." I waved my hand toward the road, the fields, and the woods beyond. "The kids are down there, catching lightning bugs. Benny never saw any before, so Katie and Roy, Jr. are educating him."

Simon looked where I pointed. The kids were still running back and forth along the fence line, trying to catch more bugs. "You got a city kid, huh? Who would have ever thought?"

"Roy keeps calling him a Yankee, like we're still fighting the Civil War or something."

Simon chuckled. "Aw, don't pay any attention to Roy. He always liked to torment you and Neva." He rolled the cigarette carefully, licked one edge to seal it, and reached into his shirt pocket for a pack of matches.

"Mama will sure be glad to find out you're home. She's been worrying over how to contact you."

"It's just as well I was gone. I never could stomach the smell of hospitals."

"Aren't you going to visit him?"

Simon lit his cigarette, then blew out the match and tossed it into the shrubbery beside the steps. "I'm off again early in the morning on another run, so I guess not. Besides, we don't have that much to say to each other any more."

"I thought I was the only black sheep of the family." I watched Simon take the first long drag on his cigarette and blow smoke into the air. Did his distaste for hospitals have to do with the war? I wouldn't mention any of what Mama had told me earlier, but I had given Simon an opening if he wanted to talk. I had so much I wanted to ask him about—the letters he'd written home, how the war had affected him, what Daddy had said to him when he'd told him to leave—but I didn't know how to approach such subjects. Simon had lapsed into silence.

"So you're living in town now," I finally said. "Don't you get lonesome all by yourself?"

"You don't have to live by yourself to be lonesome. Anyway, I like my own company, most of the time anyway."

"You've got a point there," I agreed. "Hey, you remember a poem from high school that ends with the line, 'All's right with the world'?"

"Yeah, it's from 'Pippa Passes,' by Robert Browning. Let's see. 'The lark's on the wing/ The snail's on the thorn/ God's in his heaven/All's right with the world.' There's more, but I don't remember all of it."

"That's a lot more than I remembered. I was sitting here earlier, listening to the frogs and whippoorwills, and that line came back to me. You still read a lot?"

"When I can. Not much time for it any more, though."

"I remember the letters you wrote home during the war— how you described everything so well I felt like I was there myself, experiencing it with you. You made it sound so brave and patriotic. I bragged about you shamelessly to all my friends. It was nothing like you wrote, was it?"

Simon took another long drag on his cigarette. The first stars were out. He pointed upward. "See up there? The evening star. See how she shines?"

I looked where he pointed. "Yes."

"That's not a star at all, you know. It's Venus. From this distance, though, she looks bright and twinkly, just like a star, doesn't she?"

"I'd never know the difference."

"You're too far away. Everything looks better from a distance. Especially war."

I hesitated, studying Simon's profile. "Remember Clancy? From Tennessee?"

Simon didn't answer.

"I remember crying over your letter. He was just nineteen. Neva thought it was silly, crying over somebody I didn't know, but I felt like I knew him, from your letters. I just bawled and bawled."

Simon blew a puff of smoke. "Europe was full of Clancys, young boys fresh off the farms and coal mines, straight from school books to mortar shells." He walked to the edge of the porch and flicked his cigarette ash into the shrubbery.

I wanted to ask more questions, but Simon kept his back to me as he stared off into the dusk. "That's some rig you got there," I said finally. "You must be doing okay for yourself."

"Can't complain. It's a living." Simon brightened at the change of subject. "Want to see her?"

I followed him down the steps and tried to pay attention to his descriptions of horsepower and instrument panels and hauling capacity, but the words all jumbled in my head.

"Very nice," I managed at appropriate intervals. The kids had come back and gathered around the truck, and after I introduced Benny to Simon, both he and Roy, Jr. had to climb into the cab and take a turn at sitting behind the steering wheel and pretending to drive. Remembering Mama's words from earlier in the day, I peeked behind the seat for whiskey bottles. Nothing but an empty Coca-Cola bottle and a couple of Baby Ruth candy wrappers. I felt mildly disappointed, as if Simon had let me down.

Ruth Rodgers

Chapter 14

Wednesday, July 16, 1952

On Wednesday, when we came back from our afternoon visit with Daddy and Julia in the hospital, Mama went off to her bedroom while I got Benny's crayons and drawing tablet and put them on the dining table. "Why don't you draw a picture for Grandpa?" I suggested. "Something happy to cheer him up and make him feel better? I can take it to him next time we visit. Don't you think he'd like that?"

With Katie and Roy, Jr. spending the day again with Julia's mother, Benny had followed me around the house and yard all morning, but now I wanted nothing more than to sit and rest for a few minutes. The visit with Daddy had been the same as the one the day before. When I'd tried to talk to him, he had closed his eyes and turned his head away as if to shut me out, to pretend I wasn't even there.

"He'll never change his mind," I'd told Mama on the way home. "I'm dead to him, and so is Benny. We might as well go back to New York and stay there."

"Oh, Honey, don't say that." Mama had looked at me beseechingly. "You don't know how much having you back here means to me—and to Daddy, too. It's just hard for him to show it, hard for him to back down after all the hurt you caused him."

"His hurt? What about my hurt? And Benny's the innocent pawn in all this. It's not his fault—" Remembering Benny in the back seat, I'd stopped myself from saying anything further.

Mama had changed the conversation then to Simon. "I was hoping to see Simon at the hospital after what you said last night about him being back from his trip."

"He was leaving again early this morning," I'd reminded her, not mentioning what Simon had said about him and Daddy not having anything left to say to one another. I'd feel the same way as Simon if it weren't for Benny. I didn't care so much for myself, but to have Daddy punish Benny for my mistake, to not even acknowledge him as his grandson—that hurt more than I could ever express. Maybe if Benny drew a picture, made a get-well card for Grandpa, it might be a crack in Daddy's armor.

Busily at work on his drawing, Benny was concentrating, the tip of his tongue between his lips. I walked quietly to the bedroom I'd once shared with Geneva, unlatched the double doors of the cedar wardrobe, and felt along the top shelf for the cigar box that Mama had handed me on Monday. It was still there—all that money still inside—all those bills I'd earned one by one with my sweat, all those hours of bending and stooping and scrubbing during that first terrible New York winter. How dare Daddy refuse it, call it tainted money?

I replaced the rubber band and returned the box to where I'd found it.

"Mommy?" Benny stood at the open door of the bedroom. "I finished my picture." He held it up.

I reached for the paper. "Let's see." It was a drawing of the oak tree with the tire swing hanging from the limb. Three stick-figure children were standing beside it. "Which one is you?"

Benny pointed. "And this one's Roy, Jr. And that's Katie."

"You did a good job," I said. "Grandpa will like seeing the swing Uncle Roy made for you. You want to write your name at the bottom?"

"No. It's for Katie." Benny took the picture back. "She gave me this." He pulled a silver whistle from his pocket. "See." He put it in his mouth and blew.

"She did? When?" I reached for the whistle. "Let me see that.

136

Did you wash it off? There's no telling where it's been or what kind of germs are on it."

"It's mine. Katie said it was." Benny gripped the whistle tighter. "She said if I ever got lost in the woods, I could blow it and she would find me."

"Well, that's nice, but you don't want to be going in the woods by yourself, ever. There are snakes and all kinds of dangers you don't know about. Katie and Roy, Jr. know what to watch out for, but you don't. Promise me you won't go anywhere out of my sight by yourself." I looked Benny in the eye and held his gaze until he promised. Then I took the whistle and swished it under hot water before returning it to him. I was happy that Benny was getting along so well with Roy's kids, but I felt a twinge of loss, too—of something changing in our relationship. Yesterday, when the three of them had come back from playing after the afternoon rain, Benny had been as muddy and barefoot as the other two, Katie cheerfully carrying his wet shoes and socks. I had immediately taken him into the bathroom and washed his feet with soap. With the polio virus an epidemic across the country, you couldn't be too careful. Nobody knew where it might be hiding or who might catch it next.

Benny tested the whistle with a piercing blast before returning it to his pocket. "Uncle Roy's taking us fishing on Saturday. He's gonna show me how to catch a fish."

"Whoa," I interrupted. "Don't you think you'd better ask me for permission before you go making plans?"

"Uncle Roy said it was okay. And Roy, Jr.'s gonna help me look for my daddy. He says we need a picture. Do you got a picture, Mommy?"

"No, Benbo. No picture." I scooped him up in a hug. "Not everybody has a daddy, you know. Look at Tony at home. There's just him and his mommy. And Brian's got just a mommy and a little sister."

"You got a daddy. He's sick, in the hospital."

"Yes. Your grandpa. You can't see him right now, but a picture would really cheer him up, don't you think?"

Benny held tightly to the drawing he had made of the tire swing. "This is for—"

"I know. That one is for Katie. But you can make another picture for Grandpa. First, though, do you want to take a walk? There's somebody I promised to visit. You can do another drawing for Grandpa later."

After telling Mama where we were going, I headed off with Benny for the Hardisters' house. With the road still damp from yesterday's downpour, our shoe prints left plainly visible tracks in the soft clay sand. Benny made a game of following me and trying to step in my footprints, but his legs were too short to match my strides, so he soon tired of that and ran ahead of me instead, investigating the chirps and rustles in the brush line along the fence, stopping periodically to wait for me to catch up.

As we approached Neil's trailer on the left, I dawdled, waiting for Benny to finish examining the Prince Albert can he had picked up from beside the road. "That's a tobacco can," I said, checking to make sure it was empty. "You can play with it if you want."

Benny squatted in the road, snapping the lid open and shut. I studied the closed windows of the trailer. Of course Neil wouldn't be home in the middle of the afternoon; he'd be off on the tractor somewhere.

"Come on, Benny, we're almost there. See?" As I pointed to the house on the right, Mrs. Hardister stepped onto the porch and shook a cloth over the shrubs beside the steps. A fine white dust of flour settled over the bushes. I waved and called out a hello.

"Lacey, is that you? Gracious sakes, it's been a long time. Neil said you hadn't changed a bit. Come here and let me look at you." Mrs. Hardister reached out her arm as I started up the steps.

I caught her hand and squeezed it. "How are you? This is Benny. Benny, can you say hello to Mrs. Hardister?"

Benny mumbled a hello and resumed playing with the lid of the Prince Albert can.

"Come on in." Mrs. Hardister led us to the front door. "I just put a blackberry cobbler in the oven. You'll have to stay till it's done so you can have a taste."

"Um. It smells delicious." I sat on the soft, rose-colored sofa, the same sofa I remembered from years before, and looked around at the familiar furnishings: the white lace curtains, the crocheted doilies on the backs of the chairs, the corner whatnot stand filled with ceramic dogs. A framed picture of Neil in his army uniform stood on the mantel above the fireplace. Stuck into one corner of the frame, outside the glass, was a small snapshot of a girl, a young woman perhaps. I couldn't see it clearly from where I was sitting on the sofa, but I kept glancing over that way, trying to make out the features of the snapshot.

Mrs. Hardister wanted to know all about New York. Benny, bored now with the Prince Albert can, kept walking around the room, looking out the window, returning to the whatnot stand with its shelves of ceramic dogs.

"Look, but don't touch," I kept reminding him.

"I'm afraid I don't have any toys around any more," Mrs. Hardister said. "But maybe there's something in Neil's old room. Let me see."

I used her absence as an opportunity to examine the photo on the mantel more closely. Neil looked so young in his uniform, so clean and fresh-scrubbed, his eyes bright blue against the olive drab of his army cap. I studied the snapshot. The girl, who couldn't have been more than eighteen, looked pleasant enough, but there was nothing glamorous or sophisticated about her. She had a round face surrounded by dark, curly hair, thick eyebrows, and serious brown eyes that seemed shy of the camera. There was no sign of makeup. She looked like a country schoolgirl. Surely this couldn't be the preacher's daughter. I was still standing by the mantel when Mrs. Hardister returned.

"Here, Benny, look what I found." Mrs. Hardister held out a balsa wood model airplane. "You can play with this."

"Be careful," I warned. "Don't break it."

"Oh, don't worry about that," Mrs. Hardister said. "It's been sitting on Neil's dresser for years gathering dust. When he moved into that trailer, I told him to take all his clutter with him, but he took just his clothes and necessities and told me to throw the rest away. Benny, you can have it. Take it with you when you go." She looked at me. "If that's all right with you."

"Thanks," I said. "He loves airplanes. Benny, what do you say?"

"Thank you." Benny sat on the floor and began to zoom the plane over his head.

I gestured at the photo on the mantel. "Neil looks so young in this picture. When was it taken?"

"Goodness, let me see. It was right after he finished basic training. That would have been '42. He enlisted right after Pearl Harbor."

"Ten years ago," I said. "Who's the girl?"

"Oh, that's Agnes, a girl he met in France. From what he wrote us about her, we thought for a while he might marry her and bring her back to the States, but nothing came of it." She shrugged. "He keeps after me to take her picture out of there, but I told him I wasn't going to take her down until he gave me a picture of another girl to take her place." She laughed.

I laughed with her, politely. Maybe this was why Neil had never married; he'd never gotten over Agnes, his first love.

"So far," Mrs. Hardister continued, "he hasn't brought me anybody else's picture. His daddy and me keep telling him he's the only male to carry on the Hardister name, but he don't seem to be doing much about it."

I didn't know what to say. "Maybe he'll surprise you one day."

"Maybe."

Before we left, Mrs. Hardister insisted we have some of the warm blackberry cobbler fresh from the oven. Benny didn't like it, so I ate his bowlful as well as my own. I had forgotten what a wonderful cook Mrs. Hardister was. No wonder Neil had teased me about my lack of biscuit-making skills.

During the walk home and for the rest of the day, I kept thinking about Agnes. Did she speak English? If not, how had she and Neil communicated? Did Neil still dream about her?

I hadn't dreamed about Dwayne for a long time now. I hadn't even thought much about him lately, not until this trip home had thrown the past so painfully back into my face. And now Benny wanted to see a photo of him, and I didn't have one. Neil had that, at least, for whatever it was worth.

Ruth Rodgers

Chapter 15

Friday, July 18, 1952

On Friday morning, I was sitting on the porch shelling peas when Roy's truck stopped in front of the house. "I'm going into town to bring Julia and the baby home," Roy called. "Be back in a little while. Keep an eye on these rapscallions, will you?"

"Sure. They'll be fine."

Benny and Roy, Jr. ran off to play, but Katie stayed on the porch. "I can help you shell peas," she said.

"Thanks, but I'm enjoying it. It's been a long time since I did this. You can go play with the boys if you want."

"They just want to play stupid stuff." Katie got another pan from the kitchen, filled it with unshelled peas, and pulled one of the rockers closer to me so that we could both throw our empty hulls into the galvanized tub on the floor between us. Katie was eager to talk about Zach, about how soon they would be back from the hospital, about how her mother had promised that she could help take care of him. I listened to her excited chatter, pleased that she had stopped worrying about Grandpa and had so readily accepted Benny and me into the family.

The two boys came running around the house and headed for the tire swing. "Hey, Katie, look at me," Benny called as he scrambled onto the tire ahead of Roy, Jr.

I winced, a twinge of jealousy suddenly spoiling my mood. Ever since our arrival, Benny had been doting on Katie. On

Sunday when he'd fallen and scraped his knee while I was at the hospital, Katie had comforted him. Then her cheerful carrying of his shoes and socks so he could play in the rain puddles, the gift of the whistle—all these tender little maternal acts—piled up in my head. And Benny went around saying "Katie this" and "Katie that" all day long. I threw a handful of empty pea hulls against the side of the tub, scolding myself silently for being jealous of an eight-year-old child. Anyway, now that Julia was coming home, Katie would transfer all her attention to the new baby, and Benny would have his first lesson in the fickleness of women.

"Hey, Katie, come on. Push us real high," Roy, Jr. called.

Katie looked questioningly at me.

"Sure, go on and play. I'll finish these up." I transferred the last handful of peas from the bucket into my pan. Another weekend was coming up. Grace would be back tomorrow, maybe Neva and Tom, too. The week I'd promised Neva was up. Time to think about returning to New York and my job. But Benny was beginning to enjoy himself; he hadn't asked lately about going home, and I was settling into the quiet routine myself, savoring the time I spent with Mama, reconnecting with Roy and Julia, and, yes, looking forward to more visits with Neil. Remembering our conversation on the porch when I'd told him he'd be a great catch for anyone and his answering grin and arm thrown around my shoulder brought a sudden warm flush to my face and neck.

Making peace with Daddy was another matter, but last night Benny had made a picture for his grandpa—a drawing of himself with a "Get Well" balloon coming out of his mouth. I had put it in my purse to give to Daddy later today. Maybe that would be a turning point, a beginning of a truce, at least.

※　※　※

By the time Roy returned with Julia and Zach, I had finished shelling the peas, had dumped the empty hulls into the hog pen, and was sweeping off the front porch. "Mama, they're here!" I called through the screen door.

Katie ran to the truck, with Roy, Jr. and Benny on her heels. I waited on the porch for Mama to join me while Katie stepped up on the running board for her first look at Zach. I could see Julia whisper something to her, and as Mama and I approached, Katie reached through the open window and gently touched Zach's arm and then his cheek. Zach yawned and turned his head toward her finger, and Katie's mouth and eyes widened with delight. Then Julia called to Roy, Jr., who was hanging back shyly, an uncertain grin on his face. Katie scooted over and I lifted him up so that he could peek in the window. Julia pulled his hand toward Zach's, and Zach opened his eyes and closed his fist over Roy, Jr.'s finger. Roy, Jr. beamed from ear to ear.

"Just one quick peek," Mama said to Julia. "I know you're ready to get home. We'll let you rest today and then we'll come over tomorrow so we can fuss over him some."

"He's so beautiful," I added. I couldn't wait to hold him against my shoulder, inhale his new-baby smell, feel him wriggle against my neck as he adjusted himself to the contours of my body. It had been so long since Benny had been an infant, depending on me to meet his every need. "Come here, Benny. Want to see the baby?" I lifted Benny up to look as Katie and Roy, Jr. scrambled into the back of the truck for the ride home.

❈   ❈   ❈

"You should learn to drive, Mama," I said as we headed to the hospital after dinner. "Especially now. It's not hard. I could teach you."

Mama sat stiffly, one hand against the dashboard. "I'd be scared to death. I'm too old to learn new tricks."

"You're not old. You're in the prime of life. Times are changing, Mama. Everybody drives now, men and women. You and Daddy need to buy one of them television sets, too, see how the rest of the country lives."

"No, thank you. Your daddy says he wouldn't have one of them things in the house. Geneva's got one, and she told me about some of the shows. There's this one with Ed Sullivan. She says he has all these colored singers on it every week and after they sing, he comes over and hugs and kisses 'em on stage. She says it's sickening to watch."

"Neva's offended, huh? Then why does she watch him? Did you ask her that?"

"Well, he has white people on too, I guess."

I laughed. "You should live in New York, Mama. I never knew there were so many different people in the world. Neva teaches Sunday School, right? Ask her if she remembers that song we used to sing, 'Jesus Loves the Little Children of the World.'"

"Children are one thing, but a white man kissing a colored woman, that's another kettle of fish. Just stirring up trouble, if you ask me."

I sighed and changed the subject.

❊   ❊   ❊

"You go first," I told Mama as we entered the hospital lobby. "Stay as long as you want." I had brought along a couple of Benny's books to read to him while we waited.

Mama was gone a long time. "He's lots better," she said when she returned. "The nurse says he sat up in a chair for nearly an hour this morning. And he's trying to talk more. He kept saying 'Home' over and over. I think he's tired of that hospital bed."

"I imagine so." I handed Benny the book we'd been reading. "I'll just say a quick hello."

When I entered the room, Daddy was half-sitting up in bed, looking more alert than I had yet seen him. He looked at me and then away, his eyes settling on the view outside the window.

"Hi, Daddy. Mama says you're doing better. Even talking about coming home." I kept my voice cheerful. "You don't need to worry about a thing. Mama and I have been doing the chores. And Neil's been coming over and milking the cow every morning. He said to tell you your corn's looking good. And his folks send their regards."

Daddy eyes turned back to me. He remained silent, but I could tell he was listening. I stepped closer to the bed and took a deep breath. "I brought you something. Benny made a present for you. He drew this last night to cheer you up."

Daddy's cold stare seemed to harbor the same stern rebuke that had been burned into my memory for the last six-and-a-half years.

"It's a picture of him, saying 'Get Well, Grandpa!' And he signed his name." I held out the drawing, but Daddy made no move to take it. *Keep calm*, I told myself. I'd promised Mama and Roy that I wouldn't say anything to upset him. I laid the drawing on the bed beside his right hand. "Okay, Daddy, if that's the way you want it. I'm going now. But I'm leaving the picture your grandson made for you here on your bed for you to look at whenever you're ready."

As I turned toward the door, I heard the word "No" spoken firmly and clearly.

I stopped and swiveled back to face him. "No? You don't want the picture? Or no, he's not your grandson? Well, Daddy, he is, much as you don't want to admit it, and there's nothing you can do to change that. Benny worked hard on that drawing, and he wanted you to have it." I felt the old anger rising again and I hurried out of the room without saying goodbye.

Ruth Rodgers

Chapter 16

Saturday, July 19, 1952

On Saturday Grace arrived, alone, about an hour before noon, explaining that Pete had remained home again with the girls, something about a church youth group picnic at Wakulla Springs that they didn't want to miss. "I can stay only a few hours," she said, reaching for my hands. "I promised Pete I'd be home before dark. Lacey, I'm so glad you're still here. I was afraid you'd take off before I got to see you again. Where's that big boy of yours? Benny, come on out and give your Aunt Grace a big hug."

Benny ducked behind me, and Grace laughed heartily. "I'll get my hug yet," she told him. "Just you wait. You can't hide from me all day. How's Daddy doing?"

Mama emerged from the kitchen, her face flushed with heat. "Better. They're starting to get him out of bed to sit up some, and he's talking more now. Raring to come home."

"That sounds like him." Grace put one arm around Mama's shoulder. "He's a tough ole geezer, all right. He don't let nothing stop him."

By lunch time, no one else had arrived. "I'm still waiting for my hug," Grace reminded Benny as we sat down to eat. Benny sidled his chair closer to mine.

"This is your Aunt Grace," I told him. "She's my big sister. She took care of me when I was a little baby, like Zach." I turned to Grace. "Julia and Zach came home yesterday. We're going over later this afternoon to visit."

"Ooh, I can't wait to see him up close," Grace answered. "He was all swaddled up in the hospital, so I didn't get a good look."

After exhausting the subject of Zach, Mama turned her attention to Geneva, saying how she really hadn't expected her to come again so soon, how difficult it was to make such a long trip with two small children.

"We can call her from the hospital," Grace said. "You can tell her how Daddy's improving."

Mama put up her hands. "I'm scared of them contraptions. I can never understand what people are saying over them anyway. You can do the talking."

After dinner I shooed Mama and Grace off to the hospital while I took care of all the cleaning up. Roy had promised to take Benny fishing this afternoon, and Benny didn't want to miss out on the trip. I'd just finished in the kitchen and gone out to the porch to cool off when Roy pulled up with Roy, Jr. "Nobody came back?" he asked me. "I thought Mama was expecting another houseful of company for the weekend."

"Grace is here. She and Mama just left for the hospital."

"Pete didn't come?"

"No. Just Grace. The girls had something to go to today, and Pete was driving them."

"Shoot. I was counting on Pete helping me catch a mess of fish for supper. Looks like it's gonna be up to us, boys. Benny, you ready to catch some fish? We brought you a pole."

Benny clambered into the bed of the truck beside Roy, Jr., a big smile on his face. I frowned at Roy. "Thanks for asking my permission."

"Ease up, Sis. I ain't lost a young'un in the river yet. I'll bring him back safe and sound, I promise."

"It's just that you could have asked first."

"Maybe I'll go see if Neil wants to go." Roy got into the truck. "Relax, will you? We'll be back in time for supper, with some fish to fry up, I hope."

"Be careful. Mind Uncle Roy," I called to Benny as Roy drove off. I hadn't seen Neil since Tuesday, the night the kids were catching lightning bugs. If Neil went with Roy, he'd spend some time around Benny and get to see what a great kid he was and how good a job I had done as his mother. But it was Saturday afternoon, so maybe he had better things to do, such as getting ready for a night out on the town with the preacher's daughter. After all, hadn't I encouraged him to do just that?

After Roy left, I was alone in the house. Feeling at loose ends, I wandered through the rooms, examining the pictures on the walls, the knickknacks on the shelves, the stack of quilting magazines on the hall table. In the little alcove that used to be Simon's private domain, I straightened the covers on Benny's bed and positioned Dog back on his pillow. When this was Simon's room, he had been such a stickler for neatness. This little space had always reminded me of a monk's cell in a monastery—bare and sterile. Maybe if we'd been Catholic instead of Baptist, Simon would have become a monk. Then he wouldn't have gone to war or had to turn to whiskey to get him through the nights.

The next room down the hall was Mama and Daddy's bedroom. It looked the same as always, the double bed with its heavy rolled iron headboard and footboard, the huge mahogany wardrobe, and the lighter oak dresser with Mama's delicate hand-crocheted runner across the top. On the other side of the room was Daddy's gun rack with his shotgun and hunting rifle. And still on the table beside the bed, standing on a stiffly starched crocheted doily, was Mama's ceramic figurine of a shepherdess with a staff, one hand up to shade her eyes from the sun, turned to look at the lamb trailing behind her. As a child, I had loved this figurine—its soft pastel colors, its cool smoothness, its intricate design. I picked it up, ran my finger along the folds and curves of the shepherdess's dress, the bumps of the white, wooly lamb, the thin cylinder of the brown wooden staff. So delicate. How had it survived all these years? I set it back on the table.

Beside it was the black family Bible, the same one Daddy had read from at night when I was a child, the same one he had thundered from when I came home pregnant from Jacksonville, his finger jabbing at the pages for emphasis—all those passages about fornication and lust and the wages of sin. Even now, I could feel myself trembling at the memory.

Fleeing back to the living room, I examined the two old sepia-toned family photographs on the walls. First the oval one of Daddy with his first wife and family—Daddy young and dashing in his striped suit—his dark, slicked-back hair parted in the middle, a swashbuckling handlebar mustache curling around his mouth. He faced the camera with a stern, austere gaze, one hand on the shoulder of delicate, dark-haired Elizabeth, who was seated in a white wicker chair, slim and beautiful, her hair piled on top of her head in a cascade of curls. A chubby, blonde Grace leaned against her, and the round-faced baby, Simon, stared solemnly from her lap. I wondered how Mama felt about having that picture in her living room all these years. What had it been like for her, taking Elizabeth's place? Had Daddy's second marriage been strictly a matter of convenience for him? Had his heart died with Elizabeth? So many questions I'd never considered. It was hard to associate the rakish young man in the picture with the staid, gray-haired father I'd known, the father who was now a frail old man in a hospital bed.

Grace and Simon weren't in the second picture, the one of Daddy and Mama and the three younger children, although both would have been still at home then, teenagers by that time, but still part of the family. Whose decision had it been not to include them? Mama's? Not likely. Mama thought of Grace and Simon as just as much hers as the other three. Daddy's? Did he want to record the true family situation for posterity? Or did Grace and Simon opt out themselves? Had there been a big family disagreement? I had been too young to remember any of the circumstances. Daddy was some fifteen years older in this picture, patriarch of a new wife and family—his temples beginning to gray, his mustache thinner and salted with white. His eyes were the same, though, that same fierce, concentrated stare for the camera, as if it were an enemy to be stared into submission. He was standing behind Mama, who was seated in a dark, high-backed chair, looking pinched and uncomfortable in a tight-waisted, high-necked dress. Neva was on Daddy's right, smiling demurely for the camera, and Roy, on his left, looked serious and sun-toughened already at ten. I was in front, standing beside Mama, one of her arms around me. I had been about five when this photograph was taken—thin and gangly, my hair lighter and curlier, forming a frizzy halo around my face.

I looked from one picture to the other. How much didn't I know about Daddy's life as a young man? About his and Mama's marriage? Mama said she'd been happy, but what did she mean by happy? Was it enough to have the security of marriage, to have a man obligated to take care of you for the rest of your life? My own fantasy of living happily ever after with Dwayne had turned out to be a flimsy, transparent bubble that had dribbled away into a sticky residue that I was still trying to scrub away. Maybe it was best not to depend on anybody else for happiness. That was my philosophy, anyway.

The hum of an approaching motor and the crunch of tires on the driveway announced someone's arrival. I looked out the window. Tom and Geneva in their wood-paneled station wagon. So Neva had come, after all. Before I could get to the front door, Tommy had bounded out the back seat and headed for the tire swing. Then Tom stepped out and stretched both arms above his head.

As I walked onto the porch, Neva emerged from the car, a sleeping Sarah in her arms, moist strawberry-blonde curls clinging to Neva's neck.

"Hi," I called. "Looks like you've got a sleepy little girl there." I reached out to touch Sarah's soft curls as Geneva came up the steps.

Neva formed a "Sh-h" sound with her lips, and I held the screen door open for her as she disappeared into the house, emerging in a minute without Sarah. "If she doesn't get her nap out, she'll be cranky the rest of the day," she said. "Where's Mama? I didn't see anybody inside."

"Grace came over this morning. They went to the hospital."

"You didn't go?"

"I've already been every day this week, driving Mama back and forth, and Roy had promised Benny a fishing trip to the river, so we stayed here to wait for Roy. Roy picked him up a little while ago."

Geneva turned to Tom. "You hear that, Tom? Roy took the boys down to the river. You should take Tommy and join them. Tommy, you want to catch a fish?"

Tommy, still trying to get himself going on the tire swing, didn't answer and Tom walked over to give him a starting push. "Hey, buddy, you want to catch a fish?" But Tommy was interested only in the swing.

"You didn't ask about Daddy," I said to Geneva.

Geneva took a seat on the glider. "Oh, we stopped at the hospital already on our way here, and I ran in to see him. I could only stay a minute, for Sarah was getting fussy, and Tommy was tired of being cooped up in the car. We must have just missed Mama and Grace. Daddy's looking better, don't you think? He even talked to me a little."

"Roy wants to bring him home next week," I said, "if he keeps improving."

"That soon?" Geneva looked alarmed. "How will Mama take care of him? She'll need somebody—"

"Roy's worried about how much all this is costing. He says his sharecropper knows someone who can come over every morning for an hour or so and help Mama with getting him bathed and dressed and such."

"A colored person? No. That's out of the question." Neva lowered her voice to a whisper. "Daddy would be so humiliated, having a Negro undressing him, seeing his privates."

"Well, if that doesn't meet with your approval, you'll have to take it up with Roy. Or you can come help Mama. I've already missed a week of work, and I can't afford to miss too much more."

"But can't he just stay at the hospital a while longer?" Geneva asked. "Poor Mama, to put all that burden on her."

"Mama's stronger than you think." My mind went back to

the two portraits on the living room wall—Elizabeth with her delicate features and dark curls; Mama's short, sturdy build, her clear eyes looking straight at the camera, one arm circling a five-year-old me. "She may worry about everything, but she makes the best of whatever life throws at her. Always has."

"Me, too," Neva agreed. "That's what I'm always telling Tom. Look for the silver lining in every cloud. Aren't I always saying that, Tom?"

Tom grabbed the tire swing to slow it to a stop. "Sure. Accentuate the positive. Come on, Tommy. Let's go see if we can find the fishermen. I'll bet they have an extra pole just for you."

After they left, Neva and I continued to sit on the porch.

"Oh, shoot," Neva said. "We bought some more sodas in town and they're still in the car. And now Tom's gone off with them."

"There's tea inside in the refrigerator." I said. "I'll get some for both of us."

"I'll go," Neva said. "I need to go to the little girls' room, anyway. And check on Sarah." She returned in a few minutes with two glasses of iced tea, handing one to me.

"Thanks. Oh, the other big news is that Julia and the baby came home yesterday. We're going over later to visit, when Mama and Grace get back."

"Oh, goodie." Geneva's face lit up. "I just love babies. Don't you? I've been thinking about having another one, but I don't know. Tom says if we have another boy, I'll want another girl to even things up, and if I have a girl, he'll want another boy, so maybe we should stop with two. Two's plenty, don't you think?" She laughed and took another sip of her tea. "Of course, it's not exactly up to me, I guess. Whatever happens, we'll be happy with it. Only thing is, I wouldn't want to have an only child. Tom was an only, you know, and he keeps saying how lonesome he was growing up, how he'd have given anything to have a brother or a sister."

I bristled. "Benny isn't lonely. He's around other kids his age every day."

"Oh, my goodness." Neva slapped one hand over her mouth.

"I was speaking in general. I didn't mean you. I wasn't even thinking about your boy."

"His name is Benjamin."

"Yes, Benjamin. I know that. He seems very polite and smart, but awfully quiet, don't you think?"

"You haven't seen him since last weekend, and that was when he was still adjusting. He's doing great now. Katie and Roy, Jr. are teaching him all about farm life."

"Well, that's good to know. Raising a child without a father must be hard, though, especially a boy."

"We're doing just fine." I pointed to the north to change the subject. "Look at those dark clouds. We're going to get a good soaking if we stay out here."

A brilliant flash of lightning lit up the sky, followed by a loud crash of thunder, and both of us hurried to get inside to safety.

Chapter 17

The rain had begun by the time Grace and Mama returned from the hospital. "Looks like a gully-washer," Grace said as she and Mama hurried inside.

"Sure does," I agreed. "Roy and Tom and the boys are down at the river fishing. I hope they didn't wander too far away from the truck."

"They'll be okay," Grace said. "Roy's got enough sense to get out of the rain, at least."

"Did you say Tom?" Mama asked. "Neva's Tom?"

As if on cue, Geneva entered the living room, balancing Sarah on her hip. "Hey, Mama. I told you we'd come, didn't I? You didn't believe me?"

"It's such a long way, and I know how busy you are." Mama put out her arms to Sarah. "And here's my little angel. Are you going to give Grandma a hug?"

As Geneva and Mama compared notes on Daddy's improvement, I paced the floor. The lightning strikes were getting closer, the thunder booming as if the house were under artillery attack. Where was Benny? Was he out in this weather? Surely Roy would seek safe shelter, wouldn't he?

"Gracious, Lacey, you're making us all nervous," Grace said. "Come sit down and join the conversation." She patted the sofa cushion beside her.

Within half an hour the rain had stopped and the sun was shining again. "Well, are we going to see the baby?" Grace asked. "I promised Pete and the girls I'd be home by suppertime."

Geneva and I sat in the back seat of Grace's car, Sarah between us. Mama was up front with Grace. Sarah cocked her head and smiled at me, obviously wanting to make friends, and when I smiled back, she held up three fingers. "I'm this many."

"Gracious. You're a big girl," I said. "Three years old."

"Almost four." Neva pulled Sarah into her lap. "Remember, you have a birthday coming up next month. Can you tell everyone what kind of party you're going to have?" Geneva raised her voice so that Mama and Grace in the front seat could hear.

"Princess!" Sarah answered, and Geneva was off and running, relating her elaborate plans for the party.

When we reached Roy's, Neva caught Sarah's hand. "You must be very careful around the new baby," she told her. "And if the baby's sleeping, we'll have to be very quiet."

Katie opened the front door to our knock. Julia was in the rocking chair nursing Zach. Out of modesty, I stopped a few steps inside the doorway, but Mama and Grace went right over to exclaim over the baby.

"Look at that red hair!" Grace touched the top of Zach's head with her fingertips.

Neva had averted her eyes and was trying to divert Sarah's attention from the scene by encouraging her to go play with Katie, but Sarah was interested in the baby. She squeezed past Mama and Grace until she was pressed against the rocking chair.

Julia smiled and put her free arm around Sarah's waist. "Hi, sweetie. You want to see your newest cousin? This is Zach."

"What's he doing?"

"He's eating," Julia explained. "He's getting milk. See him swallowing?"

"Sarah, come on away," Neva said. "Don't bother the baby while he's eating."

"She's fine," Julia answered. "She's not bothering him."

I sat on the sofa. Geneva would have given both her kids

bottles, of course—no uncouth breast feeding for her. I had tried nursing Benny in the hospital after he was born, but I didn't have enough milk to satisfy him, or else he wasn't sucking properly, so the nurses had given him a bottle. Unsure of myself, I had followed their lead and put him on formula. It had been expensive, though, and a pain to sterilize the bottles and heat formula in the middle of the night. I envied Julia's self-assured nonchalance.

Zach's sucking slowed and his eyes began to close. When his mouth went slack, Julia lifted him to her shoulder, gently patted him on the back, then continued to rock as he opened his mouth in a wide yawn and settled his head into the curve of her neck.

"He's asleep," Sarah whispered.

In the quiet that settled over the room, I could hear Zach's soft breaths. How many times had I stood over Benny when he was a baby, listening to make sure he was still breathing? And where was he now? Why hadn't Roy and Tom returned when the storm came up? Should someone go looking for them?

Half an hour later, after we'd returned to Mama's and Grace had left for Tallahassee, the men still hadn't come back. I reached for Daddy's car keys. "Mama, I'm going to check on the fishermen, see if they're catching anything for supper."

"I'll go with you," Geneva said. "Maybe Sarah can watch Tommy catch a fish. Would you like that, Sarah?"

We found Roy's truck and Tom's station wagon parked at the end of the first turnoff to the river. I pulled in behind them and led the way down the trail to where it opened onto a bar of sugar-white sand. "There they are!" I called with relief as I spotted the back of Benny's striped shirt. Tom was standing between Tommy and Benny, who both had bamboo poles in their hands. "Catching anything?"

Tommy turned around first. "Mommy, I caught a fish!" he yelled.

"That's swell," Geneva called back. "You must be quite the fisherman."

I walked over and put my hands on Benny's shoulders. "Did

you catch a fish yet?" I asked.

"Three!" Benny held up three fingers.

"Sounds like you've been having fun." I tried not to feel smug.

"Anybody for a fish fry?" Roy appeared from around the bend of trees at the edge of the sandbar, followed by Roy, Jr. "We got a good mess of 'em today. That little shower stirred 'em up." He dropped another fish into the bucket at my feet.

"Hey, no fair," another voice called from the tree line. "No women allowed at this fishing spot. It's off limits."

"Neil!" Neva squealed and ran over to greet Neil as he came toward us.

I looked at the two of them, Neil laughing now with Geneva, who was holding onto his arm, her face turned up to his, saying something I couldn't hear. Tom had turned his attention back to Tommy, who was tugging at his pole as if he had another bite.

Apparently something Neil said made Geneva let go of his arm and give him a playful push as they approached. "No wonder you're still an old bachelor—saying a thing like that to a married woman!" She flounced away from Neil and walked over to Tom, putting one arm possessively around his waist.

Neil laughed. "You asked for it!"

"Did not!"

I fussed with helping Benny with his line, keeping my back to Neil.

"Hey, Lacey," Neil said behind me. "You ladies checking up on us, huh?"

"You got him!" Tom yelled. "Bring him in now."

In the commotion, I was spared from answering Neil as Neva rushed over with Sarah to look at the fish on Tommy's hook and tell Tommy what a great fisherman he was. Then Tom tried to interest Sarah in fishing, but after seeing the wriggling worm that Tom was attaching to the hook, she was having nothing to do with it. The boys weren't ready to leave, so after a few minutes of standing around feeling ignored, Geneva and I started toward the car.

"Hey, can I hitch a ride?" Neil called after us. "I need to get home, and if I wait around for Roy, I may be here all night."

"A hot Saturday night date, I bet." Geneva wagged her finger at him. "Come on. You can ride with us girls if you promise to behave yourself. But you have to sit in the back with Sarah."

I put the gear shift of Daddy's car in reverse but then let up on the clutch too fast, and the car lurched backwards, almost hitting a tree. Then I stalled it in first gear before finally getting onto the road. My face and hands were drenched with sweat. Neil, thankfully, had no teasing remark about my lack of driving skill. Probably already thinking ahead to his date tonight. The preacher's daughter? Well, so what? What difference did it make to me who Neil did or didn't go out with? Benny and I would be going home to New York in a few more days, and I wished him well, whoever it might be. I concentrated on my driving.

Ruth Rodgers

Chapter 18

Sunday, July 20, 1952

"Mama, you go get ready for church now. I'll finish up in the kitchen." I untied Mama's apron. Tom and Geneva and the children had spent the night with Tom's mother but had come back over in time to take Mama to Four Corners Baptist. "Go on with Tom and Neva."

"You all go on without me," Mama protested. "I'll stay and have dinner on the table when you get back. It don't seem right, nohow, without Daddy there in his Sunday hat."

"Now, Mama, you know everybody is going to want to know how Daddy's doing," Geneva insisted. "And they'll want to talk to you. So just go get ready. We don't want to be late for Sunday school. If the kids bring back a note or a Sunday school paper, they get a sticker to put on their chart back home."

"I'll finish up dinner," I said. "You go on, Mama, with Tom and Neva."

"But what about you?" Mama asked. "We can't go off and leave you here. You and Benny come with us. We can finish dinner when we all get back."

"That's okay. You all go ahead. We didn't bring any Sunday clothes." I didn't want to tell Mama or Neva that Benny had never been to Sunday school, wouldn't have known what to do or how to behave. Besides, I could never enter Four Corners Baptist again. When I'd first come home from Jacksonville,

I'd dutifully resumed going to church with Mama and Daddy, praying earnestly week after week for a miracle to occur—either to hear from Dwayne or for my pregnancy to be only a nightmare from which I would awake one cool fall morning in giddy, goose-bumped relief. But once I began to show and Daddy had to be told, my private agony became a dirty, sinful embarrassment to be hidden from the neighbors. Daddy had forbidden me to step outside the house, said he could no longer hold up his head in church and in the community if my condition became known.

I didn't know what the neighbors and the people in the congregation had been told after I left home. The previous Sunday at Roy's, Neil had asked if I had married again, so apparently the story I'd told them about leaving to marry Dwayne was the story Mama and Daddy told to the community. But what about later, after they had learned the truth? Had they then conveniently killed Dwayne off somehow? I had no idea what sort of history they had invented for me. Anyway, I was in no mood to discuss the matter with anyone.

But a more immediate and compelling reason I couldn't go was that Neil would be there, along with the preacher's daughter, fresh from their Saturday night date. The preacher's daughter would be dressed in the latest collegiate fashion, of course, her long blonde hair curled under in a smooth pageboy style, and her eyes would be on Neil, who might even be sitting beside her, sharing a hymnbook, their arms touching as they stood and sang. "Benny and I will have our own Sunday school here," I told Mama, "just the two of us."

After the others left for church, I went into Mama and Daddy's bedroom and picked up the heavy, black family Bible. It didn't seem quite as threatening as it had the day before—just a book, after all. I shoved aside the last images of Daddy during those terrible weeks before I left home—the hurtful words, the jabbing, stabbing finger as he thrust the pages into my face. I sat on the bed and began to flip through the Old Testament, looking for a suitable story to begin with. Creation? The flood? David and Goliath? Maybe the birth of Jesus in the stable in Bethlehem would be the best place to start. Benny already knew some of the details from Christmas songs and stories. I turned to the center, and the Bible fell open to the page marked by the faded purple ribbon—the Family Records section.

At the top of the page was the wedding date of Grace Elizabeth McCormick and Peter Louis Chapin, followed by the birthdates of their two girls, Sharon Marie and Rebecca Elizabeth. Then came the wedding date of Roy Edward McCormick and Julia Ann Potter and the birth dates of Katherine Ann and Roy Edward, Jr., followed, in fresh, new ink, by Isaac David, born July 13, 1952. On the back of that page was Neva and Tom's marriage date and the birth dates of Thomas Earl, Jr. and Sarah Elaine. The bottom half of the page was empty, as was the facing page. I turned to the next page. It was also blank. Where was Benny? I flipped backwards, running my eyes down the faded lines. Here were the birthdates of Grace and Simon—their names embellished with fancy, curlicued lettering that Daddy's first wife Elizabeth must have taken such pains with, followed by the plainer, rounded letters of Mama's handwriting—first the death date of Elizabeth and baby boy McCormick—March 11, 1919, then the birth dates of Roy Edward, Geneva Corinne, and me, Lacey Louise, born May 8, 1927.

I flipped through the pages once more, rereading all the names. There was no entry anywhere for Benjamin Lee McCormick. Slamming the Bible shut, I placed it back on the table. I should have expected as much. From the bedroom window, I could see Benny outside, stomach down on the tire swing, pushing himself with his feet. I watched for a minute, my throat tight, my eyes stinging, then went to the kitchen and savagely stirred the peas that were cooking on the stove, jabbed a fork as hard as I could into the pot roast, and threw some potatoes into the sink to peel. Benny didn't need any lesson from that Bible.

❅   ❅   ❅

By the time everyone returned from church, my anger had settled into a hard, tight knot in my throat. I was determined not to make a scene in front of Neva and Tom; I would take up the matter of Benny's omission with Mama after they had gone home, so as not to give Neva the satisfaction of knowing that her kids counted and Benny didn't.

The business of getting the food on the table, filling glasses with ice, and pouring tea kept my mind occupied for the first few minutes of the churchgoers' return, and later, at the table, when I barely touched my meal, unable to swallow past the tightness in my throat, nobody even noticed. All through dinner Geneva kept up an animated discussion about the people at church— how Margaret had gained so much weight, how tall little Curtis had turned out to be, how much like her mother Carolyn was.

After dinner, left alone in the kitchen with Geneva, I took my pent-up anger out on the dishes, banging a stack of dirty plates down hard on the counter, shoving a pot out of the way so that it clattered across the floor.

"Goodness," Neva said, "you declaring war on these dishes or something?"

In answer I threw a handful of silverware forcefully into the sudsy water, splashing the front of Geneva's dress. Geneva jumped back and wiped herself with the dish towel.

"O-ooh! Now look what you did. My Sunday dress, too. What on earth is the matter with you?"

I didn't answer, just picked up a plate and attacked it with the dish rag.

"These are Mama's good plates, too," Geneva said. "She never uses them when it's just Tom and me and the kids. Wonder what the special occasion is." She paused. "You, maybe. Long lost Lacey."

"The prodigal daughter." I forced the words past the lump in my throat.

"I never understood that parable," Geneva said. "The good son gets no reward or recognition, and the bad one, the wastrel, gets treated like a king."

I attacked another plate. "Don't worry. Nobody's giving me the royal treatment. I'm still the black sheep of the family."

166

"Come on, now," Neva said. "Mama was floating on air when she found out you were coming home. You were all she talked about. And now the good company dishes."

"I set the table, if that makes you feel any better. And Mama hasn't accepted me and Benny any more than the rest of you have. And she never will. None of you ever will."

I saw a smile of triumph flit across Geneva's face. "Well, you knew when you ran off to New York how it would be. Having, and keeping, an illegitimate child just isn't done—not around here, anyway. Daddy gave you the option of staying with Grace and putting it all behind you so nobody would have to know, but you refused. So what do you expect?"

"None of this is Benny's fault."

"Nobody's saying it is. But still, you knew how it would be. People are going to talk."

My face burned. "Who's talking?"

"Oh, I don't know. I just meant people in general. When folks at church this morning found out you were home, they all wanted to know how you were, where you lived now, stuff like that."

"And you filled them in, I suppose?"

"I didn't spill any family secrets, if that's what you're worried about. I just told them that you and your little boy were living in New York. They all wanted to know why you didn't come this morning with the rest of us."

"And put Benny on display for them to point fingers at. No thanks."

"You can't keep people from talking. It's their constitutional right. Think about it, honestly. Wouldn't you be curious, too, if you were in their shoes?"

"Benny's done nothing wrong. It's not fair to hold him up to idle curiosity for my mistake. Besides, doesn't the Bible say, 'Let him who is without sin cast the first stone'? I suppose everybody else in this family, in this entire county, is perfect." I reached for another plate, but my wet hand slipped and the plate crashed to the floor, shattering into dozens of fragments.

Geneva jumped back and I could hear Mama in the living

room calling out to ask what happened, but before she could get to the kitchen, I ran out the back door and across the screened-in porch, my eyes stinging with tears. "I don't know," I heard Geneva saying behind me. "She was mad as the dickens about something, throwing things every which way. Look here, where she wet the whole front of my dress."

Not sticking around to hear more, I continued outside toward the pecan grove. Benny and Tommy had climbed into the wagon beside the corn crib, so I skirted them and headed toward the privacy of the pond, a small, natural swamp on the lowest section of the farm, surrounded by a shady wooded area of water oaks and cypresses. I followed the familiar footpath through the trees until I was out of sight and hearing of the commotion I had left behind.

Coming back had been a mistake. What had ever made me think that things would be, or could be, different? I should have stayed in New York and forgotten I even had family in Florida. Daddy had disowned both me and Benny, so I owed him nothing, and now I'd come to find out that Mama, who had seemed to want to know Benny, who'd seemed to treat him as another grandchild, had been too ashamed to write his name in the family Bible.

It was quiet out here, peaceful. I leaned against a cypress tree and let myself become absorbed in the slow rhythms of the pond's surface. The trees diffused the sunlight, and the dark water reflected the white clouds of summer sky. An occasional splash from a frog would send out a widening eddy of circles that would make the mirrored trees sway as if from a breeze and then grow still again.

I listened for sounds of someone coming after me, or at least calling my name, but I heard nothing. Benny and Tommy had seen me head this way, so it wasn't as if I couldn't be found. I could hear Neva now, telling Mama what happened: *I don't know what in the world got into her; she just got in a huff about something and started throwing things around. All I said was that people at church asked about her, and she started talking*

*about how it wasn't fair to punish Benny for her mistake and
how everybody up here thinks they're so spotless. Then she
threw that plate on the floor and ran out."*

I felt the anger begin to build again and made a conscious
effort to push it away. I'd concentrate instead on pleasant
thoughts, on how happy I'd be to get back to New York, back to
my own little room in the boarding house, just Benny and me,
the welcome we'd get from Dorothy and all the kids at the day
care, the late-night quiet talks with Rita across the hall after our
boys were asleep, the energy of the city surrounding me—the
dim little Italian deli down the street, the Greek pastry shop
around the corner, the crowds of people always in a hurry to
get somewhere—constant movement, constant noise, constant
distraction that left me no time to worry about people more than
a thousand miles away who'd already disowned me, who had
shut Benny out of the family history as if the last seven years
could be erased like a simple mistake, a smudge that could be
cleaned up so well nobody would ever know it had been there.
I heard a truck go by on the road and glimpsed a patch of dark
blue through the trees. Roy, maybe. Did it stop at the house or
go on past? I wasn't sure. I stayed where I was.

"Mommy?" The voice was so close it startled me.

"Benny? I'm over here. Be careful. The ground's slippery when
it's wet."

Benny came into view down the narrow path, followed by
Tommy, who was swinging a stick in front of him like a machete.
Benny ran toward me. "We were looking for you."

"I came down to look at the pond for a while. See how the
trees are upside down in the water, and the sky's at the bottom?
Isn't that nifty?"

Tommy continued down to the water's edge. "Hey, Benny,
come here. A turtle."

"Where?" Benny ran after Tommy.

"Don't get too close," I warned.

As the two boys got nearer, the turtle drew into its shell.
Tommy tapped its back with his stick.

"Don't bother him," I said. "Come on away from the water. There might be snakes. Or an alligator."

"At Silver Springs I saw an alligator this big!" Tommy spread his arms wide, and Benny looked at him admiringly.

Tommy squatted and poked at the turtle with his finger. Benny bent forward, hands on his knees. "Hey!" I started after them. "Don't touch. He might bite." Where was Neva? It wasn't my job to discipline Tommy. If something happened to him, guess who'd get blamed? And Benny was picking up bad habits. It wasn't like him to disobey.

"They're all right, Sis. That turtle ain't coming out for nothing till they stop pestering it." Roy was grinning as I turned at the sound of his voice. "What's this I hear about you getting mad at Neva and wetting her dress, then throwing one of Mama's good plates on the floor? Neva said you ran off in a temper fit, so I figured I'd better come find you. But I see you already been found." Roy, Jr., behind him, ran to join Tommy and Benny in studying the turtle.

"It was an accident. My hands were wet, and it slipped. I set the table with the good company plates, then Neva accused me of getting special treatment—killing the fatted calf and all just 'cause I came home, and—" I felt the sting of new tears behind my eyes and turned my face away from Roy.

"Same old story," Roy said. "What is it with you two? Don't let Neva get under your skin so."

I took a deep breath. "That's easier said than done. Anyway, it's not even Neva this time. It's Mama."

"Mama? Aw, don't worry about the plate. Mama said tell you she didn't care about that. It ain't the first plate that's been broke around here. They sent me to get Tommy and tell you to come on back. Neva and Tom are getting ready to go to the hospital and then head home from there. Come on and tell 'em bye, at least."

"I was looking at the family Bible this morning," I told Roy. "Benny's not in it."

Roy looked puzzled. "I thought we were talking about plates.

What's the Bible got to do with it?"

I lowered my voice. "Benny's not in it. Zach's already listed, along with Katie and Roy, Jr. And Grace's two girls, and Neva's two. But not Benny."

"So? Did you say anything to Mama about it?"

"In front of Neva? Are you kidding?"

"Well, Sis, I think you're making a mountain out of a molehill myself. I wouldn't worry about it if I were you. He's got a birth certificate, don't he?"

"Of course."

"Then what's the problem?"

"It's not that; it's knowing Mama can't soil her Bible with Benny's name. She's ashamed—of me and of him. That's what hurts." I raised one hand to dab at my wet eyes.

'Aw, Sis." Roy laid a hand on my shoulder. "You're just working yourself into a stew. Forget it. You think you can come back here and open up old wounds without nobody bleeding? Mama's got enough to worry about without you giving her any more grief."

"Fine. That's just fine." I twisted away from Roy's hand. "I'm supposed to wear sackcloth and ashes for the rest of my life, I suppose."

"See. That's what I mean. You're persecuting yourself. Ease up. Look at Benny down there. He's doing just fine, ain't he?"

I looked down the slope. All three boys were squatting over the turtle, their heads together, oblivious to the grownups.

"I guess." I felt empty. Even Benny was getting away from me.

Ruth Rodgers

Chapter 19

After Geneva and Tom left , planning to stop by the hospital on their way, and Roy drove off with Mama, also headed for the hospital, I took the Sunday paper out to the porch swing so that I could keep an eye on Benny and Roy, Jr.

"You sit down and relax; take it easy," Roy had told me pointedly as he left.

But that was easy enough for him to say. His kids were the pride of the family, the ones to carry on the McCormick name to future generations. They didn't have to get on their knees to beg forgiveness for being born. Daddy didn't turn his head away whenever one of them came into sight or refuse to let their names be spoken in his presence. They hadn't been denied existence by Mama and Daddy like Benny had.

I scanned the front page of the paper. The fighting was continuing in Korea, more people had been called to testify at the McCarthy hearings in Washington, the latest statistics on polio victims for the first six months of 1952 had passed 26,000, with hundreds of new cases every day. I laid it aside.

Geneva had gone home without another word spoken between us. After I had reluctantly followed Roy back to the house, she had bustled self-importantly from living room to kitchen to bedroom, looking for Sarah's special Cinderella drinking cup. I had given her a wide berth, not trusting myself to speak, afraid I'd blurt out something I'd later regret and open myself up again to her self-righteousness.

At least Tommy and Benny had gotten along great together, probably much to Neva's dismay. No telling what she was saying to Tommy now in the car about associating with somebody with such a problematical pedigree.

Roy, Jr. and Benny were in the middle of the road, rolling an old tire back and forth between them.

"You guys watch out for cars," I called.

"Yes, ma'am," Roy, Jr. answered.

"Yes, ma'am," Benny echoed.

I laughed. Benny was definitely acquiring a Southern drawl. Everyone would tease him back at home.

❈ ❈ ❈

"Daddy was sitting up in a chair when we got there," Mama reported excitedly when she and Roy returned. "He's talking more, too, though it's still hard to make out what he's trying to say."

"He can sure say *home*," Roy said, "plain as day. He's raring to get out of there."

Mama went inside to change out of her Sunday church clothes. "You think he's ready to come home?" I asked Roy.

"It's where he wants to be. And that hospital bill is adding up. Hey, I gotta get on back. You okay?"

"I'm fine. Actually, I was thinking about coming over to see Julia and the baby for a little while. You think she's up to company again? Just for a few minutes?" Now that the first heat of anger had passed, the prospect of confronting Mama with my discovery was making me more and more nervous. Visiting with Julia would give me a little more time to think it through.

"Sure, come on over. She'll be glad to see you."

I waited for Mama to finish changing and emerge onto the porch. "Mama, you want to go see the baby, just for a little while?"

When we arrived, Benny immediately ran after Roy, Jr. into the back yard, but Katie remained in the living room, not getting too far away from Zach's side. Awake and freshly fed and changed,

Zach was in a good mood. Mama held him first, propping him on her knees so that he was facing her. "Such a good baby—yes, you are," she said to him in a high-pitched voice. "Grandma's going to spoil you rotten—yes, she is." Occasionally she would lift Zach into the air and then settle him onto her knees again. Her entire attention was riveted on him. Katie, beside her on the sofa, also kept touching a hand or a leg, smiling and cooing at this new baby brother.

From my chair beside Julia, I watched with growing jealousy. I had left the hospital with Benny completely alone—no welcoming committee, no relatives waiting with open arms, nobody to tell me how to be a mother—nobody except Dorothy. Apparently, the nurses on the floor knew about Dorothy and her boarding house for young women and children, for, upon learning that I had no family in the area and no place to go except back to my tiny attic room in one of the grimiest sections of town, they had contacted Dorothy. Suddenly, there she was—her cheerful, pink-faced, ample presence appearing to me like an angel from heaven. She'd sent a cab to the hospital to pick us up, had moved me into a vacant upstairs room and stocked it with formula and diapers, and had even offered me a job, doing the bookkeeping and helping out in the children's nursery. Dorothy had been like a mother to me, when my own mother didn't know where I was or how I was faring.

What wouldn't I have given for Benny to have had the loving welcome home that Zach was getting? Only one week old, and Zach was already in the McCormick family Bible; Benny, age six, wasn't. My throat grew tight again, and when I opened my mouth to answer a question from Julia, nothing came out but a croak, which I quickly turned into a cough.

"Here, Lacey," Mama said. "You want to hold him? I've been hogging him something awful, but I just can't help it." She looked back at Zach. "No, I can't. You're such a sweet thing—yes, you are. Wait, I've got to get some sugar before you go." She nuzzled his neck. "Go on and see your Aunt Lacey for a while."

I took Zach from Mama's arms and returned to the chair

beside Julia, holding him on my knees the same way Mama had. Katie followed, leaning over the side of the chair, reaching down to stroke an arm or wrap her fingers around a tiny foot.

"Hi, Zach." I jiggled him a little. He was heavier than I had expected him to be. His eyes, two round, deep pools of cobalt blue, seemed to be studying me expectantly, alert for my next utterance. He looked like Roy already—the same high McCormick forehead, the twist of reddish hair spiraling into the precursor of a cowlick. Something about the mouth too, one corner turned up a little more than the other. I held him quietly, too self-conscious to use the babbling, repetitive baby talk that Mama had been using.

Zach opened his mouth in a wide yawn, and I lifted him to my shoulder, cradling the back of his head. As I rhythmically rubbed his back, the warmth of his pliable body wriggling against me, stretching into a more comfortable position, coursed through me like an old, familiar song.

※　※　※

Hours later, after afternoon chores and a cold supper of leftover pot roast, I sank tiredly onto the living room sofa. I still hadn't brought up the subject that had been on my mind all day. Benny slipped out the front door. "Stay in the yard," I called. "It'll be getting dark soon."

Mama picked up a stack of quilt pieces from the table and spread them in her lap, moving them around and trying out different arrangements. I watched her for a few minutes before speaking. "What are you making?"

"Just a little quilt for Zach. Each square is a different vehicle. This one's a train. See?" She pointed at the square she had laid out in her lap. "I made a baby quilt for each of the other grandkids, so this is going to be Zach's."

"Oh?" I asked. "I don't recall Benny getting any quilt."

Mama looked up at me, then back down at her lap, her fingers continuing to arrange the quilt pieces. "Well, I mean the ones close by. You were so far off up there in New York. And the three

176

boys all being so close to the same age—Roy, Jr. and Benny are only a week apart, you know, and Tommy came along a few months later. A Christmas baby, but the same year. I remember I had started the quilt for Roy, Jr. when you wrote that first letter to Grace. It took me a while to get it finished, for it was almost summertime by then, you know, and the garden was coming in and the tobacco was ready for picking, and I got swamped with canning vegetables and cooking for all the hired help. I was going to make Benny a quilt later, for Christmas, but then Tommy came along, and Neva wanted one just like Roy, Jr's except in different colors to match her nursery, she said, so I got busy with that one. I didn't have time to get one made for Benny by Christmas, so I decided it might be better to send you some money instead to buy whatever you needed. That was more sensible, don't you think?"

"Sensible? What's sensible got to do with it?" I couldn't keep the hurt out of my voice. "I got the family Bible out of your bedroom this morning. I was going to read Benny a Bible story while everybody was at church." I glared at Mama, waiting for a reaction.

But Mama only looked at me. "And...?"

"And it just happened to fall open to the Family Records section."

"Oh, I guess I left the marker there. I was writing Zach's name in a day or so ago, that's why."

"Writing Zach's name? Is that all you have to say, Mama?" Was Benny's omission from the McCormick family records of such insignificance to her that she had no clue of what I was getting at?

"Say about what?" Mama looked puzzled.

I went to the bedroom and returned with the Bible, flipping it open and slinging it into Mama's lap. "Look at it, Mama. Where's Benny? Tell me that. In the same place as his quilt, I suppose. And his picture that's not on the mantel. Every other grandchild is there except for Benny." Hot tears stung my eyes.

Mama looked at the open page as though studying it herself,

looking for Benny's name.

"Where's Benny, Mama? You couldn't stain your Bible with his name, could you?"

Mama looked at me, her mouth set in a frown of disapproval. "You see what it says right here? Roy Edward McCormick joined to Julia Ann Potter in Holy Matrimony on June 13, 1942, at Shiloh Methodist Church. Then the births are listed underneath. Same with Tom and Geneva. And Grace and Pete. Holy Matrimony. What was I supposed to do? With no marriage to record? I didn't even know Benny's last name. How was I supposed to put him down?"

"His last name's McCormick, same as mine. That's all you need to put."

"McCormick? But what about his father?"

"I put Fortrell on the birth certificate, but he's always gone by McCormick. Earlier this spring, I had it legally changed so it would be McCormick on his school records. He's mine, Mama, and nobody else's."

Mama's frown deepened. "And how is that going to look, with his last name McCormick, and no marriage to record? Think about it, Lacey. Your father reads from this Bible every night before he goes to bed, or did before he had the stroke. Every single night."

I stood over Mama, hands on my hips. "That's all you care about, isn't it? Not upsetting Daddy. You don't care about me and Benny. You think you can just omit Benny from the family tree so as not to cause anybody any embarrassment. Well, if you want to pretend he doesn't exist, then fine. Erase me, too." I flipped the page back to where my own birth was recorded. "Here, scratch me out." I picked up a pen that was lying on the table and uncapped it.

"No!" Mama grabbed for the pen in my hand. "Calm down, now." She closed the Bible and laid it aside. "When you get married, why, of course I'll write it in, and then there'll be children. You're still young. You've got time yet."

"Married? Children? Mama, don't you see? I already have a

child. He's real, and his name is Benjamin Lee McCormick, and he was born April 26, 1946. And there's nothing you or Daddy or anybody else can do to change that fact."

"But when you marry, he can take the name of your husband, can't he? Can't you see how that would be better, especially if there are other children?"

"And we can change his birth date too, I suppose? Make it 1956 instead of 1946? And he can start school in 1962 with the other six-year-olds. Don't you think the teacher and the other kids would be a little bit suspicious—a six-foot first grader who had to shave every morning before school?" I returned to the sofa and leaned forward, elbows on knees, chin propped on my hands. "You're no more accepting of Benny than Daddy is, are you? And all this time, I thought… I'll pack up all our stuff tomorrow and we'll go home soon as Roy can give us a ride into town to the bus station."

Mama picked up the quilt pieces from her lap that I had displaced with the Bible and laid them on the table beside her chair. "Honey, please listen to me. You don't know how many nights I sat up wringing my hands and crying over you. I'll tell you why I didn't make Benny a quilt, if you really want to know. After I got your letter, I started one for him, but every time I'd go to work on it, my eyes would get all teary, and my hands would go to trembling." Mama lifted her hands, shaky even now, six years later, at the memory. "And I just couldn't do it."

The tears in Mama's eyes brought tears to mine, too, and I began to sob, burying my face in my hands. I cried for myself, for Benny, for all the hurts of the last seven years I'd saved up to torment myself with. At some point, Mama had taken the Bible back to the bedroom, then come back and put her hand on my shoulder, but I had twisted away and flung myself down on the sofa, face buried against a pillow.

Sometime later—I had no idea how much later—I sat up and glanced out the window. It was dark outside. Where was Benny? What time was it? I looked at the clock. Ten minutes after nine.

I pushed open the front door. "Benny?"

There was no answer. I turned to Mama. "Did Benny come in?"

"Maybe he came in the back door and we didn't hear him." Mama headed toward the bedrooms.

I went outside. "Benny?" No answer. No sign of him. My panic mounting, I went back inside.

"He's not in the house," Mama said.

"Where's the flashlight?"

"I'll get it." Mama hurried into the kitchen. "He couldn't have gone far."

"Do you suppose he overheard us talking?" The thought made me go rigid with fear. I grabbed the flashlight from Mama's hand. "You stay here, in case he comes in. I'll be back when I find him."

Chapter 20

"Benny?" I checked all around the house and then the wagon where Benny and Tommy had been playing earlier, shining the flashlight up and down the wagon bed, into all the corners. Had he overheard Mama and me arguing? What exactly had I said? I tried to replay the conversation in my mind. How much of it would he have understood?

"Benny! Answer me. Where are you?"

Night sounds were all around me: the frogs from the pond, the crickets, the far-off barking of a dog. But there was no answer from Benny. I moved the flashlight back and forth, sweeping the area in front of me—the corn crib, the chicken yard, the pecan trees. If he'd gone back to the pond and gotten caught there by darkness, a wrong step. . . . I headed down the narrow trail, dense summer growth pressing in on both sides. "Benny? Can you hear me? Answer me."

As I approached the spot where the path zigzagged into a sudden, steep descent, the toe of my sandal caught on a root and I started to fall. Grabbing at a bush to steady myself, I heard a rustle in the underbrush and something large and dark ran past my legs. I screamed, let go of the bush, and toppled forward, landing on my hands and knees, the flashlight flying out and away.

"Benny! Are you down there?" My right hand stung, and as I touched it gingerly with the fingers of my other hand, I could feel the sticky wetness of blood. I stood, pressing the cut against my skirt to stop the bleeding, and looked down the path for the light. It had rolled up against a cypress tree, but its beam at least made it visible. I picked it up and shined it into and across the water.

"Benny! Are you here? Answer Mommy!"

All was quiet except for the chorus of frogs. I walked around the near edge of the pond, shining the light into the black water, peering along the edges for footprints. I called until I was hoarse. Nothing. Where else would he have gone? I retraced my steps to the house. Maybe he'd wandered up the road, chasing lightning bugs again. I called through the screen door to Mama. Benny hadn't come back to the house.

"I'm going to search the road," I said. "Turn all the lights on, in every room, so he can see them." I checked the yard again and then headed up the road toward the Hardisters'. Benny hadn't been in this direction except for the afternoon we'd visited Neil's mother and she had given him the model airplane. But after our visit, he'd mentioned that the lady there smelled like Dorothy back home, and if he had overheard Mama and me arguing, the Hardisters' house lights, shining in the blackness of the moonless night, might have led him to seek comfort there. I continued up the road, waving my flashlight in an arc that took in the fields on either side, repeatedly calling Benny's name and straining my ears for an answer.

I tried to stay calm, not to panic. I'd find him. He'd be okay. He couldn't have gone far. The whistle that Katie Ann had given him would be in his pocket. He carried it everywhere. Maybe if he was too frightened to call out, he would remember to blow it. "Benny. Blow your whistle so I can find you," I called. I stopped, listening hard for the sound of a whistle. Nothing.

I rounded the curve. All was dark at the Hardister house. I'd forgotten how early bedtime was in the country. Across the road, a light was on in Neil's trailer. I let myself have a moment of hope. Benny had seen Neil's light. I'd find him there, safe and sound. As I started toward the door, a big black dog ran toward me, barking, and a porch light was flipped on.

Neil opened the door, clad only in a pair of jeans. "What's the matter, boy?" he said to the dog. "Lacey? What is it? My God, what happened?"

In the glow of the porch light I could see the wine-colored smears of blood on my faded denim skirt. A line of dried blood ran down one of my legs, and when I lifted my skirt to check, I saw an angry red scrape across my right kneecap that I hadn't even felt. I could only imagine what my face must look like, still red and blotchy, my eyes swollen from crying, my hair full of twigs. I put my hand up to smooth my hair, then winced as a bramble scraped against the cut on my palm.

Neil held the door wide open. "Come inside. What on earth?"

"It's Benny. He's disappeared. Have you seen him?" I stumbled on the narrow step, and Neil caught my arm.

"Easy, now. Come on inside. Benny's missing?"

"I can't find him anywhere."

Neil led me inside and closed the door, one hand still holding onto my arm. "Don't worry. We'll find him. Let me get my shoes and shirt. You sit down for a minute, okay?" He disappeared down the hall, returning with his socks and shoes, a white tee shirt thrown over one shoulder.

"Now, tell me what happened." Neil sat on the sofa, putting on his socks. "Where did you last see him?"

I paced the floor, too upset to sit. "He went outside to play after supper. He was right out front on the tire swing. I told him to stay in the yard. Then Mama and I got to talking and I lost track of time, I guess. When I looked outside it was dark. I called him, but he didn't answer. I went all around the yard, even down to the pond, but he wasn't there. I don't know where he could have gone."

"Hey, he's okay." Neil slipped his feet into his work shoes and tied the laces. Then he stood and pulled the shirt over his head. "He couldn't have gone far. I'll get my flashlight."

I felt some of the tension go out of my shoulders and neck. Neil sounded so capable, so sure of himself. My scraped hand was stinging, and I held it up to examine it. A jagged red line ran diagonally across my palm, its edges already raised and swollen.

Neil returned with a huge flashlight and a set of keys. "If he'd come this way, ole Ranger would have let me know about it. We'll take my truck down the road a piece in the other direction, toward Roy's. He probably just got to chasing after a lightning bug and got farther than he meant to. I bet he's back home by now."

"Thanks, Neil. I hope you're right." I hurried ahead of him to the truck. If Benny had come back, scared and crying, and me not there... I crossed my fingers tightly for good luck.

But the only person standing at the front door was Mama. I jumped out and ran toward her. "Is he here?"

Mama shook her head. "You didn't find him?"

"Not yet. Neil's helping, though. If we don't find him soon, we'll get Roy."

"Lacey, honey, I feel just awful. Do you think he heard—?" Mama's voice wavered.

I turned away. A little late for apologies now. "Let's get Roy," I said to Neil as I got back in the passenger seat. I needed Roy's level-headedness to make everything all right, give me some perfectly rational explanation that would make everything fall into place.

"Sure you don't want to check around here again?" Neil asked.

"I already did. I shouted myself hoarse. Let's go. Please."

"Whatever you say." Neil put the truck in gear. "I'll go real slow, and we'll both call for him, okay?"

"He's got a whistle. Katie gave it to him a few days ago. Told him if he ever got lost in the woods to blow it, and she'd come find him."

"Maybe we should go get Katie, then."

I stiffened. Maybe that's exactly where he had headed, to Katie. "She's asleep by now. Roy, too. What time is it, anyway?" I rolled my window all the way down and aimed my flashlight toward the side of the road.

"I don't know. Maybe nine-thirty? I was about to turn in when Ranger started barking." Neil crept along, stopping every few yards for us to call and listen for a reply.

"Benny. Are you there? Blow your whistle," I called over and over. The cab of the truck filled with mosquitoes, and I kept slapping at my arms and face. Poor Benny would be covered with bites.

We continued creeping along, the blackness of the night swallowing up the brush line along the fences, the fields, even the trees that grew right beside the road, their moss-laden branches occasionally scraping against the top of the truck. We'd never get to Roy's at this rate.

"Go faster," I told Neil. "No. Stop! I hear something!" Was that a whistle off on Neil's side of the road? "Listen. Over there." I pointed out Neil's window.

Neil stopped the truck. "Benny?" he called. "You out there?"

I listened, straining my ears for the faintest sound, but I didn't hear anything except a cacophony of crickets in the nearby trees. Bending forward, I stretched one arm in front of Neil to catch hold of the driver's side window ledge, my hair brushing against Neil's face. "Benny?" I called. "It's Mommy. Blow your whistle."

I heard it. A faint, tentative note, then a longer, louder one from somewhere in the distance. "Hear that?" I laughed in dizzy relief. "It's him!" I grabbed Neil's door handle.

"Easy, now. Here's the lane to the old Carson place. Sounds like he's up this way." Neil pulled into the overgrown lane and shifted the truck into park, leaving the engine running and the headlights on. Then he scrambled out, pulling me behind him. Transferring his flashlight to his left hand, he caught my uninjured hand in his right. "Watch your step here. This road ain't been used for ages." He aimed his light ahead of us down the path. "Hold on, sport. We're coming to get you. Blow that whistle again."

"Mommy's right here," I added. "I'm with Neil. We're almost there."

The whistle sounded again, somewhere ahead and off to the

right. I stumbled on a pine branch that had fallen across the path, but Neil's hand steadied me. Why would Benny have gone this way? He must have thought, in the dark, it was the turnoff to Roy's house. "Benny? Where are you?" I called.

The whistle sounded again, closer now. I let Neil pull me along the path. Briars scratched my legs and caught in my skirt, but I paid attention to nothing but the repeated notes of the whistle.

The clearing where the Carson house used to stand was just ahead. Nothing was left of it now except a pile of bricks from the fireplace chimney; everything else had burned to the ground the night of the big fire—a log rolling out of the fireplace, the family stumbling into the frigid January night in their bedclothes, escaping with nothing but their lives. The spot had always seemed to me like a tragic scene from one of those thick Gothic novels that Neva was always bringing home from the school library, and as a child I had stepped carefully around its edges, feeling it sacrilege to tread on hallowed ground, like walking on top of graves in a cemetery. I shined my flashlight around the clearing. "Benny?"

"Mommy!" The voice was nearby.

As I turned in the direction of the sound, Neil's flashlight pinpointed him huddled beneath the big oak that had once shaded the Carsons' front porch. Benny shielded his eyes from the bright light, and I ran to him.

"Benny. Oh, Benny. Benbo." I wrapped my arms around him and lifted him off the ground. "Are you okay? You scared me so much. I've never been so scared before in my whole life." I kissed the top of his head, his cheek, his ear.

Benny clung to me, his chest heaving with sobs.

"Did you get lost?" I asked.

I could feel Benny's nod, his chin going up and down against my neck.

Neil led the way back to the road, keeping his flashlight aimed at the ground ahead of us. I followed with Benny in my arms. About halfway back to the truck, as I staggered under his weight, Neil tried to take him from me, but he would not be pried away from his grasp around my neck. I carried him over to the beam of the truck's headlights. "Are you all right?"

Neil put one hand on Benny's back and examined him from head to toe. "He's fine. Probably covered with mosquito bites, but no cuts or scrapes. You're the one in need of medical attention. Let's get you both home, out of these infernal bugs." He slapped at his arm and walked to the passenger door to open it for me.

I had trouble stepping into the truck with Benny's weight still hanging like a stone around my neck, so Neil helped to boost me in.

"You gave me and your mother quite a scare," Neil said to Benny after he put the truck in gear.

"Promise me you'll never do that again," I said. "Were you scared?"

Benny tightened his grip on my neck and began to cry.

"Poor kid," Neil said. "It's pitch black out there tonight. Good thing he had that whistle." He backed up and pulled into the road. "Next time, sport, you go chasing a lightning bug, you tell somebody where you're going. Okay?"

Mama ran outside when we pulled up.

"We found him!" Neil called.

"Thank the Lord! I was so worried." Mama ran to the passenger side of the truck and reached for Benny as I opened the door. "Benny, honey, what happened? Did you get lost?"

Benny clung more tightly to me, and Mama settled for rubbing his back. "Where was he?"

I stepped down from the truck and twisted my body so that Mama's hand fell away from Benny. "Just down the road a ways. I guess he went off chasing lightning bugs and got too far."

"Well, come on inside, out of these skeeters." Mama reached again to rub Benny's back. "You nearbout gave me a heart attack, you know that?"

I deliberately moved away, around the truck to Neil's open window. Mama wasn't getting off this easy. "Neil, I don't know how to thank you. If it hadn't been for you—"

"Forget it. Glad to be of help." Neil reached for the gear shift.

"You go on and take care of this kid of yours. And doctor that cut. You don't want it to get infected."

I stepped back as the truck started to move.

❀   ❀   ❀

An hour later I crept exhaustedly into bed, my body itching all over from mosquito bites and my hand still burning from the cut and the iodine I'd put on it. After Benny had been safely accounted for, I had busied myself with getting him cleaned up, tending to his mosquito bites, and putting him to bed, ignoring Mama's overtures at making amends. Her pretense of concern about Benny didn't fool me. The fact that she hadn't made him a baby quilt or written his name in the family Bible or put his photo on the mantel with the photos of the other grandchildren meant that it was more important to her to keep the peace with Daddy than to do what was right for her own grandson.

I still didn't know exactly what had happened—Benny had said nothing to my questions, only continued to cling to me until he fell asleep, but I was sure he had overheard at least some of my angry words to Mama. Only after I was positive he was sleeping soundly had I allowed myself to bathe and tend to my own injuries, brushing off Mama's hovering attempts to help.

I turned onto my side, but sleep wouldn't come. I found myself replaying the evening in my mind—the argument with Mama, the realization that Benny was missing, the frantic search, the comfort of Neil's calm assurance that we'd find him, the warmth of his hand clutching mine as we stumbled along the overgrown lane in the pitch-black night. Tonight was the closest I'd been to a man since Dwayne, and the memories of the evening stirred me with an old arousal that I hadn't let myself feel for nearly seven years.

Later, though, when we'd returned to the house with Benny safely found, Neil had seemed curt with me, anxious to get away. When I'd tried to thank him, he'd brushed me off, as though wanting to make sure I hadn't drawn the wrong impression from his earlier actions. Had he somehow picked up on the feelings that I was having and pulled away? *Careful now—don't want to give little Lacey Lu any romantic illusions.* All week he'd been treating me as just what I was—the little sister of his best friend, the childhood pest whom he'd put up with for Roy's sake—nothing more. Any attraction beyond that was nothing more than a figment of my imagination.

I shifted my position, but nothing felt comfortable. My hand hurt. I got up and felt my way into the alcove where Benny was sleeping soundly, his breathing soft and regular. I walked into the living room, fumbled in the dark until I found the dangling cord for the overhead light, then got a drink of water from the kitchen. It was almost eleven. Neil would have fallen directly into bed and into a sound sleep after his long workday. I pushed open the screen door and stepped onto the front porch. The black, cloudless sky was filled with stars—their brightness and sheer quantity still startling to me after living in the city for so many years. I walked to the edge of the porch and halfway down the steps so I could see higher into the sky.

A light flashed down the road toward Neil's. Then a whistle—a two- syllable bob-white sound—a pause, and a repetition. It sounded as if it came from the road, somewhere near the light, which seemed to be moving in an up-and-down motion. I hurried up the steps and to the safety of the front door. Something about the whistle seemed familiar. What was it? I searched my memory. Childhood, summer nights, bob-white whistles, signals. Roy and Neil. They had worked out this elaborate signaling system with whistles and flashlight movements—up, down, left, right— something like Morse code. The whistle came again, closer this time. Neil? What would Neil be doing out in the road at this hour of night? And here I was in my thin nylon nightgown. I reached for the screen door handle.

Ruth Rodgers

Chapter 21

Keeping my hand on the door handle behind me, I looked again at the light, now making circles in the air. What did that mean? I had no idea: Roy and Neil had never shared their code with anyone else; it was their big secret. If it was Neil, for whatever unfathomable reason, I couldn't let him catch me out here in nothing but a nightgown. I slipped inside, pulled the cord to turn off the living room light, and from the safety of darkness peeked out the front window. One last drawn-out, mournful sounding whistle was followed by silence. What was going on? I felt my way to the bedroom, groped in the dark for my robe and sandals, then made my way back to the front window.

No light. Nothing but silence. I listened carefully. Was that the crunch of footsteps in the road? If it was Neil, what was he doing here? I couldn't just go back to bed, with Neil out there practically in the front yard. I'd better see what he wanted before he woke up Mama or Benny. Feeling again for the dangling cord in the center of the room, I found it, pulled the light on, then quickly off again. On, off; on, off; on, off. I had no idea what I was signaling, except that Neil would know I had heard him. I went back to the window. The light came on again, almost directly in front of the house, aimed low now, its beam moving across the front yard. I quietly inched the front door open and tiptoed across the wooden floorboards of the porch. "Neil?" I called softly.

The flashlight's beam moved in an arc from the road to the porch, finding my feet, then moving up my body to my face. I covered my eyes with one hand.

"Sorry." Neil lowered the flashlight as he came toward the porch. He stopped a few feet away and caught the rope of the tire swing in one hand. "How's Benny?"

"He's fine. Sleeping now."

"Did I scare you?" Neil asked. "I couldn't sleep."

I put one finger to my lips. "Sh-h-h." I went down the steps toward him. "You want to wake up the whole house?"

"Sorry. I'll be quiet," Neil whispered. "How's your hand?"

"It stings, but it'll be okay in a day or two."

"Let's see."

I held my hand out. "You can't see in the dark."

Neil put his hand beneath mine and aimed the flashlight so that its beam shone on my palm. "How'd you do this? And your knee? You looked like you'd been in a fight earlier when you came to my door, all scraped up and bloody. Like some wild thing."

"I fell down at the pond looking for Benny. My sandal caught on a root and sent me sprawling. That's all." Neil was still holding my hand in his. *No romantic illusions, remember?* I pulled my hand away, took a step backward and gave the tire a push toward Neil. "What was all that foolishness with the flashlight and whistling? I didn't know what was going on."

Neil turned off the flashlight and leaned it against the tree. "Oh, that. Remember mine and Roy's top-secret code? I hadn't thought about it for years till the incident with Benny and the whistle tonight. I'd gone to bed when Ranger started barking like crazy, so I took the light out to see what was going on. I thought maybe it was you again." He pushed the tire back toward me.

I returned it. "Me? No, I've been inside. I tried to sleep but couldn't, so I got up for a drink of water. What were you signaling just now?"

"Oh, I dunno. I walked out to the road and down a ways to see what Ranger was barking at, and then I saw a light come on in your house, and that made me think about mine and Roy's old signals. I forget what they were now. Anyway, when I saw the light, I figured you might still be up, wandering around like me. So I moseyed down this way. Some scare Benny gave you, huh?" Neil sent the tire in my direction.

I caught it with my uninjured hand, wrapping my arm around it. "You can say that again. Thanks for helping me find him."

"Glad I could help. He's a swell kid." Neil grabbed hold of the other side of the tire. "Well, I better get going and let you get some sleep. Just wanted to check on you, make sure everything was okay. Sorry for scaring you." He laughed sheepishly and gave the tire a tug.

With my arm still around the tire, I was pulled off-balance, falling right into Neil's arms in the dark. "Oops." I put out both hands to push myself away, but Neil caught me and pulled me against him.

"I've got a boy." His words were thick, muffled, aimed into my shoulder.

"What?"

"I've never told anybody, not even my folks. Tonight, that was him I was looking for."

I could feel Neil's arms trembling as he held me, pulling me so tightly against him I could scarcely breathe. Was he crazy? Should I be afraid? None of this was making any sense.

"He's eight now." Neil's voice was hoarse with emotion, his words coming out in short staccato bursts. "His name's Jean Philippe. Some name for a kid of mine, huh? That's John Philip in English, like that bandleader John Philip Sousa."

Neil was talking about a real child, a boy somewhere in Europe. I finally managed to loosen his grip enough for me to catch my breath. "Here. Let's sit down." I led him to the steps and sat beside him, linking my right arm inside his left one and moving my unhurt left hand up and down his arm in a gentle stroking motion. "Tell me about him."

"Would you believe I've never seen him?" Neil said. "I've got a kid I've never even seen."

"Where is he?" I asked.

"Little town in northern France, near Belgium. It was during the war. Things were crazy then; none of us knew if we'd live through the next day, much less ever get back home. We were young, scared, homesick, taking comfort wherever we could find it."

"Agnes?" I asked.

Neil looked at me, his face a dim outline in the dark. "You know about Agnes?"

"I saw her picture on the mantel at your mother's. She said you'd met her in France. That's all I know."

"My folks don't know about the baby. Nobody does. Not even Roy. You're the first person I've told, ever. Tonight I couldn't get him out of my mind. It was him I was looking for, him who was lost and scared in the dark, crying for his daddy."

"Oh, Neil. Neil, I'm so sorry." I squeezed his arm before resuming my gentle stroking. "That must be so terrible, knowing he's there, growing up, doing all the things little boys do, without you."

Neil took a deep breath, blew it out. "My division got moved south before she knew she was pregnant. Before she told me, anyway. By the time her letter got to me and I found somebody to translate it into English, she was four, five months along. I wanted to do the right thing, but there was no way I could get back there without going AWOL. I wrote, telling her to wait for me. We'd get married and I'd bring her back to the States soon as the war was over. Even sent her a ring. But her folks couldn't wait. Next thing I heard, she was married. Some guy her parents recruited. Or maybe she'd been seeing him all along. I don't know."

"Do you still love her?"

Neil laughed ruefully. "Love? Heck, I hardly remember her. She didn't speak much English, and I didn't speak any French."

"Maybe the baby wasn't—"

"Oh, he's mine, all right. I got a picture. She's got two more kids now. She gave John Philip her husband's last name. He thinks that's his daddy."

I couldn't see Neil's face, couldn't tell what he was thinking, but the anguish in his voice was clear. Giving up Benny, never seeing him grow up, knowing he was out there somewhere being raised by someone else, calling someone else Mommy, was more than I could bear to think about. And Neil was so good with kids; his affection for Katie and Roy, Jr. was obvious.

"She sent you a picture?" I asked.

"It's an old one now." Neil reached around to his back pocket, pulled out his wallet. "I used to send her money for food, clothes, toys—that sort of stuff. And presents for Christmas and his birthday. She asked me to stop doing that, though. With the other two kids, it's too confusing, and he don't even know who I am. I'm just some American guy his mother knew during the war. I'm supposed to bow out of the picture, forget I ever had a son. That's probably the best thing for him." Neil opened his wallet, reached deep into an inside slit.

"It must be hard, living with that every day." I slapped at a mosquito on my leg.

"Yeah, well. It came to a head tonight, with Benny getting lost like that. Here's his picture. He was about five here. It's the last one she sent me."

I reached for the flashlight as Neil pulled out a grainy photograph. John Philip did look like Neil—the same fine, light-brown hair falling over his forehead, the mischievous grin lighting up his face. But his eyes were serious and dark, like Agnes's in the schoolgirl picture.

"He looks like you. Look at that grin. And the hair and ears. Oh, Neil, he's so cute."

Neil put the picture back into his wallet. "Hey, enough already. Let me get moving so you can get in out of these infernal skeeters."

I touched his arm. "I'm glad you told me about him."

Neil stood and shoved the billfold back into his pocket. "Hey, like I said, nobody else knows."

"I won't tell a soul. Cross my heart." I made the old childhood sign.

Neil pulled me to my feet. "Thanks for listening, Lacey Lu. I thought I was gonna go crazy tonight unless I told somebody." His arms circled my back, squeezing hard. I returned the hug, letting myself enjoy for this brief moment the warmth of his body against mine, the sinewy muscles of his arms around me, his cheek pressing against my hair. But just for a moment.

"Well, goodnight." I lifted my head and pushed my hands against his chest, but Neil didn't let go. Instead, his lips brushed my forehead, and when I looked up at him, trying to read his expression in the dark, his mouth moved to my lips, kissing me lightly and then more firmly, a real kiss that signaled desire. And danger.

I stumbled backwards, but Neil held onto me, grabbing for my wrists. "Sorry," he whispered, pulling me toward him again. "I didn't mean to take advantage, but I've been wanting to do that all week. Since that night the kids were out with their jars catching lightning bugs."

"You have?" Neil was still holding my wrists. "What about the preacher's daughter?"

"Oh, her." Neil's chuckle lightened the mood. "Nah, she's not my type. Roy's been egging me on to ask her out, but I ain't got nothing to talk about with somebody like that."

"What about last night?"

"Last night?"

"At the river. You said you had to get home early. Neva was sure you had a date."

"And you thought so, too?" Neil laughed again. "Nah, nothing like that. I was just ready to leave, that was all. I had evening chores to do, and I didn't know when Roy would be ready to go. And riding with a car full of women, well, I couldn't pass that up, could I? You really thought I was out squiring around the preacher's daughter?"

"Well, you certainly gave that impression."

"That was show for Geneva. And you wouldn't even talk to me."

"You were too busy flirting with Neva."

"Me?" Neil dropped my wrists and raised his hands in mock protest. "She was flirting with me is more like it. Anyway, I had to do something to get your attention. The way you were ignoring me, keeping your back turned, your hair all mussed up in them little curls that were sticking to your neck. I just wanted to..." Neil stepped closer, lifted one hand to the back of my neck, and ran his fingers through my hair. Then he kissed me again, lightly, playfully. "Just wanted to do that," he finished.

I could feel the blood rushing through my body, racing for the skin, making my nerve ends tingle. Wanting more. Wanting...

Neil released me. "Hey, I'd better get going, hadn't I? You get some rest. Okay?"

"Okay. You, too." I took a step backward toward the porch.

"Okay. Deal. See you later." Neil picked up his flashlight, aimed it at the road, and disappeared into the darkness.

Ruth Rodgers

Chapter 22

Monday, July 21, 1952

The bedroom was bright with morning sunshine when I awoke. Perspiration beaded on my upper lip, and I brushed at it with my fingers, my lips tender from last night, from Neil's mouth against mine. What had I been thinking—letting Neil kiss me like that, letting my body relax against his? But he had clung to me like a child. For eight years he'd lived bottled up with his secret, then entrusted it to me—nobody else. I couldn't very well have refused him the same comfort he'd offered me earlier when Benny was lost. I turned my back to the window and closed my eyes. Thankfully, he hadn't been able to see me very well in the dark, but he must have felt every curve of my body as he pressed me against him, nothing between us but my thin nylon gown and matching robe. And I had cooperated fully, had let myself lean into him, had let him kiss me, had let him run his fingers through my hair.

I sat up and rubbed my eyes to dismiss the image. Best to remember what I'd told Benny when he'd asked about his daddy. *It's just me and you, kiddo. We don't need anybody else.* I got up to check on him. He was still sleeping, his toy dog clutched tightly under his chin. I brushed his hair off his damp forehead and stood for a moment, just watching him breathe, before returning to my own room to get dressed and gather our dirty laundry.

On the back porch, I sorted the laundry into two piles, gingerly handling the stiff, smelly clothes I'd been wearing the night before. A wild thing, Neil had called me. I'd probably smelled like a wild thing, too. I filled the machine and started the first load.

"Mommy?" Benny stood at the kitchen door.

"I'm right here." I scooped him up in a hug. "Did you get a good sleep?"

"I want to go home. I don't like it here."

I gave him a squeeze. "You and me both. Last night was pretty scary, huh? I'm washing all our dirty clothes right now, and later tonight we'll talk to Uncle Roy about giving us a ride into town to the bus station. Okay?"

"We're going home today?"

"Not today. But soon. I promise." I lowered Benny to the floor, but he kept right beside me, a handful of my skirt in his hand. I knelt so that my face was level with his. "Can you tell me what happened last night? How you got so far away from the house?"

Benny's lower lip trembled. "You said I wasn't in Grandma's book. And everybody else was, everybody but me."

"Oh, honey, don't worry about that." I brushed at his hair with my uninjured hand. "It doesn't mean anything. We'll go home soon and you can forget all about it."

"You were crying."

"I was tired, that's all. It's nothing for you to worry about. Did you hear me and Grandma talking?"

Benny nodded, tears puddling in his eyes. "Grandma said when you got married I'd get a different name and belong to somebody else."

"No, honey, she didn't mean it that way. You'd still belong to me." I put both arms around him and pulled him tightly against me. "Nobody's ever going to come between us. Nobody. I promise."

"I don't want you to get married. I don't want to belong to anybody else."

"Oh, Benbo. You don't have to worry about that. I have no intention of getting married, not now or ever." I gave him a reassuring squeeze, then stood and took his hand. "Come on, now. Let's get some breakfast."

"Well, there's my lost boy." Mama came in the back door with a basket of eggs. "You sure gave Grandma a scare last night." She put one arm around Benny's shoulder, but he pulled away and edged closer to me, wrapping himself in my skirt.

"What's the matter?" Mama looked at me.

"He overheard us talking last night. He thinks somebody is going to take him away from me."

"Why? Whatever gave him—?"

"Never mind. We were about to have breakfast."

"Benny, honey, nobody said anything about..." Mama appealed to me with her eyes, but I didn't answer, only put one arm around Benny and pulled him closer to me.

Mama set the basket of eggs on the counter. "All these years, it's like I was being tore in two, between you and your daddy—him pulling one way and you the other. Now with you back, I was hoping—"

"Hoping what, Mama? That you'd wake up and Benny would be nothing but a bad dream? There's nothing left to say, to you or to Daddy. We'll be gone soon and you won't have to think about us any more."

After breakfast I dawdled with the job of running the clothes through the wringer and hanging them on the line, not wanting to go back inside and deal with Mama again. Maybe I'd just drive Daddy's car into town and leave it at the bus station for somebody to pick up later. Or keep driving all the way to New York. Take the cigar box with the five hundred dollars, too.

But I knew I couldn't take Daddy's car or his money, couldn't give everybody the satisfaction. *Well, what did you expect*, Neva would say, *after what she did before?* I wanted nothing more from any of them.

As I hung the wet clothes, Benny stayed right beside me, getting in my way and causing me more than once to stumble. "Why don't you go play in the wagon?" I asked. "Or throw some corn to the chickens? You know where it is, in the crib over there."

But Benny continued to dog my steps, unwilling to leave me for even a second. I hung the last item on the line, then walked to the corncrib and sat on its step. Benny sat beside me, one hand resting on my scraped knee.

"Ouch, honey, don't do that. Mommy's knee is all scraped up." I held out my right hand to examine it. "My hand, too. See?"

Benny looked at my hand, then up at my face. His lower lip quivered.

"Hey, it's okay," I reassured him. "I fell down last night when I was looking for you, but I put some medicine on it, and it'll be all better in a day or so. You shouldn't have run off like that, you know. I'll never let anything bad happen to you. You know that, don't you?"

Benny nodded obediently.

"Where were you going? To Uncle Roy's?"

"I don't want to belong to somebody else. Grandma said—"

"Grandma didn't mean it like that."

I ran the second load of clothes through the wringer and hung them on the line, still avoiding going back into the house. Mama would be in the kitchen now, putting peas on to cook, flouring chicken to fry for dinner. When I'd first arrived in New York, it had seemed strange to hear people talk about eating dinner at night, and now dinner at noon seemed strange to me. Funny how quickly I'd adapted. I'd be glad to get back to my old routine—the kids in the nursery school, my own cozy little room, the summer nights spent sitting on the stoop with my girlfriends, watching the kids play in the alley while we gossiped about everybody's lives, the stacks of old movie magazines that everyone passed around until they were ragged, the latest Frank Sinatra tune on the radio, the hum of human voices surrounding me, making me feel safe—a place where I was welcomed, where I belonged.

When Mama called us in to eat, I was pushing Benny on the tire swing, and his excited squeals of "Push me harder, Mommy!" brought tears of giddy relief to my eyes. After the panic of last night, I'd never let him out of my sight again, not for a minute.

At the table, Mama tried to get back into Benny's good graces. "I made fried chicken," she told him. "And you get both drumsticks."

But despite her efforts at conversation with Benny, the meal was strained and quiet, and I was in no mood to help the situation. It wasn't until we were clearing the table that Mama brought up the subject of going to the hospital. "I hate to ask you, Lacey, but I promised Daddy I'd be back to see him today," she said finally. "The doctor was going to check him this morning and leave word about when he could come home. I don't want to put you to no trouble on my account."

"I'll take you, but don't expect me to see him, all right? While you're there, Benny and I will go by the bus station and check the schedules."

"I thought you were staying till the end of the week," Mama said. "You haven't changed your mind, have you?"

"What do *you* think?" I spun on my heel and went outside to retrieve the clothes from the line. There was still a noticeable tea-colored stain on the denim skirt where the blood had streaked it. Oh, well, it was old anyway, one of my second-hand purchases. Benny's few clothes were limp and faded from wear, and I could see new stains from the last time I'd washed them. When I got home, I'd have to make another subway trip to the Salvation Army thrift shop to pick through other people's castoffs. Each trip there left me feeling more shamed and depressed, but at least I paid for my purchases; it wasn't like I was accepting charity.

Taking the clothes inside, I tossed them onto the bed and began to fold them, avoiding looking at the shopping bag across the room, one of those upscale department store bags with the reinforced handles and the store's initials in fancy script. On Saturday, while the men cleaned the fish for supper, Geneva had gone out to her and Tom's station wagon and returned with that bag, plunking it into my arms with a flourish.

"Here, Lacey, I brought these for Benny. It's just a few things of Tommy's that he doesn't wear any more. They grow so fast at this age, you know. Some of these are practically brand new."

I had reflexively taken hold of the bag when it was thrust into my hands. "You didn't need to—"

"Oh, it's play clothes mostly, nothing much. I've been getting Tommy outfitted for school starting next month, you know, so I was cleaning out his dresser drawers, and there's so much he's hardly worn at all. I was telling Tom last week that somebody ought to get some use out of them. And then I thought of Benny." She smiled triumphantly.

I flinched. As a child, I'd always gotten stuck with Neva's hand-me-downs, and now here was Neva pushing Tommy's castoffs on Benny. And not even hand-me-downs. Benny was older and taller than Tommy, even if he wasn't as hefty. Some nerve.

Neva had chattered on and on. "Tommy's such a fussbudget about clothes, a regular little rebel about what he will and won't wear. I'll declare, I never know what to buy him, and he hates to go shopping with me, all that trying on and such. So I just buy and take my chances. I bet Benny's not so fussy, is he? I mean, he can't afford to be, you know."

I still hadn't looked inside the bag. After yesterday's upheaval—the accident with the plate, the argument with Mama, and then Benny's disappearance—I'd forgotten about it until now. Well, I still wasn't touching it. I didn't need charity from anyone, least of all Neva. Once Benny was in school all day, I could get a better job and buy nice things for him and for myself.

I picked up another skirt from the bed, one of my Salvation Army finds, a gauzy print of tiny yellow and purple flowers on a navy blue background. I'd been wearing it the night the kids were catching fireflies, the night I'd encouraged Neil to ask out the preacher's daughter, the night he'd jokingly put his arm around my shoulder and I'd first imagined what it would feel like to be kissed by him.

And now I knew. It had been so sweet, had felt so right. Why, then, was I feeling so threatened by it? Neil wasn't Dwayne. I folded the skirt and laid it on the pile. It didn't matter, anyway. Benny and I would soon be on our way back to New York, and Neil would be nothing more than a memory.

Chapter 23

I pulled up to the front door of the hospital to drop Mama off. "We'll be back in about an hour."

"Aren't you coming in?" Mama looked at me in surprise.

"I told you we were going to check the bus schedule. It's time for me and Benny to get back home, back to people who care about us." I looked at my watch. "It's two-thirty now. I'll be back here in the parking lot at three-thirty. I'll wait for you in the car."

"Honey, I already told you how bad I feel about all this. I don't want you to go off this way."

I waited in silence for Mama to close the car door before pulling off and driving the few blocks to the bus station. Two buses a day departed heading north—to Valdosta, Macon, Atlanta, Chattanooga, one at 9:40 a.m. and the other at 4:20 p.m. I'd have to change buses again in Valdosta if I wanted to head up the East Coast toward Savannah and points north. If Roy couldn't take us for the morning bus, maybe he could run us into town at noon, and Benny and I could wait for the afternoon one. At the window I asked about prices and transfer schedules, adding figures in my head. I'd have just enough to get us home again, with precious little left over.

As we walked outside, Benny pointed across the street at the large neon ice cream cone at the Dairy Delight. "Mommy, look. Ice cream."

"I see. But we need our money for the trip home, for the bus tickets." I caught Benny's hand and started for the car just as a young woman turned away from the serving window with two cones swirled high with vanilla ice cream. She held one out to a boy about Benny's age and handed the other to a slightly younger girl with blonde curls. Then she turned back to the window, counted out some coins from her purse, and accepted another cone for herself. I watched her put one hand on the little girl's shoulder as they walked away, licking their ice cream cones with obvious delight.

"Maybe just a small one," I told Benny. "A ten-cent one." I opened my coin purse and pulled out a dime and a penny.

After getting Benny's cone, we were waiting at the curb to cross the street back to the car when someone called, "Hey, Lacey." I looked around, startled. Simon was striding toward us, one hand lifted in a wave.

"Hi! What are you doing here?"

"On my way downtown." Simon motioned down the street. "Got in late last night from south Florida and I'm leaving first thing tomorrow for Pensacola, so I need some more tobacco for the trip." He tapped at his shirt pocket and then made as if to reach for Benny's ice cream cone. "Hey, Benny. You gonna give me a bite of that?"

Benny took a step backward, out of Simon's reach, and I laughed. "Benny, you remember Uncle Simon, don't you? He's the one with the big truck. You sat in it and blew the horn, remember?"

Benny nodded but kept his distance, protecting his ice cream cone.

"What brings you two into town?" Simon asked.

"I dropped Mama off at the hospital to visit with Daddy. We were checking bus schedules. It's time for me to get back to work. And Benny's eager to get back to his friends."

"That's a long trip on a bus. Too bad you're not closer."

"It's close enough, the way things are going."

"Oh?" Simon pulled his Prince Albert can out of his pocket. "How's he doing?"

206

"Okay, I guess. Roy's pushing for him to come home, to save money."

"Mama can't take care of an invalid; you know that."

"Roy's got it all figured out. He says he can hire somebody to come in and help out cheaper than paying for a hospital room. You been to see him yet?"

Simon concentrated on rolling his cigarette. "I've been on the road."

"You're here now. You should go for Mama's sake, at least."

"Yeah, I know." Simon lit his cigarette, took a long puff. "Tell you what, I'll do it today. Then I'll come out to the house tonight and visit with you and Mama for awhile, if that's okay. You and Benny can take a ride in my rig."

"Mama would like that. Come for supper."

"Okay. Visit the old man, get a home-cooked meal in return. But you have to promise to go for a ride in my truck. Benny can blow the horn again. What do you say?"

Benny looked at me. "Can we, Mommy?"

"Sure. That sounds like fun." I looked up the street at the courthouse clock. "I told Mama we'd pick her up at three-thirty. I'll tell her you're coming for supper. Even better, you can ride with us and tell her yourself before you go in to see Daddy."

"Nah, I'll walk. Give me time to work up my courage. 'Screw it to the sticking point' as Shakespeare said."

"How do you remember all that stuff?" I asked. "You're a regular walking encyclopedia."

Simon tapped his cigarette to knock off the ash and took another puff. "Nothing to it. See you tonight."

❋ ❋ ❋

"What did the doctor say?" I asked after Mama settled herself into the car.

"A few more days, if Daddy keeps improving. By the end of the week, for sure."

"Roy will be glad to hear that." I turned the car onto the highway. A few more days. That would give me time to talk to

Roy and for Benny and me to make our escape back to New York before Daddy was released. "We ran into Simon downtown. He's back from his south Florida trip but off on another one early in the morning. He said he'd go see Daddy this afternoon, and then come out to the house tonight. I told him to come for supper. I hope that was okay."

Benny leaned forward from the back seat. "He's taking me for a ride in his truck."

"He is, is he? That'll be nice." Mama smiled at Benny, then turned back to me. "I know Daddy will be proud to see Simon. You don't know how much it means to him, and to me, too, having you all come home to see him like you did—Grace and Geneva coming two weekends in a row, you coming all the way from New York. It's such a blessing to have all my children around me. Just like it used to be, when you all were still at home."

"You can't turn back the clock, Mama, much as you'd like to. Those days are long gone."

"I know." Mama sighed. "But still it's good to see all of you coming together again. Family is important. Friends come and go, but family is forever."

"Hah! That's funny, Mama. My friends accept me for who I am. And they accept Benny. Not like certain family members I could name."

"Sh-h-h." Mama motioned her head toward Benny in the back seat.

I told myself to stay calm, to not say any more in front of Benny, but the anger wouldn't be tamped down. "It's time you faced up to facts, Mama, you and Daddy both. You can't change the past, much as you want to. All you can do is admit your mistakes and keep plugging along, making the best of today. That's all I'm trying to do, and all I'm getting is people throwing my past back into my face, rubbing it into my skin like sandpaper. I've had it, Mama, up to here." I held my hand up under my chin.

Mama looked intently at the road ahead of the car. "Not here, Lacey, not now. Not in front of him."

"Why not?" I asked. "He's what this is all about, isn't it? If I'd just gone to Tallahassee for a visit with my big sister, come home five or six months later as the same skinny Lacey, got a job in the dime store downtown, then married some red-necked farmer, everything would be hunky-dory now, wouldn't it? Nothing to embarrass the family name." I jerked the steering wheel around a curve without slowing down, causing Benny to slide across the back seat. Mama let out a gasp and grabbed at the dashboard. "That was my great sin, wasn't it, Mama," I continued, "embarrassing the family name? And now, here I come, dragging home the visible evidence, having the gall to think he might be treated like just another grandchild. Well, now I know just how wrong I was, don't I?"

I blew the horn, louder and longer than was necessary, at a dog that had run barking into the road, then looked back at Benny, who was cowering in one corner of the back seat, hands over his face. I let out a deep breath. I'd better get hold of myself.

"Hey, Benny," I called, forcing my voice to be calm, "everything's okay. I'm just tired, that's all. I didn't get much sleep last night, what with you disappearing on me like that. My hand hurts, too." I lifted it off the steering wheel to examine it. "How are those mosquito bites of yours? We'll put some more salve on them when we get home."

Benny, reminded of the bites, began to scratch at one of his arms, his face still hidden from view.

I reached behind me with one hand and felt for his leg. "Don't worry, Benbo. We're going home soon. Everything's super duper. Okay?"

I took Benny with me to do the evening chores while Mama started cooking supper for Simon's visit. "I'm not mad at you, Benbo," I tried to explain as we walked out to the pasture to drive the cow up to the barn. "What I said in the car to Grandma, it doesn't have anything to do with you. It's just that coming back here brings back a lot of sad memories, and I can't deal with them right now."

Benny said nothing, but I could see the puzzlement in his eyes.

"Someday, when you're older, maybe you'll understand. It's just too complicated to try to explain."

"Is it 'cause I'm not in the book?" Benny asked.

"That's part of it, but it's a lot more complicated than that."

"Doesn't Grandma like me?"

"Of course she likes you, honey. What's not to like? You're a super duper kid, and don't you ever let anybody tell you any different." I caught Benny's hand. "And guess what? Uncle Simon's taking us for a ride in his truck tonight. Aren't you excited?" I used my most enthusiastic voice, hoping to erase the memory of my angry outburst at Mama in the car. Okay, I wasn't the perfect mother, but it wasn't for lack of effort. Benny and I were a family, and nobody else's opinion mattered.

Chapter 24

Simon had arrived and we were eating supper when I saw Neil's truck go by toward home. Today was Roy's tobacco gathering day, so Neil had been helping him since early this morning, and tomorrow Roy would be returning the favor by helping Neil. Both of them would have been up since at least five a.m., and Neil couldn't have gotten to sleep last night before midnight. Poor guy. I wasn't likely to see him again before I left for New York, but that was all for the best, anyway. After our late night encounter and his startling confession of a son in France, seeing him again would be awkward. The embrace and the kisses that followed had been nothing more than physical need—a raw hunger for human contact that I knew all too well. Once Benny and I were back at home in New York, I could write him a long letter of appreciation for helping me find Benny and let him know how deeply I empathized with him for the huge emptiness in his life of having a son he'd never seen.

"Lacey, can you pass me another biscuit?" Simon took two off the platter that I handed him. "Mama, you still make the best homemade biscuits I ever tasted. And I'll have another piece of that fried steak. Anybody else want more mashed potatoes before I clean out the bowl?"

Mama beamed and passed the potatoes. "Finish 'em up. But save some room for dessert. Peach cobbler. Your favorite."

Simon cleaned his plate, then sat back and patted his flat

stomach. "Whew. That was good. I don't get many home-cooked meals these days, being on the road all the time."

I smiled at Simon's obvious enjoyment of the meal. Having him over was a nice diversion; it kept my mind off Neil and provided a buffer between Mama and me. "I'm surprised you're still single," I said. "All my friends used to think you were so handsome. And smart."

Simon shook his head. "I like my independence just fine, thank you. I'll leave the marrying to the rest of you."

"Not me." I looked pointedly at Mama. "If you ask me, marriage is highly overrated. Who needs it?"

"My sentiments exactly," Simon answered.

Mama looked from me to Simon, a frown of disapproval on her face. "I don't know what this world is coming to." She stood and began to clear the plates away, and I jumped up to get dessert bowls and spoons. Mama set the dish of peach cobbler down in front of Simon. "You didn't finish what you were saying earlier about your visit with Daddy in the hospital. Did he say anything to you? I know he was just tickled pink to see you."

Simon took a big helping of the cobbler. "Um-m, this looks good."

"I bet he talked about coming home, didn't he?" Mama asked.

Simon lifted a spoonful of cobbler to his mouth. "Um-m." He chewed and swallowed. "I saw him only for a minute. The nurse was putting him back to bed. Said he'd been sitting up for a while, so he was pretty tired."

Mama nodded. "He was up in a chair while I was there. But didn't he look good? He's got so much of his color back since last week. But then you didn't see him when he looked so pale."

"He looked okay." Simon took another bite of cobbler. "I didn't stay long. He looked like he needed some rest."

"I know he was glad to see you just the same," Mama said. "It's good you went. I know how much you hate hospitals, being around sick people."

"Yeah, I already saw enough dying to last me the rest of eternity." Simon put down his spoon, which was halfway to his mouth, and pushed his plate away. "Whew, I'm full."

"But you didn't finish your cobbler," Mama protested.

"It's good. I'm just stuffed, that's all."

After the dishes were done, Benny and I climbed into Simon's truck for our promised ride. "Just a short one," I said. "It'll soon be Benny's bedtime. Mine, too."

Simon turned the ignition switch. "We'll just go out to the highway for a ways so I can get her up to speed and then come back. I got an early day tomorrow myself."

Benny sat in the middle between us, fascinated with all the gauges on the dashboard. I crooked one elbow out the open window. The last streaks of pink and purple sunset tinted the low clouds on the western horizon, while behind us, to the east, the sky was darkening into twilight. Last night I'd been in Neil's truck, wild with fear about Benny's disappearance, and now here was Benny beside me, bouncing on the seat with anticipation, gingerly reaching with one finger to touch first one thing and then another, wrapping his small palm around the gear shift knob, making motor noises under his breath, completely absorbed in the moment. He seemed to have forgotten my earlier outburst in the car.

"Here, Benny, you want to shift the gear? Put your hand right here and when I give the word, we're going to push her up into second." Simon put his hand over Benny's. "Now." He pushed the gear shift up. "Hold on. Now we're going to pull it down." Benny followed Simon's directions, his eyes dancing with excitement.

"Thanks," I said to Simon over Benny's head. "He's in heaven."

"Maybe he'll be a truck driver, like me. Benny, you want to drive a rig like this when you grow up?"

Benny looked at me as if asking my permission.

"Sure, if you want. You can be whatever you want to be."

"Okay," Benny said.

I laughed. "You've made an impression. He'll talk about this for months."

Benny resumed his examination of the dials. I leaned back into the seat and let myself relax. My eyes were getting heavy, and I put one hand up to stifle a yawn.

"Ready to go back?" Simon asked. "We haven't got her up to highway speed yet."

"No, don't mind me. It's been a long day. You really go see Daddy this afternoon?"

"You doubt my word?" Simon arched his eyebrows at me.

"At supper, what you said about seeing enough dying, I didn't know."

"Yeah, I went. I figured it was the least I could do, with you coming all the way from New York like you did."

"He looks so old, not like I remember him."

"He did look bad. But don't tell Mama I said that, okay? I apologized for not seeing him earlier, told him I'd just got back from a trip was the reason I hadn't been, but he didn't say anything, just kept lifting one hand and saying "Home," like he wanted me to take him out of there right then. It was kind of creepy, seeing him like that, so I left, told him I'd see him again soon."

"All he's said to me so far is "No," like he's still disowning me."

"You made Ma happy, anyway, coming home like you did."

"You think so? You should have been here yesterday. Mama and I had a big argument last night. That's why I was at the bus station today, checking schedules."

"You and Mama?" Simon's voice was sharp, like Roy's had been that first night when we got off the bus. "Arguing about what?"

Stung by Simon's tone, I looked over at him. He was staring straight ahead, hands clenched tightly to the steering wheel. I'd been counting on Simon to be the one family member who could share my feelings of being an outcast, and now he was attacking me, too. "Never mind. It's between her and me."

Benny, alert to the suddenly charged atmosphere of the conversation, pulled his hands away from the dials and put them in his lap.

I patted his leg. "This is fun, huh, Benny? Wasn't this nice of Uncle Simon, to take us for a ride?" I wanted to tell Simon about my discovery yesterday, about last night's argument. *Benny's not in the family Bible,* I wanted to scream; *Benny didn't get a baby quilt like all the other grandchildren; Benny's picture isn't on the mantel with the photos of the other grandkids. Benny doesn't exist.* But here was Benny sitting between us, looking up at me, curling himself up already for further blows. I couldn't do that to him again. I changed the subject. "How long have you had this truck? Where all have you been in it? I guess you see a lot of the country, don't you, traveling all over like you do?"

Simon, eager to talk about his rig and his travels, launched into an account of his adventures over the last few years. I leaned back and willed myself to relax.

As we passed Neil's trailer on the way back, I didn't see any lights on inside. Neil was probably asleep already. Had he spent the day regretting that he'd told me his secret, kicking himself for kissing me and saying all those things? He had been overwrought last night, holding onto me like a man clinging to a cliff by his fingernails, crushing me so tightly I could scarcely breathe. This morning, in the clear light of day, had he been embarrassed about baring his emotions so nakedly?

As Simon parked the truck and got out, Benny slid behind the steering wheel, gripping it in his small hands. Simon laughed as he closed the driver's side door, talking through the open window. "Hey, Benny, you gonna drive this rig back to New York?"

I opened the passenger door. "Come on, Benny, time to get out. Uncle Simon has to go home."

"He's okay. Nothing he can hurt in there." Simon held up his keys and then stuck them in his pocket. "Let him drive for awhile. I could use something cold to drink, if you got anything."

I jumped down from the cab, casting a quick glance behind the seat before closing the door. Sure enough, the narrow neck of an amber-colored glass bottle was visible under the back of the seat, sealed with a cork stopper. I could see only the top inch of the bottle's neck, but the cork was enough to confirm my suspicions. I walked around the front of the cab to join Simon on the other side. "Want a Co-Cola? Tom and Neva brought a whole case with them this weekend."

"That'll hit the spot. Thanks."

When I walked inside, Mama was sitting in the living room in semi-darkness, one of the quilt squares she was piecing together for Zach's quilt in her lap.

I pulled the cord hanging from the overhead light. "You can't sew in the dark, Mama. Why didn't you turn on the light?"

"I was just about to. My eyes ain't as good as they used to be. I guess I'm getting old." Mama blinked and rubbed her eyes in the sudden brightness of the bare bulb.

I looked at her, sunk into the old flowered armchair. She looked tired. The light revealed dark crescents beneath her eyes and glinted off the silver-gray hairs streaking the auburn waves that I had inherited. I calculated in my head. Mama had turned fifty-two this year.

"Simon wanted a cold drink. You want anything? A glass of tea?"

"No, nothing for me. Ain't Simon coming in?"

"I don't know. Benny's still in the truck, pretending to drive. Simon's keeping an eye on him right now."

I popped the caps off two bottles of Coca-Cola and took them back outside. Simon was standing beneath the oak tree, one arm wrapped around the tire swing. The same spot Neil had stood last night.

"Thanks." Simon took the bottle I handed him. "Ma still up?"

"Yes. She asked if you were coming in."

"In a minute. How's she holding up?"

"Okay. She's excited about Daddy coming home."

"She looked tired tonight, more than usual. I hope she doesn't run herself down, trying to take care of him."

Simon sounded like Roy, worried over Mama. Why did men think women were so weak, so in need of masculine protection? "She'll manage okay. She always has."

"She's had more than her share of grief."

"You mean me, I suppose?"

"That's a big part of it. You nearly killed her when you ran off like you did, her not knowing where you were, or if you were alive or dead. If you don't believe me, ask Roy."

I bristled. "From what I hear, you contributed some, too."

Simon looked toward the corn field across the road. "I'm no saint, but at least I never deliberately set out to hurt her. When you kids were little, all of you, Roy especially, used to taunt me about how she wasn't my real mother. Remember that?"

"No." I shook my head.

"It was Roy, mostly. Just childish possessiveness. But it made me feel like dirt. I don't remember my real mother, so Mama's the only mother I've ever known. One day—I was about ten, I guess—she overheard Roy saying that and she took me aside and told me I was just as much her son as Roy was, that when she married Daddy, I became her son just as sure as Daddy became her husband, that God gave Grace and me to her, and nobody could break a bond that God himself had forged. I'll never forget that day." Simon's voice cracked with emotion. He took a long sip of his soda and wiped the back of his hand across his mouth.

I was quiet. As the youngest of the family, I'd never thought of Simon and Grace as stepchildren. Was that how they had regarded themselves? And the family portrait on the wall, the one with Mama and Daddy and the three younger kids. How had they felt, looking at that every day? I wondered again whose idea that was, why Simon and Grace were not included. It had to be Daddy. Some rigid idea of keeping things separate for posterity. Mama would never have excluded them. I could picture the scene Simon described, could hear Mama's voice telling him about God giving him and Grace to her. Mama could work God into any conversation. No wonder Simon was so defensive of Mama. She'd treated him with more kindness than Daddy ever had, encouraging him in his schoolwork, running interference for him with Daddy. Even after he'd come home from the war, when Daddy told him to leave because of his drinking, Mama would have been in the middle, taking his side.

"Well, I need to get going." Simon said. "If you're still around when I get back, maybe I'll see you again. If not, take care. Send me a postcard from New York."

"What you said earlier—I didn't set out to hurt her either."

"Tell *her* that." Simon handed me his empty Coca-Cola bottle. "I'll just step in and say good-bye."

❉   ❉   ❉

After Simon left, Benny and I sat on the porch steps, watching the lightning bugs and counting the stars as they popped out of the darkening sky. If Simon had still been here he could have identified each constellation and told Benny the story of how it got its name. "There's the bear," he used to say, or "There's Orion, the hunter," but all I ever saw was a jumble of stars. Only the Big Dipper actually looked like a dipper. What admiration I'd had then for my big brother; he was the smartest person in the whole school, maybe even the whole world. But tonight he'd sounded sharp and angry with me: *You hurt Mama. You nearly killed her, running away like you did, her not knowing where you were, if you were alive or dead.*

But Simon didn't know about Benny's omission from the family Bible. Nobody understood why I was so upset. *Forget it,* Roy had said when I'd tried to tell him. *Let it rest. Take it easy.* I'd already told Mama I was sorry for worrying her; what more could I do? What else did the family expect from me?

"Come on," I said to Benny. "It's getting late. Time for bed." I stood and reached for his hand.

"I'm gonna be a truck driver, like Uncle Simon."

"That's nice. Will you take me with you on your trips?"

"You can go, but I get to drive."

"That's a deal." I pulled open the screen door. "Come on now. Bath time for you."

"Me and Roy, Jr.'s gonna build a fort in the woods at his house tomorrow. His daddy said we could."

"Whoa, I thought you couldn't wait to go home."

"And Uncle Roy's taking us fishing again on Saturday. Last

time I caught three fish." Benny held up three fingers, spreading them as wide apart as he could.

"Bath time. We'll talk about it tomorrow."

Benny insisted on bathing himself, wanting me to leave before he completely undressed. This was new; he'd never demanded privacy before when it was just the two of us back home. Had he gotten the notion from Roy, Jr., maybe? Last night, I had bathed him and doctored his mosquito bites, and he hadn't protested. Nevertheless, I left him alone, after testing the water to make sure it wasn't too hot. His sudden modesty didn't surprise me, exactly, but it was faintly disturbing, a clear message that soon there would be other secrets, other facets of his life I would be utterly left out of; soon I would look at him and see a stranger.

"Benny didn't want any help with his bath," I explained to Mama as I returned to the living room.

"He's a big boy," Mama answered. "That's how you know you've done a good job, when they don't need you no more."

"I guess. It's hard, though."

"Seems to me he's growed a mighty piece just since you been here. That first night, he had hold of your skirt, wouldn't turn loose for nobody. Now he's playing with Roy, Jr. like he's knowed him forever, and him and Tommy hit it off right away. Thick as thieves."

"Yeah. I bet that got Neva's goat—Tommy and Benny."

"She gave you all them nice clothes of Tommy's."

"Ha! I don't need her charity. Next time she comes, you tell her to take them back and give them to some of her country club friends."

"All you children wore hand-me-downs. Believe me, I was grateful for anything anybody gave me in them days. That was back during the Depression, and—"

I resigned myself to another lecture. At least Mama and I were talking again, even if we were disagreeing. Maybe I did owe Mama an apology for blowing up at her on Sunday night. But Mama owed me something too, so that made us even.

After tucking Benny in, I took a quick shower, leaving the

bathroom door cracked so that I could hear a knock on the front door or Neil's bob- white whistle from the road. Foolish, I knew; he'd probably been asleep for hours already.

I toweled myself dry and pulled on my nightgown. Was that a noise from outside? I tiptoed in the dark to the living room and peeked out the front window. Nothing there. No flashlight beam from the road. Quietly, I pushed open the screen door and stepped onto the porch. All was quiet. After a few minutes, I went inside and pulled the cord on the living room light, three times on and off in rapid succession. No response. I went to bed and tried to sleep.

Chapter 25

Tuesday, July 22, 1952

I awoke sometime before dawn with sure signs of my period coming on—my stomach cramping, my back aching. After rummaging through my suitcase for the necessary supplies, I made my way to the bathroom and then to the kitchen, where I ran a glass of water and shook two aspirins out of the bottle on the counter. The first pale streaks of morning light through the back window revealed a low ground-fog hanging over the pasture, enveloping everything beyond the boundaries of the back yard fence in a pinkish haze.

As I set the empty glass on the counter, a figure emerged out of the fog, opened the gate of the cow lot, and started toward the house. It wasn't Mama—too tall and thin. Roy? No, I could see now that it was Neil, carrying a pail of milk. Mama had mentioned that Neil had been coming over every morning to milk the cow, but up to now I'd never been up early enough to have seen him.

Remembering the thinness of my gown, I backed away from the window and hurried to the bedroom for some clothes. As I stripped off my gown and fumbled into a bra, I heard the ping of the back screen door opening and closing, then the soft thud of the refrigerator door. I stepped into the first skirt I saw and grabbed for a blouse, buttoning it as I headed back to the kitchen. I'd be just getting up, coming into the kitchen to start a pot of coffee; I'd give a start of surprise to find him there, put my hand up to my chest, say, "Goodness, Neil, you're up early, aren't you?"

He was gone. I walked to the back porch and peered into the fog. He had disappeared. I considered running outside barefoot, calling after him, but then stopped myself. What was I doing, running after Neil like some silly, love-struck teenager? Let him go. At least the activity, or the aspirin, or both, had caused my cramps to temporarily disappear. I looked at the kitchen clock. Five-forty-five. I'd go back to bed, try to get another hour's sleep.

In the bedroom, I caught a glimpse of myself in the mirror as I picked up my gown from the floor. Something looked funny, off-kilter. I straightened and looked closer at my image. The buttons and buttonholes of my still untucked blouse were mismatched; I'd gotten off crooked, one button off all the way down, and one side hung down longer than the other—the way Benny buttoned himself sometimes. I looked like a six-year-old—my hair mussed from sleep, my blouse crooked, my nose and cheeks newly pink and freckle-splotched from unaccustomed exposure to the sun. It was a good thing Neil hadn't seen me. I began to laugh, the first real laugh I'd had since arriving home. It felt good. The more I laughed, the more ridiculous the whole thing became; I laughed until I had to wipe my eyes with my fingers.

"Lacey?" Mama knocked on the door. "Are you all right?"

"I couldn't sleep. Cramps. I got up to take some aspirin."

"I thought I heard crying."

"No, Mama. I'm fine, really."

"Okay." Mama sounded doubtful. "But stay in bed and get your rest. And let me know if you need anything."

"Thanks. I think I will sleep a little longer. Just until Benny gets up." I lay back down in my clothes and curled up on my side. Just a few more minutes, till the fog lifted.

※　※　※

When I woke again, it was after eight. I stretched my legs and turned onto my back. I felt better, except for the heavy, achy feeling in my lower torso, as if I had a ten pound weight sitting in my lower abdomen.

I found Benny in the kitchen, eating a bowl of corn flakes.

"I didn't want to wake you," Mama said. "I tried to get him to eat an egg and some toast, but that's all he wanted."

I scrambled myself two eggs and mixed them into a plate of grits. "You ought to at least try some grits," I told Benny. "As Roy would say, this is the test of whether or not you're a real McCormick." I held a forkful toward Benny's mouth, but he pulled back and grimaced. I laughed and continued eating. Now that I had made the decision to go home, I felt light, a bubble floating above all the detritus that had surrounded me this past week.

Another cramp gripping my midsection made me rethink that plan, remembering those long hours on the hard bus seat, Benny whining and wriggling against me for hours on end, the stifling, sweaty odor of all those bodies, the jarring, jerky starts and stops through clogged city traffic, the diesel fumes. I put one hand on my stomach, feeling queasy at the thought. Roy would be working at Neil's all day today, so the earliest I could talk to him would be tonight. I'd wait and see how I felt then.

After breakfast, Benny renewed his pleas to go over to Roy, Jr.'s to build their fort in the woods. "Mama," I asked, "anything you need me to do here?"

"No, go ahead and visit with Julia. Go have some girl talk and let Benny build his fort."

"Okay, if you're sure." I swallowed another two aspirins before taking Daddy's car key off the hook.

On the way over Benny talked nonstop about the fort. "Roy, Jr.'s got a hammer," he said, "and his daddy's got lots of nails."

"Nails?" I asked. "A hammer? I don't think so. What if you hit your finger instead of the nail? What if a nail flew up and hit you in the eye? I don't want you going anywhere near a hammer, not without adult supervision."

"Uncle Roy said—"

"Sometimes Uncle Roy needs to mind his own business."

※　※　※

"They're not getting any hammer or nails," Julia reassured me when I expressed my reservations about the boys' project. "Roy drove some stakes into the ground for them in between some of the pine trees and told them they could use any old boards around the yard they could find. Roy, Jr.'s got a pile gathered up already. They'll have to lean the boards against the stakes and trees and see what they can come up with." She handed Zach to me. "Let me go throw a load of clothes in the washing machine," she said. "Beat the afternoon rain. I'll be right back."

Relieved that no hammer or nails would be involved in the boys' project, I sat on the sofa, jiggling Zach in my lap. His dark blue eyes studied me intently for a moment; then he began to fret, and by the time Julia returned, he was crying in earnest, in spite of all my efforts to soothe him.

"He's hungry," Julia said. "He'll go to sleep after his feeding, and then we can sit and visit awhile."

"Is there anything I can do for you?" I asked. "Hang some clothes on the line? Wash the breakfast dishes?"

"Goodness, no," Julia said. "You did enough while I was in the hospital. You just sit and talk to me. My mother's been coming over every day, taking charge of the kitchen and shooing me out every time I put my foot in the door." She laughed. "She's grocery shopping right now, with Katie along to tell her what to get. I appreciate everybody's help, but I'm ready to reclaim my own house."

"If you're sure."

"Positive. Tell me what's going on in your life. What are the men like in New York?" Julia looked at me as eagerly as if we were two girls at a pajama party, sharing secrets.

I laughed self-consciously. "I wouldn't know. I haven't met any."

"I don't believe that. In six years? Come on, now. Surely—"

I shook my head. "Honest. Not a one. Looking for a man hasn't been on my list of priorities."

"You're as bad as Neil," Julia said. "I keep after him all the time to get busy and find himself a wife before it's too late. He's going to end up a lonely old bachelor if he doesn't watch out."

Julia's mention of Neil sent a flush creeping up my neck, and I stood and walked to the window, keeping my back to Julia. "I wonder how the boys are doing."

"They're fine. We can go check on them as soon as I finish feeding Zach. Now what were we talking about?"

"Neil," I said more quickly than I'd meant to, blushing again at the little thrill of pleasure that coursed through me. "I was surprised to see him still single."

"He'd make somebody a marvelous husband; I keep telling him if Roy hadn't asked me first—"

I turned, surprised, searching the expression on Julia's face.

"I'm kidding." Julia laughed. "Teasing him. But enough about him. We were talking about you."

"I told you. Nobody." I searched for a way to turn the conversation back to Neil. "Benny got lost the other night," I said. "Neil helped me find him."

"I heard about that. Neil was telling Roy. Something about running off after lightning bugs and getting lost."

"He was just down the road a ways, but it sure gave me a fright. If it hadn't been for Neil..." I returned to the sofa and sat. Zach was still nursing, but his eyes were closing.

Julia lifted him to her shoulder and patted his back. "Here come our groceries," she said as a car turned into the driveway. "Stay for dinnner. We'll make baloney sandwiches. Roy's eating at Neil's folks; today is Neil's tobacco gathering day, you know."

"Thanks, but Mama will be expecting us. I promised her I'd take her back to the hospital this afternoon to see Daddy."

"Then let Benny stay. He and Roy, Jr. are having a good time."

"Thanks, but he'd better go with me."

✳   ✳   ✳

Back at Mama's, Benny chattered excitedly all through dinner about the fort, and as soon as he finished eating, he ran outside to search the yard for scrap lumber.

"Julia wanted me to let him stay over there all day," I told Mama as we sat finishing our meal, "but I told her I'd promised to take you to see Daddy this afternoon."

"You and Benny go ahead with your plans. I don't want to be a bother; I feel like I've imposed on you enough already." Mama got up and began to clear the table. "Anyway, Roy said he'd drive me later tonight. He wants to talk to somebody about Daddy coming home."

"It's no bother." I hadn't been to see Daddy since I'd given him Benny's "Get Well" drawing and he'd told me "No" and refused to look at it, but I could at least say good-bye before I left, at least remind him that I had tried to make amends and he had refused to accept them.

As Mama lowered glasses into the sink to wash, I looked at her slumped shoulders, her bent head. What Simon had said last night, *Tell her that*, rang in my ears.

"I'm sorry, Mama." I stood behind her, talking to her back. "About the other night. I shouldn't have lost my temper like I did. But where Benny is concerned, I guess I go a little bit crazy. He's all I've got."

Mama dried her hands on her apron and walked out of the kitchen. In a minute she came back with a small bundle and held it out to me.

"Here's Benny's quilt," she said, "what I got done of it."

I unfolded the bundle. Four quilt squares had been completed, sewn together in two pairs of two each. Instead of being a baby design, like the quilt she was making for Zach, each square was a fan shape, alternating solids and prints, and I recognized some of the fabrics as remnants from my old dresses—going all the way back to elementary school. All were feedsack cotton. "Oh, Mama, it's beautiful!" I traced my fingers over the different prints. "I remember this dress. And this was Roy's shirt."

"I wanted to give you something to hold on to, to remind you of home. But that's all I got done. Every time I'd sit down with it, I'd fall apart. Seems like piecing that quilt just brung everything down on me. It got so I couldn't even take it down from the shelf without starting to cry."

"Can I have this, Mama, to keep?"

"If you want it. But I'm afraid it won't do Benny much good now, big as he is." Mama gave an apologetic laugh.

Benny burst through the screen door. "Mommy, can we go back over to Uncle Roy's? I found some boards outside. Can I have 'em?"

"You'll have to ask Grandma about that."

"Let's see what you found." Mama reached for Benny's hand. "See if it looks like fort material."

I hugged the quilt squares to my chest as Benny dragged Mama out the front door.

Ruth Rodgers

Chapter 26

"Sure is hot," I said to Mama as we bounced along the washboard ruts of the dirt road after I had given in to Benny's pleas and dropped him and his collection of boards off at Julia's again. I was uneasy about leaving him there without me, but Julia had promised to keep a close eye on him. "They're having fun," she told me. "It's not that often Roy, Jr. gets to play with other little boys his age."

"But what about...?" I started but didn't finish my sentence. Last week when I'd gone over to do Julia's laundry, I'd seen two little boys playing outside near the sharecropper's cabin. Katie and Roy, Jr. had been spending that day with Julia's mother, and Benny, excited to see other kids, wanted to run over and play, but when he started in that direction, someone inside the house had called to them, and they had disappeared. I'd had to explain to him that it wasn't because they didn't like him; it was probably because their mother needed them, or she had a snack for them or something. I didn't want to get into the sticky subject of race relations in the South with a six-year-old. Roy certainly would not have considered them appropriate playmates for Roy, Jr.

"What about what?" Julia had asked.

"Oh, nothing, never mind. We'll try not to be gone too long."

❄ ❄ ❄

"Hey, Miz McCormick," one of the nurses called as we entered the hospital. "He's sitting up in his room, waiting for company. Even got a shampoo this morning. Go on in."

At first I didn't see anyone in the room, my eyes resting first on the empty bed, but Mama went to the chair beside it that seemed to be holding a pile of wrinkled laundry.

I looked closer. Daddy seemed dwarfed by the white blanket wrapped around his shoulders and draped over his lap, hiding everything except his head and one wrinkled hand. "Hi, Daddy," I said. "I see you're getting better."

Mama laid her hand over his. "Roy's coming tonight to see about how soon you can come home. It won't be much longer. You eat your dinner?"

"Home," Daddy said.

Mama nodded and patted his hand. "That's right. Another day or two. We can't stay too long. Lacey left her little. . ." she paused, looked at me, and continued, "her little boy over at Roy and Julia's. Him and Roy, Jr. are making a fort in the woods."

Daddy's eyebrows lowered and his mouth pulled down into a deeper frown, but I wasn't going to get into another argument with him now. I walked to the window ledge, where the Get Well cards had been arranged around a vase of flowers new since the last time I'd been here. I pulled the florist's card from its envelope. "From Geneva, Tom, and family." Of course. That one bouquet of flowers probably cost as much as one week's salary for me, salary I'd given up to stay here with Mama, drive her back and forth to the hospital and the grocery store, and do whatever else needed doing while Neva got on with her country club life.

"Ain't they pretty?" Mama said when she noticed me looking at them. "They come yesterday while I was here. Purple lilies was always one of Daddy's favorites. Weren't they, Isaac?" She patted Daddy's hand.

I didn't see Benny's "Get Well" drawing anywhere. Had it been thrown away? I found it in the bottom drawer of the night stand—a single wrinkled sheet of lined tablet paper. One of the nurses had probably picked it up off the floor or the bed and put it there for safekeeping.

"Mama, did you see this? The drawing Benny made? I gave it to Daddy last time I was here." I held it up—the stick figure with the black spirals of hair and wide, smiling mouth, the balloon saying "Get Well, Grandpa."

"I saw him making it back at home." Mama took the paper, studied it, and then held it in front of Daddy. "Benny's quite the little artist. Like Lacey was at that age, remember?"

Daddy turned his face away, refusing to make eye contact with the drawing.

"Benny's been asking when he can see his grandpa," I said. "All the way down on the bus I was hoping you'd get to meet him, see what a great kid he is, but I guess that's not going to happen."

Daddy lowered his chin and closed his eyes, his entire body seeming to draw in upon itself. I looked over at Mama as if to say, *See, I told you so*, but she was still intently studying the drawing.

"Mama, we need to go. I told Julia we wouldn't be gone long."

Mama handed the paper back to me, then stood and put her hand on Daddy's shoulder. "We'll go now and let you rest. I'll come again tonight with Roy. You want the nurse to put you back in bed?"

Daddy didn't answer or open his eyes. He seemed to be already asleep again. I returned the drawing to the nightstand. "Well, Daddy, I guess this is good-bye for me. Benny and I will be going home to New York as soon as Roy can give us a ride to the bus station. We won't bother you again, ever." Hot tears blurred my vision as I followed Mama out the door.

"You saw how he was," I said to Mama as we left the hospital. "Nothing's changed. Nothing ever will. I don't know why I came back."

"Oh, Honey, he's happy to see you, to see that you're doing so well. I know he is. He just has a hard time showing it, that's all."

"Mama, you're living in a dream world if you think he's ever going to accept me and Benny into the family again." I made a mental note to talk to Roy at the first opportunity.

❁   ❁   ❁

But when Roy came by that evening, I was washing the supper dishes, and Mama was out the door and into his truck before I had time to ask about a ride. After finishing in the kitchen, I swallowed another aspirin and sank into Mama's flowered armchair, in need of a few minutes of rest.

"Mommy!" Benny pulled at my arm. "I want to go back over to Roy, Jr.'s house so we can work on our fort some more."

"It's too late for that. It'll soon be dark outside. Why don't you go out and swing?"

"I don't want to swing." Benny kept whining that he wanted to go back over and play with Roy, Jr.

"Too late," I repeated. "Besides, you were already over there all day. Tell you what. We'll go for a walk instead." Neil would be firing up the furnace at his tobacco barn right about now to start the curing process for the tobacco he'd gathered earlier today. He'd have to stay at the barn until the fire was burning steadily, then get up once or twice during the night to add more logs to keep the temperature stable. "I'll show you how tobacco is cooked over a big fire."

As soon as I spoke, though, I had misgivings. I wasn't sure how to react to Neil after our midnight meeting. Maybe he was avoiding me for the same reason, regretting in the clear light of day his impulsive actions on Sunday night. Besides, I was tired and not at my best. I felt bloated and achy all over.

But Benny was pulling on my hand. "How big is the fire, Mommy? Let's go. Where is it?"

I let myself be pulled from the chair. I'd keep it brief—tell Neil good-bye and thank him again for his help in finding Benny. Fifteen minutes, tops. Just show Benny the big furnace and the tobacco hanging on tiers inside the barn.

Benny raced into the road, urging me to hurry, but I took my time, planning in my head what I would say to Neil. Reaching down and scooping up a handful of the red clay roadbed, I squeezed it into a crumbly ball in the palm of my hand. When we were kids, Geneva and I used to gather handfuls of this clay, dampen it with water, and shape it into all kinds of things to place on top of the tobacco furnace for cooking. Neva always made plates and bowls and cups, but I'd made people—whole families of people who nearly always lost an arm or a leg, sometimes a head, when I removed them from the furnace after they'd dried. When I'd cried with disappointment, Neva had scolded me for attempting too much, for not learning from previous tries that my clay people wouldn't hold together. But I'd kept on trying, refusing to give up, believing I would finally get it right. Maybe I should have listened to Neva. Thinking about all those poor, mangled people made me sad even now.

The tobacco barn was diagonally across the road from Neil's trailer, next to the driveway leading up to his parents' house. I kept up a noisy, running conversation with Benny to give Neil advance warning of our approach. I didn't want to take him by surprise and see a forced friendliness in his expression, a cornered look that meant he had been avoiding me. This way he could prepare himself, even flee if he so chose.

When we reached the barn, no one was in sight. I led Benny beneath the attached roof and showed him the long table where the tobacco leaves had been laid earlier in the day to be handed in bunches of three to the women who stood beside the wooden horses and tied the tobacco onto sticks.

"That's not a horse!" Benny said when I pointed one out to him.

"Well, that's what they're called, anyway. See the notches here? You lay a stick across the top, like this, drop it into the notches. Then you loop your string around one end." I picked up a tobacco stick from the pile beside the barn and laid it on the horse. A ball of twine was still in the coffee can nailed to the bottom of the back of the horse. I ran it up through the eye made from a fence staple at the top of the support and looped it around the stick. "Now you hand me some of that tobacco there, and I'll show you how it's fastened to the stick." I pointed at some torn, trampled leaves lying on the ground.

Benny looked around, puzzled. "Where?"

"Those leaves down there. You're standing on one right now."

"You said tobacco."

I laughed. "That's a tobacco leaf. That's what it looks like before it's cooked and cut up to go into cigarettes." I bent to gather a few scraps of leaves.

"Hey, you're too late for that." Neil came striding across the road in white tee-shirt and faded dungarees. "You should have been here earlier if you wanted to tie tobacco. I could have used you a few hours ago."

"I was just showing Benny how it's done." I wrapped the twine around the stems of the tobacco leaves in my hand and flipped the bundle to the other side of the stick. "I still remember how." My heart was thumping in my chest, and I looked back at the ground. "Hand me some more, Benny. There's some over there. See?"

"I could use a good tyer next Tuesday," Neil said. "Pay's good. Two dollars a day, plus dinner at Ma's. What do you say?"

I wrapped the string around the bundle of leaves Benny handed me. "Sounds tempting, but I'm not planning on being here that long." I risked a look into Neil's face. "As a matter of fact, I came over to say good-bye."

"You leaving so soon? Seems like you just got here."

"I've been here a week and a half already. Daddy's better, and I have to get back to my job so I can pay my bills."

"Can't argue with that, I guess." Neil sounded disappointed, or was that just my imagination?

"Benny and I wanted to say thanks again for helping find him Sunday night. And I promised Benny I'd show him your furnace. You fired it up yet?"

"I was just about to. Come on, sport. Want to see me start the fire?"

Benny and I followed Neil around the barn to the furnace opening. We both had to step back from the heat and smoke while Neil worked with adjusting the logs and feeding the fire. Neil talked to Benny while he worked, explaining what he was doing. "Come on, and I'll show you inside the barn where the

234

tobacco is."

They disappeared inside, and I hoisted myself up onto the long wooden table where the tobacco leaves were unloaded. The first stars were beginning to appear in the twilight sky, and a sliver of a moon was visible above the pines in the distance. The fifteen minutes I'd allotted myself were already up.

As Benny and Neil emerged from the barn, Neil pulled a handkerchief out of his pocket and mopped his face. "Starting to get hot in there."

Benny ran over to me. "It's dark, Mommy, and the tobacco's up high. The man held me up so I could touch it."

"His name's Mr. Hardister," I said.

"Can I see the fire again, Mr. Hardest?" Benny asked.

Neil laughed. "Sure. If it's all right with your mother."

"Stand a long way back," I warned him. "Away from sparks."

As Benny ran around the side of the barn, Neil sat beside me. "Going home, huh? When are you leaving?"

"Tomorrow, I hope. Soon as I can get Roy to give me a ride to the bus station. I really need to get back."

"Your job and all that."

"Yes. Daddy's better. And Benny misses his friends."

"I was sorta getting used to the idea of you being around again."

I studied Neil's profile in the growing dusk, trying to determine if he was being serious or was teasing me again. *Keep it light*, I told myself. I bumped the side of my sandal against his shoe. "If you're ever up in New York, drop by for a visit. I'll cook you that meal I promised you, New York style."

Neil laughed scornfully. "Me in New York? That'll be the day."

"You and Roy are two of a kind." I jumped down from the table. "It's getting dark. We'd better head back. I'll get Benny."

Neil stood beside me. "Well, it's been nice getting reacquainted with the grownup Lacey Lu." He reached for a stray curl of my hair and gave a slight tug. "Sure wish you didn't have to rush off so soon."

I avoided his eyes. "It's best this way, Neil. Trust me. Best for me and Benny."

"If you say so." Neil stepped back and stuck his thumbs in his jeans pockets.

"You don't know what it's been like, being back here, having everybody point and stare, being reminded every minute... You know why Benny ran off the other night?" I stopped, aware that I'd said too much already. "Never mind."

"Try me," Neil said.

"Huh?"

Neil put his hands on my shoulders and turned me to face him. "I told you my secret, remember? Nobody else knows—not Roy, not even my folks." He pulled me closer, his arms locked around my back, my head resting on his shoulder. "You can tell me anything, and I won't breathe a word to anybody. That's a promise. Okay?"

"Mommy!" Benny dashed around the corner. "Mommy?"

I stumbled backwards away from Neil. "No. I can't. I have to go. Hey, Benbo, you ready to go back to Grandma's?"

Benny looked at me, then at Neil. I could see in the firelight the look of confusion on his face. I reached for his hand. "Come on, bedtime for you. Can you say thank you to Mr. Hardister for helping find you on the road the other night?"

Benny sidled against me, holding onto my skirt. "Thank you," he said obediently.

"No problem, sport. Glad to do it." Neil tousled Benny's hair. "I gotta check on the fire."

I stood with Benny, watching as Neil pushed another log into the furnace opening, causing a shower of sparks to burst around him, bronzing him like a statue.

"Well, this is goodbye, I guess. And thanks again, for everything." I waited for Neil to turn around, but he kept his back to us, busily poking at the fire as we walked away.

Chapter 27

After refusing help again with his bath, Benny went to bed willingly, full of elaborate plans for continuing work on the fort early in the morning. A few more days, and he would have all but forgotten his friends back home. I had to talk to Roy as soon as he and Mama returned from the hospital.

At the sound of Roy's truck turning into the driveway, I hurried out to the porch. "The doctor signed the papers for Daddy to come home tomorrow," Mama announced excitedly as she came up the steps. "Roy wants you to go with him in the morning to help clean out his room and pack his things."

"Eight o'clock sharp," Roy called out his truck window. "Be ready to go."

"Wait." I lifted one hand and ran down the steps. 'I need to ask you—" but the truck was already moving. I followed Mama inside. So Roy was counting on me to help him get Daddy all packed up and back at home, was he? Well, that certainly wasn't part of my plan. I'd pack up all our belongings tonight, then get myself and Benny up early in the morning and have everything ready to go when Roy arrived. Then he could drop us off at the bus station before going on to the hospital to get Daddy. If he needed someone to gather up Daddy's things, Mama could go along and do that. Roy wouldn't even have to make a special trip into town on our account. Perfect planning.

After Mama went to bed, I laid out one change of clothes

each for Benny and myself and packed the rest in the suitcase I'd borrowed from Rita. Then I went to the dining room to get Benny's crayons and tablet of paper. The crayons were scattered across the table, so I'd begun lining them up in the box they'd come in when I heard a bob-white whistle outside. Neil? What would he be doing here? I walked over and peeked through the front screen door. At first I could make out nothing but the ribbon of road in front of the house, lighter than the surrounding darkness of fields and woods, but then a circle of light moved across the yard, sweeping back and forth, low to the ground. I returned the two crayons in my hand to the table before pushing the door open and stepping outside.

"Neil? Is that you?"

"Hey, Lacey. I figured you'd still be up."

I put one finger to my lips, whispering. "Sh-h-h. Mama and Benny are sleeping." I held onto the screen door handle, letting it close quietly behind me.

"Sorry." Neil kept his voice low as he came up the steps. "I figured I owed you an apology for the way we left things earlier at the barn." He turned off the flashlight and stood it on the floor beside the top step. The overhead lights from the living and dining rooms, both still on inside, provided a dim illumination through the screen. "I guess I wasn't on my best behavior. So I'm here to renew my offer. If you want to talk, I'm here to listen. If not, hey, that's okay, too."

I crossed my arms in front of me. "Roy's bringing Daddy home tomorrow. He comes. I go. That's all there is to it."

"That bad, huh?" Neil motioned for me to sit in the swing and then lowered himself down beside me, stretching one arm across its back. "Want to tell me about it?"

"No, not particularly." I leaned forward, acutely aware of Neil's proximity.

"Okay." Neil withdrew his arm and put both hands on his knees as if preparing to stand. "Then I'll be on my way, I guess. Sorry I bothered you."

"Wait." I spoke quickly before he had time to push himself up, one hand automatically reaching for his arm before I realized what I was doing. I returned my hand to my lap. "I didn't mean to sound rude. It's just that I'm tired, and it's late, and I really don't feel like talking about it."

"Fair enough." Neil stood. "You have a safe trip home and all that. Take care of yourself and that boy of yours."

"No, you don't have to rush off." Now that Neil was here, I couldn't let him just walk away. I felt bad, too, about our awkward goodbye at the tobacco barn earlier—about how uncomfortable and flustered I'd felt when Benny saw me in Neil's arms. I owed Neil an apology, too, or at least an explanation. "I didn't mean you had to leave. I just meant it's too nice a night to spoil it with my problems." I shifted over to make more room on the swing. "Sit down and stay a while. Look at all those stars. I'm going to miss the night sky when I get back home."

"No sky there? Or no night?" Neil's teasing tone put me somewhat more at ease as he sat back down and stretched one arm across the back of the swing again.

"Not much of either. Too many buildings and lights."

"You don't strike me as a city person. Why New York?"

"I guess because it's big and anonymous, and nobody there asks questions. Live and let live."

"I get the message. So we just sit, huh? No questions."

"Benny was mighty impressed with your tobacco furnace tonight." I could feel Neil's fingertips brushing lightly against my shoulder. I didn't dare move, didn't dare risk letting him know how arousing such a slight touch could be, didn't dare risk turning it into something more intimate. "He's starting to like it here. Before, he was all set to go home and now I'm going to have to drag him away."

"Smart boy," Neil said. "Maybe he'll be a farmer."

"Not likely. He has no idea what farm life is all about; it's all fun and games to him."

"You never know how kids will turn out, what'll interest them. I'd give anything..."

I turned my face toward him, trying to read his expression in the dark. "John Philip?"

Neil shrugged. "He's better off where he is. Anyway, this was supposed to be about you. It's your turn to cry on my shoulder." He dropped his arm across my back and pulled me closer.

I stiffened, raised my head, and slid away from Neil. *No complications.* "Thanks for the offer, but it's too nice a night for crying. Listen to those frogs down at the pond. I'm going to miss all this."

Neil lifted his arm so that it stretched across the back of the swing but didn't try to touch me again. "You don't have to rush off tomorrow, do you? I was hoping you'd stick around till the weekend, at least. Matter of fact, I was planning on asking you to the movies on Saturday night. That streetcar movie with that young actor—what's his name? Marvin somebody. It's showing in Valdosta this weekend."

"Marlon," I said. "Marlon Brando. He's in all the magazines."

"So the girls like him, do they?"

"I guess so." I was glad that it was too dark for Neil to see me blush.

"You, too?" Neil poked at my shoulder with one finger. "I think we should go see what all the fuss is about."

"I won't be here, remember? But thanks for asking."

"Right. You're leaving. But if you change your mind, the offer still stands." Neil poked at my shoulder again. "Guess it's time for me to mosey on toward home."

I wasn't ready yet for him to leave. "I'd love to go out with you, Neil, but I can't. You don't know me, my past."

"I know more than you think I do. I know you never married; I know that heel you met in Jacksonville got you pregnant and then dumped you."

"How do you know that?" I stood and walked to the edge of the porch, keeping my back to Neil. I could hear the swing creak behind me as Neil also stood, but I didn't turn around, didn't dare let Neil see my face.

"How do you think? Roy told me. 'Course by the time he found out what really happened, the guy was long gone and you were in New York. Nobody knew how to go about finding him 'cause they didn't even know his last name, much less his whereabouts. Guys like that are the scum of the earth." Neil spit the words out.

I half-turned toward Neil. "But that first morning, in Roy's kitchen, you asked me—"

Neil's voice was lighter, more teasing. "What was I supposed to say? That's the standard story around here, that you married the guy and moved up to New York. After that the story gets a little fuzzy."

"No grieving war widow?"

"Nobody seems quite sure what happened afterward. Your folks have kept pretty tight-lipped about the whole thing, and nobody wants to bring it up when it's obvious they don't want to talk about it. But the story is that he did make an honest woman of you anyhow, whatever happened afterward."

"But nobody really believes it? Is that what you mean?"

"I didn't say that. I said Roy told me the real story."

"Everybody knows, I'm sure." I paced the floor, my hands clenched tightly together in front of me. "My taking off and never coming home again till now. Mama and Daddy not wanting to talk about me, like I'd died of some unspeakable disease. Did Roy tell you the rest of it—the names Daddy called me? How I stole money out of his bank account to run away? How nobody knew where I was for nearly six months afterward?" I spoke rapidly, my voice rising, the words pouring out. "Did he tell you how Mama and Daddy couldn't soil the family Bible with Benny's name? That's why Benny ran off the other night. Mama and I got into a huge argument about Benny not being in the Bible, and Benny overheard us." I stopped to catch my breath. "I'm soiled goods, Neil. I never should have come back." I returned to the edge of the porch, arms crossed in front of me, my back to Neil.

"Come here."

I didn't move. Behind me I could hear Neil's footsteps, coming toward me. He caught my shoulders, turned me around, and put his arms around me. "Don't say that," he said gruffly. "Don't think that, Lacey Lu." He rocked me in his arms, one hand gently stroking my back. "Look at me."

When I raised my face towards him, I felt his lips softly graze my forehead. I tried to step back, but he held onto me, pulling my head down against his chest. For a long moment I let myself rest against him, let myself yield to the comfort of his rhythmic stroking.

Gradually, however, I became conscious of the muscles of his arms, the growing hardness of his body against mine. I stumbled backward. "Don't," I said, "I can't. We can't."

"Can't what?" Neil tilted my chin up and kissed me again— softly, quickly, on the lips. "There, that's not a sin, is it?"

I felt the hotness of tears begin to burn my eyes, and I reached up with one hand to brush them away. Neil caught my hand in his. "Is this the one with the scratch? Let's see." He rubbed his thumb lightly over my palm.

"Ouch," I said.

"Sorry." Neil pulled my hand by the wrist up to his mouth and kissed my fingers. "The other night, when you came to my trailer, all cut up and crying, it was like I'd been expecting it, like I'd dreamed it all already. Then later, when we found Benny, and it was the three of us out there in the woods, in the dark, I know this sounds crazy, but it was like it was meant to happen, just that way. Am I making any sense?"

"No. Yes. I don't know. I can't do this, Neil."

"Can't do what? We're two grown people, and we aren't doing anything wrong. You're human, Lacey, that's all. We're all human. I'm so human right now, I could ..." Neil stepped back. "We're gonna have your Mama out here in a minute, ordering you inside and me off the property."

"Yes, you'd better go now," I agreed.

"In a minute. Come on, let's sit down again." Neil led me to the swing, put his arm around me, and pulled me against him so that my head rested on his shoulder. "Now, how's this?"

I concentrated on breathing—in and out, in and out. Neil's closeness, his masculinity, made me uncomfortable. I twisted my hands together in my lap, unsure what to do with them. I didn't want to touch Neil's leg, didn't want to arouse him as I'd done Dwayne. I'd driven him wild, Dwayne had whispered, and he couldn't help himself. It had been my fault, just as Daddy had said; I hadn't behaved like a lady.

"Remember when you were little," Neil said, "how you used to pester me and Roy to let you tag along with us? We were always telling you to get lost."

"I remember."

"You were such a feisty little cuss back then, cute as a speckled puppy nipping at our heels." Neil chuckled. "Don't lose the spirit, Lacey Lu. Don't let anybody tamp it down or walk all over it—not that crud of a sailor or your Daddy or anybody. You stand up tall and look 'em in the eye."

I raised my head from Neil's shoulder. "Easy for you to say. I can't do it any more. I thought I could, but everywhere I turn, it's like butting my head against a wall. I guess I'm not as hard-headed as I used to be."

"So it's easier to run back to strangers?"

"You sound like Roy. And they're not strangers. They're my friends."

"Sorry. No more big brother talk. Hey, look, there's a lightning bug." I turned my head to look and Neil planted a quick kiss on my lips. "Gotcha." He kissed me again, longer this time. "I gotta get home and get some shut-eye. It's a date for Saturday night, right?"

"Now wait a minute. I'm—"

"I know. But just in case you change your mind." Neil kissed me once more, his lips soft against mine, not rough and demanding like Dwayne's kisses had been. "See ya." He got up from the swing, retrieved his cap and his flashlight, and was gone before I could respond.

Ruth Rodgers

Chapter 28

Wednesday, July 23, 1952

"Lacey, Roy's here." Mama tapped on my bedroom door. "Are you going with him?"

"What? What time is it?" I sat up in bed and rubbed my eyes. I'd meant to get up early and wake Benny and have us both ready and waiting when Roy arrived. It couldn't be eight o'clock already. "I'll be there in a minute." I hadn't finished packing, hadn't checked the house for scattered belongings, hadn't made any preparations to leave. Was Benny even awake yet? I peeked into his room, where he was still sleeping. Neil's visit had distracted me from my plan, and now, with Roy waiting impatiently, it was too late to carry it out.

I gathered my clothes and headed for the bathroom. "Be right there." Last night, after Neil had gone home, I'd taken a long, warm bath to relax my cramps, and then later in bed, after the light was turned off, I'd touched myself in my private places, wondering what it would feel like to have Neil's hands on me, his mouth on me, his body pressed against mine. Sinful, I knew, but I couldn't stop myself, couldn't keep my hands from exploring and producing sensations that filled me with guilty pleasure. Daddy had been right; with Dwayne I had let lustful thoughts overpower my self-control, had given in to the temptations of the flesh, and now here I was succumbing to the same fleshly desires with Neil.

"Hey, you fall in?" Roy called outside the door. "Hurry up. We need to get a move on."

When I emerged a moment later Roy was standing in the kitchen with Mama, a cup of coffee in his hand. The clock on the wall gave the time as 7:35. "Last night you said eight o'clock." I frowned at him. "What's the big rush?"

"It'll be eight by the time we get there." Roy set down his cup and reached for Daddy's car keys. "Some of us have work to do today. You ready?"

"Sorry I overslept," I apologized to Roy once we were on the road. "Neil came over after you dropped Mama off last night, and we sat on the porch and talked for a while. It was pretty late by the time I got to bed." I gave a big yawn to accentuate my words.

"Neil? What'd he come for?"

"He'd gone out to check his tobacco barn and decided to walk on down, it being such a nice night. Anything wrong with that?"

"I just figured he'd be beat, after working all day. He walked, you say?"

"It's not that far. Benny and I had gone over there earlier while you and Mama were at the hospital. Benny wanted to see his tobacco furnace."

"So he decided to repay the visit? In the middle of the night?"

"It wasn't that late." I folded my arms and studied the scenery. Roy could be such a cynic. I didn't know why I tried to tell him anything.

"Hey, what's eating you?" Roy punched me on the arm. "Mama's gonna be tickled pink, having Daddy home so she can fuss over him."

"It'll be a lot of extra work for her—feeding, bathing, and such. And how's he supposed to use the bathroom? Remember, I have to go home—back to my job, you know. In fact, I was wondering—"

"We'll see how it goes the next couple of days, see how he adjusts to being home."

"I have to be back at work next Monday." I pushed my point. "That means I need to leave tomorrow. I don't want to put you to any extra trouble, but I'll need a ride to the bus station. I already checked the schedules, and there's a morning bus at 9:40 and an afternoon one at 4:20. You can drop us off anytime, though, and we'll wait as long as we need to."

"Tomorrow? I don't know if I can manage that. I'm already missing a couple hours of work today."

My heart lurched in my chest. "But I have to get back. I meant to ask you sooner but I hadn't had the chance until now. If you can't take us, I'll have to find another ride into town."

"Relax, Sis. Let's get through today and then we'll worry about tomorrow. I know Daddy ain't gonna be content to stay in bed all day, but the doc says if we get him a wheelchair, he can get around some by himself."

"A wheelchair? Aren't they expensive?"

"More than I can afford, I'm sure."

"You think he'll ever walk again?"

"Who knows? He's stubborn enough."

"Stubborn enough to try and hurt himself, more likely," I said. "If he falls and breaks something ..."

As Roy pulled up to the front door of the hospital, the thought of how Daddy would react to Benny—so eager to meet his grandpa—made my hands and forehead grow clammy with perspiration. I fought to keep back a wave of nausea that rose from my stomach into my throat. *Count to ten*, I told myself, taking a deep breath of fresh air as I stepped out of the car.

At the counter, a nurse handed some papers to Roy to be signed. "He's up and waiting for you," she said, "raring to go home."

Roy looked up from the papers and grinned. "I told you, didn't I? We get him home and Mama gets some of her fried chicken and biscuits in him, he'll be out plowing the field tomorrow."

The nurse laughed. "You talk like that, we'll keep him here. The doctor left a long list of instructions for you." She held out a manila folder. "Go on down. I'll bring a wheelchair."

Roy passed the folder along to me. "Hey, you all right? You look a little green around the gills."

"I'm okay." I wiped one hand across my damp forehead and followed Roy down the hall. It wouldn't do to pass out here in front of everyone.

Daddy was sitting in a chair, dressed in his own clothes, a faded work shirt and pants that hung limply on his withered frame. He looked up as Roy entered. I hung back at the door, watching the hallway for the nurse who was bringing the wheelchair.

"You ready to go home?" Roy was asking. "We're busting you outta here, right now."

"Home," Daddy repeated. I slipped quietly into the room, escaping his notice, and sank into the vacant chair by the window where I fanned myself with one of the Get Well cards on the ledge.

Roy bent over Daddy, his hand on the arm of the chair. "Yep. You're going home. Mama's waiting for you. Making you some cornbread right now."

"Home," Daddy said again.

I gathered the cards into a stack and placed them in the paper bag I'd brought with me. What did Daddy think of when he thought of home? He and his neighbors had built that house when he was a young man, right after he married Elizabeth. Every one of his children had been born there, in the front bedroom, on the same big bed with the iron railing.

Home meant something to Daddy and his generation. And it wasn't just the house, but the land, too—the land that was passed on from generation to generation, the land that provided sustenance and continuity, the land that endured. Once Daddy passed on, Roy would be the one to take over the place, add the land to his own holdings, and preserve it for the next generation.

The nurse pushed the wheelchair into the room, and I pulled open the drawer of the nightstand. I still hadn't spoken to Daddy. Like Simon had said earlier, we had nothing more to say to each other.

As I began moving around, though, Daddy looked up as if noticing for the first time that I was there. "A-ay," he said. "A-ay."

I looked at Roy to see if he understood what Daddy was saying, but he only shrugged. "Roy asked me to come along and pack up all your stuff," I said. I picked up a pair of slippers from the floor and added them to my bag.

"The water pitcher is his, too," the nurse said. "And the bathroom things. Take them along with you." She handed me a plastic bag with Pine Lake Hospital printed on it.

When we got home, Mama ran outside and hovered behind Roy as he maneuvered Daddy out of the front passenger seat and into his arms like a sleeping child. "I got the bed all turned down and ready for him," she said.

I followed Roy and Mama up the steps, Roy carrying Daddy as easily as if it were Benny or Roy, Jr. sleeping in his arms. The image was so incongruous that I felt disoriented for a moment. What had happened to the tyrant I'd fled from in terror seven years ago? How had he been transformed into this frail shadow of himself? And how could I still be frightened to the point of nausea of someone who couldn't walk, couldn't talk, couldn't feed himself? But I was. A cramp gripped my stomach as I followed Roy up the steps, and I made a detour to the bathroom and then to the kitchen for the bottle of aspirin. But as I stood in the kitchen sipping from a glass of water, a new anxiety arose. Where was Benny? I hurried toward the front bedroom where Roy had taken Daddy.

Benny was standing just outside the open bedroom door, his eyes wide with curiosity.

"Come on out of the way," I whispered, reaching for his hand.

"Is that my Grandpa? Why was Uncle Roy carrying him? Is he asleep?"

I led Benny to the living room and tried to explain to him the consequences of the stroke, how Grandpa couldn't walk or talk right now, and how sick he'd been. "So we have to be very quiet and let him sleep and get all the rest he needs. Okay?"

Benny listened solemnly. "Okay."

Roy came through the room. "He's all settled in. I gotta get back to work. Want me to get the stuff out of the car before I go?"

"No, go on. I'll get it in a minute."

"Okay." Roy tossed the car keys to me. "Mama put a rubber pad on the bed, but the nurse said to try to get him to go every couple of hours to prevent accidents. And he needs lots of liquids, she said. All the water he'll drink. I told Mama everything I could remember. I'll be back over tonight to check on things."

"Tomorrow," I reminded Roy, "Benny and I have to go home. Can you give us a ride into town?"

"We'll see. I gotta get to work." Roy didn't look back as he hurried out to his truck. Would he even consent to take us to the bus station, or would I need to find another ride? It would be just like him to expect me to stay here indefinitely and be a nursemaid to Daddy as long as he needed one. Well, it hadn't been my idea to bring Daddy home in this condition. I wasn't holding any cups for him to sip from or holding a bottle for him to urinate into. The idea made me shudder. No wonder Geneva had begged off.

"I could take him some water," Benny said.

"What?"

"My grandpa. I could take him a drink of water." Benny looked up at me, all innocence and concern in his wide brown eyes.

"Maybe later." I kissed the top of Benny's head. "Let's let him rest right now."

Mama stayed in the bedroom, fussing over getting Daddy settled, and I took Benny with me to the garden to see what needed picking, dawdling over the rows of vegetables, eating up as much time as possible.

When we returned, Mama was in the kitchen pounding some steak to tenderize it for pan-frying. "I know Daddy's tired of that hospital food," she told me. "I promised him some nice, tender steak and mashed potatoes for dinner."

"Sounds good." I put Benny to work washing the vegetables while I got out some potatoes to peel, and it wasn't until an hour or so later when Mama was dishing up food for Daddy's dinner that I remembered I hadn't brought in the items from the car.

"You and Benny go ahead and eat at the table," Mama said. "Don't wait for me. I'll stay in the bedroom and help Daddy with his food."

"In a minute. I forgot to bring in Daddy's things from the car. And the doctor left some instructions." I got the keys from the hook in the kitchen and retrieved the two bags from the trunk, carrying them to the porch and setting them down before returning for the flower arrangement that Neva had sent. I set the vase of lilies beside the bags and went back to check for anything else left behind. The manila folder of papers from the doctor was lying on the back seat.

"Yoo-hoo, Benny," I called through the screen door as I returned to the porch with the folder. "Want to help me with these bags?"

There was no answer. After taking the two bags and the folder of papers inside and then returning for the flowers, I called again. "Benny?" He wasn't in the living or dining room or kitchen. "Benny, where are you?"

Mama, of course, had taken Daddy his dinner. And Benny, doing his good deed for the day, would have trotted right along behind her with his glass of water for Grandpa. Pulse quickening, I picked up the hospital bag and hurried down the hall.

The bedroom door was open. Mama had set the plate of food on the table beneath the window and was arranging pillows behind Daddy's back to prop him up so that he could eat. Behind her, Benny was holding a glass of Mama's sweet tea, clasping it tightly in both hands. I stopped at the door, unsure of what my next move should be. Daddy didn't seem to have taken any notice of Benny yet.

"I bet this will taste better than that hospital food," Mama was saying. "You need to eat, the doctor says, to get your strength back. And I made you some extra sweet tea, just the way you like it." She turned and reached for the glass that Benny was holding.

Daddy looked over then, right at Benny.

Ruth Rodgers

Chapter 29

I stood frozen at the open doorway as Daddy's gaze took in Benny, then moved back to Mama and behind her to the familiar furnishings of the room, as if to reassure himself that he was really at home. Mama held the glass to his lips, but he pushed it away and looked again at Benny.

"This is Lacey's little boy," Mama said. "He helped me fix your dinner."

I could see Daddy's eyes narrow into a glare as they focused on Benny. I stepped forward and reached for Benny's hand. "Come on with me, Honey. Let's let Grandpa eat his dinner." I held up the hospital bag toward Mama. "Here's his water pitcher and the things he needs for the bathroom. He probably should…" I nodded toward the bag.

"I was thinking the same thing." Mama set the glass on the table and reached for the bag. "You and Benny go on and eat your dinner. I'll take care of things here."

As I hurried Benny out of the room, I could almost feel Daddy's eyes on me, hot pin-pricks of anger stinging my back, but I didn't dare turn around for a look. I hadn't spoken to him since he'd arrived home.

Benny was excited about having somebody new to break the monotony of the day. "When my grandpa finishes eating," he told me as we filled our plates from the stove and sat down to eat, "I'm gonna tell him about the fort me and Roy, Jr. are making in the woods. And about the fish I caught when Uncle Roy took us fishing."

I listened in helpless dismay at Benny's plans to make friends with a man who refused to acknowledge his existence. Two weeks ago—less than two weeks—all through those hundreds of miles from New York to Florida, I'd told myself I wouldn't let anybody hurt this child of mine—not Daddy, not Neva, not anybody. I'd come home with the intention of making Benny accepted. *When they see him,* I'd told myself on the bus ride down, *when they get to know him, see how loving and generous and trusting he is—how bright and curious and funny...* Now, here I was, wanting nothing more than to run away, letting Daddy's rigid disapproval shrivel me back into a curled ball of defeat. *Stand up for yourself,* Neil had told me last night. But I had no strength left for fighting.

"I don't think he's ready for that yet," I told Benny. "We'll let him take a nap first. Okay?" To distract him from returning to the bedroom, I suggested that we go back over to Julia's so the boys could finish the fort. Getting out of the house would keep Benny away from Daddy for the afternoon. Plus Roy had never given me a definite answer about taking me into town tomorrow. I could talk to Julia and make her see how important it was that Benny and I get on that bus. Then she could talk to Roy on my behalf, convince him to make the time to give us a ride.

❊   ❊   ❊

Julia greeted us at the front door with Zach in her arms. "Roy, Jr.'s been pestering me all day about when Benny was coming back. He's outside somewhere, probably at the fort. Go on out, Benny, and call him. Come on in, Lacey. How's your father doing? I hope Roy did the right thing, bringing him home so soon."

"So far, so good. He's sleeping, so we decided to get out of the house and let him rest." I followed Julia inside.

Zach began to fuss and Julia jiggled him in her arms. "I was just on my way to change his diaper," she explained. "I'll be back in a minute."

Katie was leaning in the doorway leading to the kitchen, one bare foot propped against the door jamb. Ashamed of my pangs of jealousy on Sunday night, I smiled at her. "Hi, Katie. Did you hear about Benny getting lost?"

Katie nodded.

"I wanted to thank you for that whistle you gave him. That's how we found him, by him blowing that whistle."

Katie smiled shyly. "It was just an old one I found in the yard."

"And a good thing for Benny. He takes it everywhere now—won't let it out of his sight."

Katie ducked her head and pulled a handful of hair across her face, hiding her mouth, but I could see that she was pleased. *A daughter would be nice to have, a little sister for Benny.* I stopped myself. *I'm not getting married, not now or ever,* I'd told Benny. *It's you and me, kiddo, you and me. We don't need anybody else.*

Julia came back with Zach and held him out to me. "Here. All nice and clean."

I positioned Zach on my legs so that he could look up at me. "Hi, Zach. Remember me?"

While Julia and I talked, Katie sat beside me on the sofa and played with Zach, stroking his legs and arms, tickling him on the tummy. Zach stretched, waved his arms, and opened his mouth. "He's laughing," Katie said. "You like that, Zachie?"

Had Benny been this content as a baby? I couldn't remember. So much I had forgotten already, in six short years, and no memorabilia to jog my recollections—no Baby's First Year book, no bronzed baby shoes or heirloom christening gown, no lovingly stitched baby quilt from Mama. Not even any baby pictures except those tiny, grainy snapshots from the Woolworth's photo booth. A lump rose in my throat, and I coughed to clear it. What had Julia said? Something about Benny blossoming.

"Yes," I answered. "He's certainly having a good time, thanks to Roy, Jr. and Katie here. But we have to get back home. As a matter of fact, I asked Roy earlier if he could give us a ride to the bus station tomorrow, but he never gave me an answer. I was hoping you could talk to him—"

Julia looked startled. "So soon? It seems you just got here."

"It's been almost two weeks. I have to get back to my job on Monday."

"Of course. We'll hate to see you go, but Roy will make time to give you a ride whenever you want. I'll talk to him as soon as he comes in from the field."

"Thanks. I'd appreciate it." I leaned back against the sofa, a weight lifted off my chest. Julia would talk to Roy, and everything would be arranged for tomorrow. Mama might get a little weepy-eyed, but she'd probably be relieved not to have to run any more interference between Daddy and me. Roy would make more cracks on the way into town about how Benny and I were turncoats, living in Yankee territory, but I could handle it. In less than twenty-four hours, we'd be on our way home, away from all the hurt and rejection of the last six-and-a-half years. I felt almost giddy with anticipation.

"Have you heard about that new movie with Marlon Brando?" I asked Julia. "*Streetcar Named Desire*? I've heard it's supposed to be good." Why was I bringing that up? I'd promised myself not to talk about—not even to think about—Neil.

"I don't know anything about the movie, but I saw Marlon Brando's picture on the cover of one of those movie magazines at the drugstore. Bare-chested. Real sexy." Julia smiled at me. "Now, that's what you need, Lacey."

I shook my head. "Not me."

"Oh, come on, admit it. Look, you're blushing."

I didn't answer.

"There's somebody in New York, isn't there?" Julia probed. "That's why you're in a rush to get back. What's his name? What does he do?"

I looked across the room at a picture on the wall. "No, nobody in New York."

Julia perked up. "Nobody in New York? Then who? Where? When?"

"Nobody, really, nobody in particular. I thought for a long

time I'd never trust a man again, but lately..."

"Lately? What?" Julia leaned forward, waiting for an answer.

"I've been talking a lot to Neil." There, I'd said it. "He's restored my faith in men, I guess you could say."

"Roy told me about him helping you find Benny that night he wandered off and got lost," Julia said. "So what have the two of you been talking about?"

"Just things. He came over last night after Mama and Benny had both gone to bed. We sat on the porch and talked. He asked me to go with him to the movies on Saturday night to see *Streetcar Named Desire*. That's why I was asking."

Julia's eyebrows shot up. "He did? You're going, of course? If you want me to watch Benny, I'll—"

"I told him I couldn't. I'll be back in New York by then."

"Oh, that's right. Golly, that's too bad. It would be good for you and Neil both to have some fun. I know he doesn't get out much, and from what you say, you haven't been exactly the social butterfly lately." She glanced at the clock, then at Zach, who was beginning to fret. "He's getting hungry. Katie, can you. . .?"

Katie carefully lifted Zach from my lap and carried him over to Julia.

"Anyway," Julia continued, unbuttoning her blouse, "count yourself lucky for the invitation. Believe me, it's not often Neil takes anybody out—in spite of my best efforts." Zach began to nurse contentedly and Julia stroked his cheek with one finger. "You hungry, huh?" She looked up at me. "Thank goodness I'm not sore any more." She put her hand under her breast to adjust it to a more comfortable position and Zach lost his hold, Julia's exposed nipple glistening with the saliva of Zach's mouth and a bubbly froth of milk. Zach protested with a howl. "There, there," Julia crooned. "I'm not taking it away. Here you are."

I looked away, feeling a flush of embarrassment creeping up my neck and face. I couldn't confide in Julia. I could imagine it now—Julia and Roy laughing over it at supper tonight—Lacey's crush on Neil. Time to change the subject. "I'd better check on Benny and make sure he's not doing anything dangerous."

"Oh, he's all right. Katie can run down and check on them. Honey, go make sure the boys are behaving themselves. And tell them to come to the house if they want some Koolaid."

I walked to the window and looked toward the woods. I hadn't really told Julia anything worth gossiping about, had I? Besides, what was there to tell? Neil had kissed me. That didn't mean a lifelong commitment. If I told Julia, she would tell Roy, and then Roy would say something to Neil. I wouldn't say another word. Instead, I'd take the memory home with me to New York, where I could safely turn it over and over in my mind, examine it from every angle, maybe share it with Rita over a cold soda on the back stoop while the kids played in the alley, the radio playing in the background—miles away from a steamy Florida night in a front porch swing.

A clatter on the front porch announced the boys' arrival.

"Mommy, we put a roof on our fort. Come see," Benny said excitedly.

I smiled at Benny's flushed face. "In a minute. Who's ready for some nice cold Koolaid?"

Chapter 30

As we left for the drive back to Mama and Daddy's, I steeled myself to getting through the rest of the day. At least my departure was settled. Julia would talk to Roy, and when Roy came over later to check on Daddy, we could make definite arrangements. Benny and I would be on the bus tomorrow. We'd resume our old life in New York and put all the entanglements of family behind us. When the next telegram came, announcing Daddy's death, I'd send my condolences, but I wouldn't return, wouldn't muddy the waters with my presence. Thankfully, Benny was too young on this visit to be aware of the stigma everyone here attached to him, and I'd have to make sure that he never became aware of it. The only way to do that was to leave and never return. The label of "bastard child" was so ugly, so freighted with loathing, that just thinking it sent an involuntary shudder through my shoulders.

"Mommy, I didn't make a happy picture yet for Grandpa," Benny was saying. "I'm gonna draw him a rainbow, and make a stripe of every color. You think he'll like that?" He bounced up and down in the front seat beside me.

I sighed and reached over to tousle his hair. "Honey, it's too late for any more pictures. When we get back, I want you to gather up your writing tablet and all your crayons and put them in your bag. Uncle Roy is taking us to the bus station tomorrow so we can go home."

"But me and Roy, Jr. are gonna play in our fort tomorrow. We're gonna pretend the Indians are attacking and shoot them with Roy, Jr.'s guns. And Uncle Roy is taking me fishing again, and—"

"I'm sorry, Benbo, but Roy, Jr. will have to fight the Indians by himself. And the fishing trip isn't till Saturday. We'll be home by then. Maybe on Sunday we can go to the playground at the park. We'll invite Tony to go with us. What do you say?"

"The park's baby stuff. I want to go fishing. And I promised Roy, Jr. So there!" Benny folded his arms in front of him.

"Well, you'll have to change your plans; that's all. When we get home, we'll go down to the corner bakery first thing and get you a doughnut, one of those with the colored sprinkles. Then you can tell the other kids about your vacation in Florida—about catching lightning bugs and going fishing and building a fort. Won't that be neat?"

"I'm not going." Benny pushed his lower lip out in a scowl. "I promised. Besides, my grandpa needs me."

If Benny only knew what his grandpa was really like... But he didn't. And he never would—not if I could help it. "Sorry, Benbo, but we have to go home, and that's all there is to it. And stay away from Grandpa, you hear? He's still very sick and needs lots of rest. I don't want you pestering him."

When Benny didn't answer, I reached over to touch his leg, but he pulled away, looking out his window away from me. "I know you're having fun with Roy, Jr.," I said, "but I have to get back to my job. No work—no paycheck, no food on the table. I told Dorothy two weeks. Time's up. Monday morning it's back to work. You understand, don't you?"

Benny didn't answer or look at me. The house was just ahead. "And stay away from Grandpa," I repeated as I parked the car. "He's not up for company quite yet. We have to let him rest and get his strength back."

I kept Benny outside with me as I did the afternoon chores, keeping him occupied for as long as I could. Both of us would keep our distance from Daddy the rest of the day, and tomorrow

I'd go into the bedroom only long enough to say good-bye.

"Want to walk down to the pond?" I asked Benny after latching the gate to the cow pen. "Maybe we can find another turtle."

"I want to take a turtle home with me for a pet. Can I, Mommy?"

"We can't take a turtle with us on the bus, but once we get back, we can go to Woolworth's and buy one of those little-bitty ones," I said. "Whichever one you like." Anything to keep his mind on returning home, on forgetting his promises to Roy, Jr.

"I want a big one," Benny said, "this big." He stretched out his arms.

At the pond we didn't see any turtles. I leaned against an oak tree and kept a watchful eye on Benny while he explored nearby. This would be my last visit to this spot, my last look back at a past I was leaving behind forever. It was quiet here, and I absorbed the silence, filling myself up with it, storing it for later. I idly plucked an oak leaf and twirled it in my fingers. Maybe I should stick it in my pocket and take it back to New York with me, a tangible reminder of this place I had once called home. Bringing it to my nose, I inhaled its faintly bitter scent, traced its thin center ridge with one fingertip. If I took it back with me, it would only dry out and turn brown, then brittle, then crumble into nothing. Better to take nothing, to go back as empty-handed as I came, as empty-hearted.

Empty-hearted. The thought hammered inside my chest. I'd been telling Benny all along we had each other, and that's all we needed, but what about when Benny grew up and struck out on his own? What would I do then? Already he was expanding his limits, moving away from me. Another month and he'd be in school, another year and he'd be better buddies with his friends than with me, another few years and he wouldn't need me any more.

I dropped the leaf and took a step toward him. "Come back, Benny. Don't get so close to the water. There might be snakes."

※　※　※

By the time Roy came over after supper to check on Daddy, I was finishing my packing. I had taken all my old dresses that might still be suitable for wear when I got a new job, then had dumped the bag of Tommy's castoffs onto the bed. Some were so new that Geneva had not even removed the price tags. No sense letting perfectly good clothes go to waste. What Benny couldn't use, I could pass on to the younger kids in the house. I packed everything back into the fancy bag and then laid Benny's books and toys on top of the clothes.

The quilt squares that Mama had given me were on the dresser. I picked them up, the cotton feeling cool and slightly damp in my hands, as if still holding all Mama's tears that had soaked into the pieces as she stitched them together. I added the squares to the suitcase. Someday, when Benny was older, he might like to know the stories contained within all those pieces of patchwork.

As I walked down the hall toward the living room, I could hear Roy clomping across the porch and could hear Mama talking as she held the door open for him to come inside. "He's been raring all day to get out of that bed. I kept telling him to wait for you to get here. He ain't gonna be satisfied to just lay there all day."

"Well, he ain't got much choice, has he?" Roy said. "Hey, Sis, I know you said you wanted to leave tomorrow, but I was wondering if you could stick around a couple more days, just till the weekend? If you could stay till Grace gets here Saturday—"

"Saturday? What about this person you're hiring to help out?"

"Well, that ain't decided yet for sure. I'm waiting to see how much help Mama thinks she's gonna need. I figured you'd be here through the end of the week." He turned to Mama. "I'm going to try to finagle a way to get a second-hand wheelchair so's he can get himself around some. I don't know where the money's coming from, on top of all the doctor and hospital bills, but I don't want you trying to lift him by yourself."

So Roy expected me to spend two more days with Daddy, did he? Two more days of Daddy shooting daggers at me with his eyes and pointedly ignoring Benny. It was too much to ask. I didn't answer Roy but went instead to the bedroom that had once been mine and Geneva's and reached one hand to the top shelf of the wardrobe, feeling with my fingers for the cigar box with the five-hundred dollars. I pulled it forward. It was Daddy's money—money I'd borrowed only because I was so desperate I didn't know what else to do. And I'd done the honorable thing by paying it back. Daddy couldn't refuse it this time. I'd cancel my debt to him once and for all—buy back my freedom and go home tomorrow with a clear conscience.

By the time I came into the hall with the box, Roy and Mama had already gone into the front bedroom. I followed them, pulling off the rubber band as I went.

"Here!" I turned the box upside down and dumped the money on the foot of the bed, not looking at Daddy but focusing on Roy instead. "Pay the doctor and buy him a wheelchair. Buy him whatever you want. Just get me to the bus station tomorrow." Dollar bills fluttered onto Daddy's legs and onto the floor.

"Hey! What's this?" Roy asked.

"Five hundred dollars, that's what. It's all his. Benny and I are leaving tomorrow. If you can't take me, I'll hitch a ride. Or walk."

Roy was scooping bills off the floor and straightening them in his hand. "Where'd all this come from?"

"It's the money I paid him back, every cent. He wouldn't take it—called it tainted money. Mama kept it all. She said it was mine, to do with as I pleased."

Mama held up one hand. "Lacey, there's no need...." She touched Daddy's arm. "It's all the money she sent over the years. When you wouldn't take it, I saved it all in that cigar box. I told her to take it and use it for her and Benny."

Roy was still collecting bills. "Hey, Pa, looks like you hit the jackpot." He turned to me. "You mean it—I can use it for a wheelchair?"

"It's his money, not mine. Do whatever you want with it." I waved one hand in dismissal and spun toward the doorway.

"Aaay," a voice behind me said. "Aaay." The same sound he

had made in the hospital this morning. It hit me now—he was trying to say my name. But what did he want? What more could he possibly demand of me?

"What?" I asked tiredly, turning to face him, looking straight at him for the first time since he'd come home. "What now?"

Daddy slowly raised his right hand, palm open toward me. "Aaay," he said again. His brow furrowed as he searched his mind for the right word. Then he looked at Mama. "You," he said, "you—"

"He wants to say thank you," Mama interpreted. At that Daddy nodded and looked again at me. His hand dropped back to the bed, and his forehead relaxed.

"Don't thank me." My voice was still sharp with anger. "It's your money. Why wouldn't you take it?"

As Daddy turned his face away, I could see a tear trace a slow path down his cheek. Roy and Mama both looked at me.

I took a step closer to the bed. "Never mind. It's yours now. Roy can get you the best wheelchair there is. Then you can sit out on the porch and watch the corn grow." I touched his hand.

Daddy closed his fingers over mine. His skin felt dry and crinkly—like wrinkled cellophane.

"I'm going now." I pulled my hand away and fled out the door, down the hall and through the kitchen into the bathroom, where I noisily blew my nose. Why, after all that had happened between us, had I let myself be moved to tears? If Daddy wanted to make amends, then let him acknowledge Benny, accept him as my son, as his grandson. Let him do that, and then—only then— would I feel satisfied.

Chapter 31

As I came back through the kitchen, Benny looked up from where he was kneeling in one of the dining room chairs, putting the finishing touches on his rainbow picture.

"Look, Mommy," he called to me. "I'm almost finished. One more stripe."

I walked over to look. "That's nice, honey, but Grandpa may not feel up to looking at it right now. Maybe you should wait until tomorrow to show it to him."

Benny's eyes were so full of disappointment that I relented. "Well, we'll see. I think Uncle Roy is going to bring him out here so he can sit up in a chair for a little while, and maybe he'll feel like looking at it then." After all, what was the most Daddy could do? Refuse to look at it? Give Benny the evil eye again? At least he couldn't yell at him or call him names. What did it matter anymore? I walked into the kitchen and ran myself a glass of water from the faucet. Somewhere in the distance, a dog barked. Was it Neil's? What was Neil doing right now? Would I see him again before I left tomorrow? Behind me I could hear Roy settling Daddy into the easy chair in the living room. I didn't turn around.

"Hey, Sis." Roy walked up behind me. "Thanks. Who'd have thought—all them dollar bills sitting around in a cigar box, like Monopoly money. If you're really set on leaving tomorrow, I'll take time off to get you into town. Katie can stay with Mama the next couple of days."

"Katie? She can't—"

"Least she can run home and find me if there's trouble. I don't want Mama trying to lift him and hurting herself."

"Why don't you call Grace and ask if she can come tomorrow? Or Neva? I've already paid my dues."

"You want to call 'em, go ahead. Closest phone is all the way in town." Roy shrugged. "You've been a life-saver, Sis, between driving Mama back and forth to see Daddy and taking care of the kids for Julia while she was in the hospital. I appreciate it. I'll knock off work early tomorrow and get you into town by four."

"All finished!" Benny stood, clutching his picture and smiling triumphantly.

"Wait," I cautioned. "Wait for me."

"What you got there, sport?" Roy asked.

Benny held it up. "For my grandpa."

"Hey, a rainbow. That's great. You gonna give it to him now?"

I shot Roy a warning glance, but he ignored it, so I followed the two of them to the living room, where Mama was still fussing over Daddy in his easy chair, propping his feet up on a footstool and making sure he was comfortable. I drew in my breath as Benny walked over and held out the picture. "Here, Grandpa. I made this for you."

Daddy looked down at the sheet of paper but made no move to take it. He didn't look at Benny, as if by not seeing him he could pretend he wasn't there, as if by sheer willpower he could blot Benny out of existence.

"He's giving you a present, Pa," Roy said. "He made it all by himself. See?" Roy turned to Benny. "His hands don't work too good right now. Just lay it in his lap."

Benny laid the paper across Daddy's legs, then scooted back to me. I put an arm over his shoulder. Daddy's right hand moved and touched the paper, knocking it off his lap and onto the floor.

"Hey, Pa, you dropped it." Roy reached for the paper and put it back on Daddy's lap. "Look here, he's even got a pot of gold at the end. See that? You know what? You just struck your pot of gold—all them dollar bills floating down on you like manna from heaven. Thanks to Lacey, we'll get you the best wheelchair money can buy. What do you say to that?"

Daddy looked at the picture in his lap. His hand moved again on top of the paper. "Aay-n-n, aay-n-n. . ."

"Rainbow," Benny prompted.

"Aay-n-bow," Daddy repeated. He leaned back in his chair as if the episode had exhausted him.

Benny, emboldened by Daddy's success at saying "rainbow," squirmed out from under my arm and approached Daddy's chair again, pointing at the top band of color that arced across the page. "Red," he said. Then he pointed to the next. "Orange. Yellow." He went through each band slowly, enunciating each word clearly. I noticed that Daddy was nodding his head slightly as Benny recited each color.

"He's so smart," Mama said from the sofa where she had finally taken a seat. "Knows all his ABC's and numbers, too. Lacey's been doing a marvelous job—"

Daddy's hand brushed across the paper again, knocking it onto the floor.

Roy bent to pick it up, handing it this time to Benny. "Maybe you better put it on the table for now. He can look at it some more tomorrow."

Benny laid the paper on the table beside Daddy's chair and looked at me for direction on what to do next. "Come on," I said. "Let's sit down for a minute." I sank onto the sofa beside Mama and motioned for Benny to join me. Roy, to fill the silence, began to tell Daddy about the crops. I half-listened, one arm around Benny. I didn't understand why Benny wanted so much to make friends with Daddy, wanted to help do things for him. He didn't know any old people in New York, had never had a man for a friend. Until this visit, his only adult influences had all been women. Why such an interest in Daddy?

❄　❄　❄

An hour later, after Roy had returned Daddy to bed and left

for home, I tucked Benny into bed after his bath.

"Grandpa liked my rainbow picture," Benny said as I handed him his stuffed dog.

"Yes," I answered. "Yes, he did."

"My grandpa doesn't want us to leave."

"Huh?"

"He needs me to stay and take care of him."

"There'll be other people to help," I answered. "Grandma and Uncle Roy are here. And Aunt Grace is coming back this weekend."

"But he wants me," Benny insisted.

"How do you know that?"

"He told me. He said I'm a good helper. He said—"

"Whoa. He said all that? When?"

Benny smiled, turned onto his side, and closed his eyes. I sat on the edge of the bed until his deep, even breathing assured me he was asleep. Where had Benny gotten such an idea? Was it another maneuver to avoid leaving? Or simply wishful thinking?

Mama peeked into the doorway. "Goodnight, Lacey. Give Benny a kiss for me. I'm gonna miss you and him both when you leave tomorrow."

I tiptoed to the door. "Goodnight. We'll see you in the morning."

Mama laid her hand on top of mine. "I wish you could stay longer. I wish you weren't so far away."

After Mama went to bed, I paced restlessly about the house. Tonight was my last chance to see Neil—to say one final goodbye and thank him once more for helping me find Benny. I could make the short walk up the road to his trailer, say good-bye, and be back in half an hour, tops. Getting the flashlight from the kitchen, I eased the front screen door open, holding onto it so it wouldn't bang closed. Down the steps, past the tire swing, out to the road. I stopped and listened. What if Benny woke and called for me?

But Benny was a sound sleeper. And I'd stay only a minute—no touching, except perhaps a quick, friendly hug just before I dashed off. No holding, no murmuring, no kissing. Nothing to indicate that I felt anything for him other than friendship and gratitude.

As I approached the trailer, Ranger began to bark—high, excited yips of greeting, and when I opened the front gate, he jumped up on me, forepaws on my stomach. I stumbled backward.

Neil's porch light came on. "Ranger. Down," he called sharply as he opened the door. "Just tell him to get down."

In the porch light, I could see that the dog's tail was wagging furiously. I put one hand between his ears and rubbed his head. "Some watchdog you got here."

"He just likes the women," Neil answered. "I got him trained good. You still here? I thought you'd left already."

"Tomorrow. I'm all packed. Roy's driving us into town. So I came to say good-bye."

Neil was shirtless and barefoot, dressed only in a pair of faded dungarees. "Come on in, out of the skeeters. Mr. McCormick come home today?"

"He's home." I followed Neil inside. "I won't stay but a minute. I just wanted to thank you again for helping me find Benny and say I'm sorry I can't go to the movie on Saturday, but I've got my job waiting for me at home, and—"

"Whoa. Slow down some. There's no dynamite set to go off anywheres. Have a seat while I go get a shirt on—make myself decent."

I remained standing. "No, you're fine. I really can't stay. I just put Benny to bed, and nobody even knows I'm gone. I came to say good-bye, that's all. So good-bye. Take care. Have a good life."

Neil had started toward the bedroom, but he turned back, a look of concern on his face. "You're jumpy as all get-out. What is it? Something wrong at home?"

"No. Nothing. I have to go now." Being in Neil's presence was making me much more nervous than I'd expected to be.

Neil came toward me and caught both my hands in his. "Your hands are shaking like crazy. Something happen today with your daddy?"

"No, nothing out of the ordinary." I pulled my hands away and crossed them in front of me. "Grace is coming for the weekend, and Roy's getting him a wheelchair to make it easier for him to get around. It's time I got back home."

"It's me, then," Neil said. "You scared of me?"

I looked toward the door. "I have to go, really."

"I won't bite." Neil took a step backward and held up both hands, palms toward me. "If going back to New York is what you have to do—you do what's best for you and Benny, that's all. Friends?"

I smiled in relief. "Friends. Thanks, Neil—for everything." I extended my right hand.

Neil caught my hand in both of his. "So long, Lacey Lu. You take care, you hear? And if you ever need anything, anything at all...."

I nodded, feeling my lips begin to quiver. I lowered my head, and Neil reached for me, pulling me toward him. I buried my face against his shoulder and squeezed my eyes tightly shut to keep the tears inside. "I'm getting you all wet."

"That's all right. You can cry on my shoulder any time. You want to talk about it?"

I lifted my head and wiped my eyes with my fingers. "No, I'm fine. Really."

"I'm gonna miss you, Lacey Lu. You know that, don't you?"

"Don't say that." I took a step backward, one hand fumbling behind me for the screen door handle.

"Hey." Neil followed me. "I can say whatever I want. And you know where I am if you ever change your mind. Write me a letter sometime, let me know how things are going. Okay?" He pushed the door open and held it for me.

"Yes, I'll do that. I'll write soon as I get home. And thanks again, for everything."

"Glad to do it." Neil lowered his arm, letting the screen door close behind me. "You take care—of yourself and that boy of yours." He lifted one hand in a final wave.

"Bye, then." I hurried away, not allowing myself to look back until I'd reached the road. When I did finally take a peek, his front door was closed for the night and his porch light had been extinguished.

Ruth Rodgers

Chapter 32

Thursday, July 24, 1952

The next morning I was outside gathering the eggs when I heard Mama calling for me. I set down my basket and came running at the sound of urgency in her voice.

"What is it? Did something happen to Benny?"

"No. It's Daddy." Mama puffed to catch her breath as she met me in the back yard and followed me up the steps. "I was in the kitchen washing up the breakfast dishes, and Daddy took a mind to get out of bed by himself. Benny heard a commotion and went in there and found him on the floor."

"Is he hurt?"

"I don't know. I was afraid of something like this happening."

I followed Mama down the hall to the bedroom. Daddy was crumpled on the floor beside the bed, and Benny was kneeling beside him, one hand stroking his arm. "It's okay, Grandpa," he was saying, "it's okay." He looked up at me. "My grandpa tried to walk, and he fell. I'm taking care of him." He pointed at the pillow he had half-nudged beneath Daddy's head.

I knelt beside Benny. "Daddy, are you hurt?" I ran my hand along his left arm and leg, the paralyzed side, checking for any sign of pain or swelling. "That hurt anywhere?"

Daddy grunted and moved his right arm. "No, I . . . , I . . ."

I moved to the other side, prodding at his right ankle, up his leg to his knee, then up to his hipbone. "Sore anywhere?"

Daddy flinched when I touched his hip. "That hurt?" I asked. "No."

I looked at Mama. "I don't think anything's broken. He'll probably have a pretty good bruise here on his hip, though."

"Did you hurt yourself anywhere?" Mama asked. "You want to see the doctor?"

"No!" Daddy spoke emphatically.

"Let's see if we can get you back in bed," I said. "Move back, Benny. Grandpa's okay." I got behind his head and tugged him into a sitting position, leaning against my legs, and then with Mama and me on either side, we were able to lift him enough to get him sitting on the bed. Benny helped with his legs and feet as we laid him down and helped him get comfortable again, his head and shoulders propped on pillows and his legs covered by the sheet. I faced him, hands on hips. "Don't go trying that again, you hear? Mama doesn't need any more worries. Benny and I are leaving this afternoon for New York, so it'll be just you and her here. She can't pick you up all by herself."

Daddy grunted and looked away from me, refusing to meet my eyes.

"You gotta rest and get your strength back," Mama said. "You know what the doctor said."

Benny touched Daddy's arm. "You want a drink, Grandpa? I can bring it to you."

"Maybe he needs to…" Mama stopped, giving a nod in Benny's direction. "You and Benny go on. I'll stay with him for a while."

I took Benny back outside with me as I finished gathering the eggs. "Why don't you go play on the tire swing?" I asked him after we'd checked the final nest. "This will be your last chance. We're leaving later today, as soon as Uncle Roy comes to take us into town." It was now mid-morning, only a few more hours before we'd be on the bus. I'd have to keep Benny busy and out of the way until then. "My grandpa," he'd said this morning, as if Daddy were a new toy that belonged exclusively to him. Maybe because while Daddy was in the hospital, I had kept referring to him as "your grandpa." Now Benny felt a sort of possessiveness toward him.

No need to burst his bubble. Let him go back to New York and tell everybody about his grandpa and his grandma and his uncles and aunts and cousins. From that distance, they could become whomever and whatever he needed them to be. Daddy seemed now to be simply ignoring Benny, as if he were a gnat he could brush away with one hand.

Benny ran off to the swing, and I took the basket of eggs into the kitchen and set it on the counter beside the sink. Mama was sweeping the kitchen floor. "He was trying to get up to use the bathroom," she told me, "but that's all taken care of now. "I'll wash them eggs if you want."

"Okay. While you do that I'll feed the chickens and then check the garden." The busier I stayed, the faster the hours would pass. I debated calling Benny to come with me, but he seemed content on the tire swing, lying across it on his stomach and pushing himself with his feet.

The heat was already settling around the day, pricking at my neck and arms. I got the bag of chicken feed from the crib and filled the chickens' feeding trough, then cleaned and refilled their water bowls, running the water from the hose until it was cool against my fingers. Back home the kids would be cooling off by chasing one another down the alley with water pistols, giggling and running in a squealing, wriggly mass. Benny wasn't too happy about leaving Roy, Jr. and the fort, but once he was back home with his friends, he'd quickly fit in again, would take his accustomed place in the beehive of activity surrounding him. And for me, too, once I was resettled into my daily routine, this two-week interlude would gradually lose its painful sting, its memory growing hazier with the passage of time as the old hurts became buried once more under the bustle of new activities and experiences.

I picked two tomatoes and a cucumber from the garden and took them in through the back door to the kitchen, then walked to the front window to check on Benny in the swing. He wasn't there.

I met Mama in the hallway leading to the bedrooms. "Where's Benny? I told him to play on the swing, but I don't see him out there."

Mama gestured behind her. "Back there."

"With Daddy?" Alarm bells rang in my head. "I'd better—"

"Sh-h-h." Mama put her finger to her lips. "Come look."

I followed Mama to the bedroom door. Benny had pulled a chair right beside Daddy's bed and had an open book in his lap.

"Lamb," he was saying, holding the book up so Daddy could see the picture. "Lamb. See? Now you say 'lamb.'"

Daddy looked at the picture. "Lam-m," he repeated.

"Good job!" Benny patted Daddy's hand and turned the page. "Monkey. Mon—key." He looked up and saw me. "I'm helping Grandpa," he said. "I'm teaching him how to read."

Daddy followed Benny's gaze and fixed on me at the door, not taking his eyes off my face. I felt exposed, as if my every past word and action were being judged. What was he thinking? As he raised one hand as if to speak, I broke the spell by hurrying to Benny. "That's great, Honey, but that's enough reading for now. You don't want to tire Grandpa out. Let him rest."

"He's not tired. Are you, Grandpa?"

Daddy didn't answer, but as I remained standing there, his eyes blinked and then closed, his face loosening and growing slack as it relaxed from the great effort of concentration.

"Sh-h-h," I whispered, indicating Daddy's closed eyes. "Let's go now, okay?"

Benny touched Daddy's arm. "After you rest, Grandpa," he whispered, "we'll read some more, okay?"

"I told you to stay outside and not bother Grandpa," I said after we were back in the living room.

"But he wanted me to help him. He said I was a good teacher. He said—"

I looked at the mantel clock. Almost eleven. Not quite five more hours to go.

"You should have seen the two of them before you came in," Mama said to me. "Their heads together, Daddy repeating all them words. Benny's being a real help. If he stayed around, he'd have Daddy talking again in no time, I know."

"Get your head out of the clouds, Mama. You saw how he looked at me just now."

"He's worried himself sick about you all these years, just like me. He just don't know how to own up to it, that's all. You know how men are. They can't swallow their pride like women can."

"When will my grandpa be rested?" Benny asked.

"We'll see," I said. "You want to read your book to me? I'd like to hear it."

"Before you do that," Mama said, "there's something I want to show you."

"What?"

"Wait right here." Mama walked toward the hall and returned with the family Bible, motioning for me to sit on the sofa. Benny stood in front of me, his eyes on the book.

As Mama laid the Bible in my lap, I glanced down at the familiar black leather cover, the words *Holy Bible* spelled out in gold lettering. I'd decided on Sunday I wanted nothing more to do with this Bible. "I don't think—"

Mama put her finger at the page marked by the faded purple ribbon and flipped it open. "Just look."

I'd already seen all I wanted to see of these pages. What did Mama mean by showing them to me again? I refused to look down.

"Mommy, there's my name. Benjamin. Right there."

I looked where Benny was pointing. At the bottom of the page, after Geneva and Tom's two children, fresh, black ink spelled out "Born to Lacey Louise McCormick," followed on the next line by "Benjamin Lee McCormick, April 26, 1946."

"Hey," I said. "That *is* you." I put one arm around Benny's shoulder. "There's your name. And your birth date." I looked at Mama. "When—?"

"It took Benny to find it." Mama laughed nervously. "I couldn't let you go off without setting things right between us. I couldn't get it off my mind, ever since Sunday when Benny got lost. You were right. I was wrong."

"Am I in the book now?" Benny asked.

I pulled him closer. "Yes, you're in the book. Grandma put you in. See, here's Katie and here's Roy, Jr. And Zach, the baby. And here are your other cousins, Tommy and Sarah." I ran my finger beneath each word, pronouncing it aloud for Benny. "Thanks, Mama."

"I'm sorry I didn't do it before." Mama pointed at the blank space beside my name. "I didn't know if you wanted me to put down a name for—"

"That's up to you. I don't care one way or the other. His name's on the birth certificate. Dwayne Franklin Fortrell. F-O-R-T-R-E-L-L."

"Who's that?" Benny asked.

"That's your daddy's name."

"He went off to the war on a big boat," Benny told Mama. "He's coming to find us when he's finished fighting."

"No," I said. "Remember what I told you? How long a time it's been? How he never even saw you, to see what a great kid you are? It's just you and me, remember?"

"But me and Roy, Jr. are gonna—"

I sighed and rested my chin on the top of Benny's head. "We'll talk about it later."

Mama laid her hand on my shoulder. "Maybe there'll be somebody else. More children, later on."

"Don't count on it." I looked again at Benny's name, spelled out in indelible black ink. "What about Daddy, when he sees this?"

"I'll handle that," Mama said. "After you and Benny are gone, and he's got more of his strength back. No need to worry him with it now in his condition."

"Is Grandpa finished resting yet?" Benny asked. "I want to help him read the rest of the alphabet book."

"Almost." Mama reached for Benny's hand. "We'll take him some dinner first. Come on. You can help me make him some cornbread."

I remained on the sofa with the open Bible in my lap, staring at Benny's name, preserved for posterity. A sudden wetness of my eyes blurred my vision. Why did such a simple act as writing a name on a page matter so much to me? I thumbed through the New Testament, scanning, as I had as a child, for the pages filled with red ink, signifying the spoken words of Jesus. From infancy through adolescence, I had been immersed in the sacredness of these tissue-thin, gilt-edged pages—the majesty of its King James English rolling from Sunday morning pulpits like the voice of God himself, washing over me like waves—rising and falling to the music of the preacher's cadences. Then, later, how I had cringed under the wrath in Daddy's voice as he growled out the words *harlot* and *whore.* I couldn't let Mama bear full responsibility for adding Benny's name. I would show it to Daddy myself, tell him Mama had done it at my insistence, try one last time to mend the broken threads of our relationship before Benny and I went home.

I got up and started quietly for the bedroom.

Ruth Rodgers

Chapter 33

I tiptoed into the room, holding the Bible in front of me. "Daddy? Do you hurt anywhere from this morning? You want to go into town and see the doctor?"

"No." Daddy lowered his eyebrows, his eyes narrowing to the Bible in my hands.

"Roy's taking Benny and me to the bus station this afternoon so we can go back to New York. Before we go, though, I wanted to show you something." I laid the Bible over Daddy's legs and opened it at the ribbon. "Mama added Benny's name to the Family Records. Right here. 'Benjamin Lee McCormick. Born April 26, 1946.' See?" I pointed at the fresh writing.

Daddy pushed at the Bible with his right hand.

"We had a huge argument the other night about him not being in there, and she did it for me, so don't go holding it against her after we're gone. You want to blame somebody, blame me. Benny's my son, Daddy, your grandson, and there's nothing you or anybody else can do to change that fact. I'm sorry for the way it happened, believe me, but I wouldn't undo a minute of it, not if it meant I wouldn't have Benny."

I pulled up a chair and sat close to the bed. Daddy's right hand was resting on the Bible, partially covering Benny's name. When I looked at him, he stared away from me, out the window. I started again. "You can't hide from the truth, Daddy, much as you want to. You can't keep pretending Benny doesn't exist. He's real flesh and blood. He's my life, Daddy. If you can't accept that, if you still want to disown me because of what I did, then that's your decision. I'm not going to worry about it any more. And I'm not going to subject Benny to any more of your disapproval. We're going away today, in just a few hours. And we won't be coming back—ever."

I stood, walked to the window, and took a deep breath before turning back to face him. "When I found out, last Sunday, that Benny's name wasn't in the Bible like all the other grandkids', I can't tell you how hurt and angry that made me feel. I guess I sorta lost my temper and said some things to Mama, and Benny overheard us arguing. He got scared and ran off in the dark, and I nearly went crazy till we found him, way off up the road at the old Carson place. He's all I have, Daddy. When I ran away, I sacrificed everything for him. Do you realize what that means? Did you ever love anybody that much, that you'd give up your own life to save theirs? If I'd been Abraham and God had asked me to sacrifice my son, you know what I'd have said? I'd have said, 'Take me, God, if you want a sacrifice.' I wouldn't have offered him Benny."

I coughed to clear the lump in my throat. Daddy was looking down at the Bible, his hand still covering Benny's name. He didn't look up or give any sign he was listening. Had he already turned me off, the way he would turn off an annoying radio program? "The reason Benny was running away," I continued, wanting to get everything out into the open before I lost my nerve, wanting to make him understand why Mama had done what she had, "the reason he was running away was because he thought, since he wasn't in the Bible, that he didn't belong here, that somebody might even take him away from me, since I was in the book and he wasn't. That's why Mama wrote it in."

Daddy said nothing, only continued to look down at the Bible. I took it out of his lap, letting the pages fall shut. "Okay, Daddy, be that way. I'm sorry I disappointed you, okay? I didn't do it deliberately. I didn't set out to make a mess of my life. But whatever regrets I have, Benny's not one of them. Your refusal to accept him is more your loss than it is his. You should hear him go on about his grandpa. I can't imagine what the truth would do to him." I laid the Bible on the table in its usual spot. "I'll be going now."

"No." Daddy reached his right hand toward the table.

"No, Benny's not worthy of being in the Bible? Then neither am I. Erase me, too, if that's the way you want it. We'll be gone soon, and you can forget either of us ever existed."

"No, I ..." Daddy waved his arm once in the air before letting it drop onto the bed.

"What?" I asked. "I've suffered enough, Daddy. I don't have anything left to give." I started toward the door.

"Me," Daddy said. "Give me..."

"Goodbye, Daddy."

"Give me..." Daddy motioned toward the Bible on the table.

"You want the Bible? Why?"

Daddy struggled to raise himself higher in the bed. "I want..."

I walked back to the bed. "Okay. Here it is." I picked up the Bible and plopped it across his legs. "Find all those verses about harlots again. I'm not staying to listen to it this time, though. I'm finished with all that."

"No," Daddy said. "Stay." His voice had some of its old commanding force. I hesitated, watching with curiosity as his right hand fumbled with the Bible, trying to open it to the page marked by the purple ribbon. I wasn't going to help him, wasn't going to wait around for any more sermons.

After finally getting it open to the Family Records section, he reached to the table and fumbled around with the collection of items on it.

"You want to scratch out Benny's name right now?" I asked. I moved some papers on the table and picked up Mama's pen. "Here. And scratch me out, too, while you're at it."

Daddy waved the pen away. His hand found what he was looking for—his glasses. He put them on and then flipped back and forth between pages, scanning with one finger, apparently looking for something.

I threw the pen back onto the table. "Forget the lecture, Daddy. You can't scare me any more with your Bible thumping or your God. I don't believe in your God any more."

"Here." Daddy put his finger on a line of the Family Records pages. The top of the page was labeled Deaths. "Ben."

I looked where he was pointing. Written in Mama's plain rounded script was "Elizabeth Mary Collins McCormick, June 11, 1919." Directly beneath that was "Baby boy McCormick, June 11, 1919." Puzzled, I looked back at Daddy. What did this have to do with Benny?

Daddy's finger remained on the line. "Ben," he repeated. "Ben-a-min."

"Benjamin?" I asked. "The baby boy. His name was Benjamin?" Daddy nodded. "Ben-a-min."

"But there's no name on the gravestone. Just Elizabeth's. And baby boy. Mama didn't know. Why didn't you…?"

Daddy had been overwhelmed when Elizabeth died. Two small children and nobody to mother them. He hadn't been thinking clearly. Or nobody had asked him for a name. Did stillborn babies even get names? Maybe giving him a name was more than he could handle at the time of the funeral. And he hadn't recorded the deaths himself. That had been done by Mama, months later—maybe even years later—after their marriage.

"I didn't know, Daddy. When I chose Benjamin, I picked it because I liked the sound of it. And I always liked Benjamin in the Bible. I didn't know I was taking someone else's name."

A movement at the door made me look up. Mama was standing in the open doorway, a plate of food in her hand.

"I never knew you had picked out a name." Mama addressed her comment to Daddy. "If I'd known, I would have written it in."

I touched the back of Daddy's hand. "I'm sorry, Daddy, sorry about the baby. And about Elizabeth."

"Ben." Satisfied now that he had been understood, Daddy leaned back into his bank of pillows, his face relaxing from the strain of talking.

I removed the Bible from his legs and laid it on the table.

"Here's them fried hoecakes you wanted," Mama said. "And some fresh string beans and new potatoes seasoned with ham hocks, just the way you like 'em."

Benny stepped forward with a glass of iced tea. "I got your drink, Grandpa."

Daddy's eyes focused on Benny, his face lighting up in recognition. "Ben," he said, reaching for the glass. "Ben-a-min." He looked back at me and nodded.

I wrapped my hand around Daddy's unsteady one and helped him raise the glass to his mouth. "Here you go, Daddy. Nice, sweet tea."

Daddy took a sip and then yielded the glass to me. "Ben," he said again, his arm outstretched toward Benny. "Ben-a-min."

Benny put his hand in Daddy's. "Are you rested now, Grandpa? You want to read some more after you eat?"

One side of Daddy's mouth turned upward into a smile. "Okay. Ben." He squeezed Benny's hand and looked at me. "Ben-a-min. Good boy."

"Yes," I answered. "He's a very good boy. The best." I put one hand on Benny's shoulder, smiling through the moistness that dampened my eyes.

"Here's your dinner," Mama said again, moving closer. "It's getting cold."

I set the glass of tea on the table and positioned Mama's chair beside the bed. "Here, Mama. We'll get out of the way so Daddy can eat in peace." I touched Daddy's arm. "Benny and I will see you after a while. We have a couple more hours before we leave for home." I ushered Benny out the door. "Come on, Honey. Let's go eat our lunch. Then you can read some more of your book to Grandpa."

Benny and I were still at the table when Mama came into the kitchen and set the empty plate on the counter. "He cleaned it up," she said proudly. "Look at that. He'll get his strength back now—now that he's got that weight off his shoulders. Now that we both have, I should say. It's been a long time coming, but sometimes things just have to work themselves out in their own good time. I'm sorry, Lacey, for me and for him. All these lost years—"

"It's all right, Mama. Come on and eat."

Mama sat at the table at her accustomed place. "Don't go yet, Lacey. Stay a few more days. Let Daddy and Benny get better acquainted. They both took to each other from the first. Benny's good for him. For me, too. There's six years worth of catching up to do."

"I can't. I have to get back to work." I'd already said my good-byes to Julia yesterday. And to Neil last night. "I'm all packed, and Roy's taking off early to drive us into town."

"Pshaw, Roy would be tickled pink to hear you'd changed your mind."

"Thanks for asking, but I can't. We really have to get back home. I promised Dorothy."

"Mommy, can I go read my book to Grandpa?" Benny asked. "He said I could after I finished eating."

"Sure you can." I smiled at him. "Just make sure you don't read too long and tire him out."

Benny ran to get his book, and I took our plates and glasses to the sink. Now that the moment of leaving was here, I was torn between what I was leaving behind and what was waiting for me in New York. Part of me wanted to stay, but the other part knew that procrastination would only make things harder.

Chapter 34

Roy pulled into the gravel parking lot behind the bus station and switched off the ignition. "You sure you're gonna be okay, going all that way by yourself?" He looked over Benny's head at me.

"Of course, we'll be okay. We got here, didn't we?"

"You need any money?" He reached for his back pocket.

"No. I'm fine. You don't need to worry about me. I'm all grown up now, in case you hadn't noticed."

Roy got the suitcase out of the truck's bed and followed us into the station. "Just don't forget where home is," he said. "Don't go turning this young'un into no citified Yankee kid."

I got into line to buy our tickets. "There you go again. We'll be back next summer for a nice, long visit. I promised Mama and Daddy."

"You hold her to that, Benny," Roy said. "Pester her every day if you have to. Don't forget you got Southern blood, boy, McCormick blood. You oughta be out in the woods, climbing trees and hunting and fishing. Here." He took off his green John Deere cap, grimy from sweat and tobacco tar, and clamped it onto Benny's head. "Take this with you to remember where you came from."

Benny reached with both hands and adjusted the cap so that he could see from beneath its brim. He grinned at Roy.

"Thanks," I said. "And thanks for the ride. I really appreciate you taking time off work to do this." I laid one hand on his arm. "And don't worry about me and Benny. We'll be fine, really. Next summer will be here before you know it."

Clutching our tickets in one hand and Benny's bag of books and toys in the other, I followed Benny onto the bus and into an empty seat. Through the window, I could see Roy raise one hand in a wave. "Wave bye to Uncle Roy," I told Benny. Saying goodbye to Mama and Daddy had been so rushed that the finality of it all had not yet sunk in. Roy had arrived late—in a huge hurry, as usual—and so Benny and I had had to leave with hardly time for a quick squeeze of Daddy's hand and a hug for Mama, our goodbyes called behind us as we raced outside to the demanding beep of Roy's truck horn.

The bus began to move, pulling out of the station. No turning back now. As Pine Lake receded into the distance, I could feel the heaviness that had been hanging over me for the past two weeks begin to lift, evaporating behind me like the bus's exhaust fumes. Finally rid of the encumbrances of the past, I was free to go wherever I wanted, do whatever I pleased—I didn't have to answer to anyone. I actually felt lighter, more buoyant, as if I'd shed a heavy suit of armor.

"Here we go, Benbo. On our way home. Are you excited?"

Benny fiddled with his cap, which kept falling over his eyes. He pushed it back. "That's a baby name. My name is Ben."

He had such a look of seriousness on his face that I had to laugh. "No more Benny?"

"Ben. That's what Grandpa called me. Benny's for babies. And Yankees."

"Okay. I'll try to remember that," I said. "Ben it is."

"Ben McCormick," Benny insisted. "And I'm not a Yankee."

"You've been listening too much to Uncle Roy. You'll always be a McCormick, no matter where you live. Place doesn't matter."

"And I'm coming back on Saturday to go fishing. I promised."

"I'm sorry, Honey, but we can't come back this Saturday. It's too far. But next summer you can go fishing again, and you and Roy, Jr. can build another fort. Look, there's a corn field. And there's some tobacco. See?" I pointed out the bus window.

"Is that Mr. Hardest's tobacco?"

"Mr. Hardister? No, that field belongs to somebody else. We can't see Mr. Hardister's field from the bus, but it's over that way." I pointed east.

"Mr. Hardister said he would give you a job. Then we could stay here."

"A job? Neil?"

"He said you could tie the tobacco onto the sticks for him, remember? You said you knew how."

I laughed. "That's not a real job. It only lasts for a few weeks in the summer, just until all the tobacco is gathered. Besides, it's hard, nasty work. I have a job back at home helping Dorothy. And you're starting school soon. You and Tony. Aren't you excited about that?"

"There's a school here, too. And a big yellow school bus picks up all the kids. Uncle Roy said Roy, Jr. and me would be in the same class if we lived here. Can we, Mommy?" He pushed his cap back again so he could look up at me.

"Uncle Roy said that, did he?"

"He said McCormicks don't belong up North in Yankee country. He said us McCormicks got to stick together. He's gonna put me and Roy, Jr. to work next summer, and pay us fifty cents a day if we work hard."

"Is that so?"

"I want to live here and work for Uncle Roy and take care of Grandpa."

"Just wait till you get back home and see all your friends again. Pretty soon you'll forget about this summer."

"No, I won't. Never. Never. Never." Benny crossed his arms in front of his chest.

"Sure you will. We both will, after a while."

❋   ❋   ❋

Fifteen minutes later, we were crossing the state line into Georgia and would soon be changing buses in Valdosta—where

Neil had said *Streetcar Named Desire* was playing. If we'd stayed, I could have gone with Neil to the movie on Saturday night. But I wouldn't think about that. I wouldn't let myself dwell on the memory of Neil beside me in the front porch swing, his lips teasingly warm against mine; Neil sitting next to me on the front steps, showing me the photo of John Philip; Neil at the tobacco barn, bronzed in the glow of the sparks from the furnace; Neil holding my hand in the dark as we stumbled down the overgrown path to the old Carson place in answer to Benny's whistle.

No more focusing on the might-have-beens; I'd think about my cozy third floor walk-up in New York—the front room with the sink, hot plate, and refrigerator that made up my kitchen, the comfy brown couch that folded out and became my bed at night, the card table and two chairs that comprised my dining room suite, Benny's little alcove bedroom behind the curtains I'd hung for privacy.

It wasn't much, certainly not by Geneva's standards, but it was home. Rita, across the hall, sometimes came over after the kids were asleep, both our doors open in case Tony woke and came looking for her, and we'd sit at the table talking quietly, the radio playing softly in the background. Most of the time, though, we did our socializing on the stoop while the kids played out back in the alley, gossiping about the other neighbors or planning our futures, complete with exciting, high-powered jobs, glamorous clothes, and handsome men falling all over themselves for our attention. Rita and I would laugh together about how we'd walk past with our heads in the air, looking neither right nor left, even if every man in New York swooned at our feet. Men were no good, not to be trusted, and neither of us ever wanted to complicate our lives with a man again.

What would Neil think of my life, if he were to come to New York to visit me? What if one morning I woke to a tapping on my door and opened it to his comforting grin? What if he held out his arms to me, and said, "Come here, Lacey Lu. I've come to take you home where you belong."

But no, here I was daydreaming again, just as I'd done with

Dwayne, fantasizing scenarios that would never happen. Neil would never come to New York. Neil and I lived in two different worlds. He was a part of my past, and the past was what I was leaving behind.

When the bus stopped at the Valdosta station, I stood and reached for Benny's bag. "Time to change buses." I let Benny go ahead of me down the aisle, Roy's cap tilted on his head at a rakish angle. Had he gotten taller since we'd been in Florida? He looked healthier, tanner. The sunshine and fresh country air had done him good. He skipped down the steps of the bus and hurried ahead, threading his way through the other passengers to be first to the outside compartment where the suitcases were being unloaded. "Wait," I began, but then stopped myself. It was time to give him some growing room. Soon he'd be away from me all day at school. I had to admit that part of me was looking forward to reclaiming the freedom of being my own person, not simply Benny's mother. Ben's mother. I'd have to get used to this new, grown-up name.

I followed at a slower pace. Soon I could make my own plans, dream my own dreams—resume a career, develop new friends, new interests. My life was about to change, to enter a new phase. I picked up my battered suitcase, which Benny—Ben!—had already claimed for me, and strode confidently into the station, conscious of the picture I made in my crisp white blouse and gauzy floral skirt. Two weeks in the Florida sunshine had done me good, too. *Don't lose your spirit*, Neil had told me. *Don't let anybody tamp it down or take it away from you.* Good advice to live by.

I checked the schedule board. Half an hour until the next bus left for Savannah, Charleston, and points north. It was hot and crowded inside the station, and I wiped my brow with the palm of my hand. "You want a Co-Cola, Benny?"

Benny put his hands on his hips. "It's Ben. Ben McCormick."

"Sorry. Ben." As I fished in my change purse for two nickels, one slipped out of my hand and rolled across the floor.

"Allow me," a voice said. A man scooped up the nickel and

held it out to me.

"Thanks." I looked up into his face. Tall, nice-looking, late twenties, early thirties—the exact type I'd shied away from for the last six years. I took the nickel, put it into the slot, and opened the door to pull out a soda. "Here you go," I said to Benny. Then I inserted the other nickel and pulled out a bottle for myself, conscious that the man was still standing right behind me.

"Mommy!" Benny held his bottle up to me.

"What's wrong?" I asked. "Don't you want it?"

The man chuckled and took the bottle from Benny's hand, stuck it under the opener and handed it back to him. "Here you go, buddy."

"Oh." I felt a trickle of perspiration run down my nose as I popped the lid off my own bottle and took a sip. The man was jingling the change in his pocket. "Oops, sorry." I stepped aside.

The man got his own Coca-Cola. "Mighty hot today."

"Yes. Yes, it is." I stole another look at his face. Blue eyes. Curly light-brown hair.

"Where you headed?" he asked.

"Home."

"And where's home?"

"New York."

"Wow, that far away? Been down here visiting?"

"Yes. My father had a stroke, but he's better now. So we're headed home—me back to work and Benny—Ben—here off to school in a few more weeks."

"Hi, Ben," the man said. "I'm Steve." He looked back at me. "Steve Boatwright. And you're?—"

"Lacey. Lacey McCormick. "

"Pleased to meet you." Steve touched the bill of his cap. "I bet your husband is looking forward to the two of you getting back home, now that your daddy's doing better."

I was conscious of my bare left hand, circled around the Coca-Cola bottle, as I lifted it and took another sip, letting the fizz of the soda linger in my mouth, enjoying the sensation of its tingle. "No husband," I said. "Just me and Benny."

"Ben," Benny reminded me.

"Just me and Ben."

"Oh?"

I took notice of the change in tone, the increased interest. I ran my tongue nervously over my lips and looked away. "What about you? Where are you headed?"

"Nowhere. I'm here to meet somebody." He looked at his watch. "Her bus is running late. Should've been here by now."

"Oh." I was conscious of a trace of disappointment. *Her* bus. Wife? Girlfriend? "I'm sure it'll be here soon."

"Yep. Me, too. It's just she's not much used to traveling. I hope she got on the right bus." He grinned. "Had a hard time getting her to go all the way to the big city of Atlanta. I bet your mama's the same way."

"Your mother?" I asked. Had my tone betrayed my relief? And why relief, anyway? What possible difference did his marital status make to me? For that matter, what was I doing standing here in a bus station talking to an attractive, eligible man—a total stranger? This was not like me at all. I put one hand on Benny's shoulder and looked away, concentrating on listening to the long list of towns as a boarding call came over the loudspeaker.

"That you?" Steve asked.

"No. We want Savannah."

"My sister just had a baby," Steve was explaining. "My mother's been up there helping out. Been gone a week now."

We continued to talk until the Atlanta bus arrived and Steve hurried off to rescue his mother. "Nice meeting you," he said as he left, lifting his empty coca cola bottle in a kind of salute before depositing it into the crate beside the vending machine. "Have a safe trip home."

"Thanks. Nice meeting you, too." I watched his back disappear into the crowd, feeling a mixture of excitement and self-reproach. Here I was, not yet thirty miles into my return journey, and already I'd talked with—some might even say flirted with—an attractive man, someone I'd never seen before and would likely never see again. I couldn't believe how easy it had been—how natural it had felt as it was happening. And I was heading back into a city full of unattached men. Always before, I'd looked at them as other Dwaynes, but maybe some of them were Steves. Some, perhaps, might even be Neils.

No, there could be only one Neil. But how would I know for sure if I didn't allow myself the chance to find out? Wasn't that what life was all about—taking chances? Anyway, I'd promised Neil I'd write to him as soon as I got home, and I would. And there was always next summer. But next summer was a whole year away. Between then and now was a clean, blank slate.

When the boarding call came for our bus, I let Benny go ahead of me. "Grab the first empty seat," I told him. "Looks like it's gonna be crowded."

The bus shifted gears and picked up speed as it left Valdosta behind and headed north into hilly Georgia farmland. Through my bus window I could see fields and pastures scrolling past in what seemed an endless patchwork sequence of greens and golds, oranges and browns—the squares stitched together with the zigzags of split rail fences. I leaned back in my seat, imagining the future—years like miles unrolling before me, holding new surprises right around the bend. Whatever the future held, I was on my way to meet it.

Patchwork

Ruth Rodgers